Ladies' Tailor

Ladies' Tailor
A Novel

Priya Hajela

HarperCollins *Publishers* India

First published in India by HarperCollins *Publishers* 2022
4th Floor, Tower A, Building No. 10, Phase II, DLF Cyber City,
Gurugram, Haryana – 122002
www.harpercollins.co.in

2 4 6 8 10 9 7 5 3 1

P-ISBN: 978-93-5629-057-0
E-ISBN: 978-93-5629-058-7

Typeset in 11/14 Minion Pro at
Manipal Technologies Limited, Manipal

Printed and bound at
Thomson Press (India) Ltd

For my paternal grandparents, Bakshi Pritam Singh (Papaji) and Beant Kaur (Biji), who left their home in Harial, Gujarkhan (Pakistan) and made a new life in Ludhiana, Punjab.

Foreword

THE PLACES I HAVE WRITTEN ABOUT IN THIS BOOK – Delhi (Nizamuddin, Patel Nagar, Khan Market, Shahdara, Kingsway Camp), Lahore, Amritsar and Sukho are all real, but many elements are fictional. I have not lived in most of these places. Some I have visited but only fleetingly. All provide the setting that I needed to tell this story. I have researched many details about the places but have shortened distances, invented streets, and reimagined architecture, all in the service of my characters. There are many details of the period related to means of transport that are minimally available and hazy at best. These, too, I have imagined and manipulated based on the needs of my characters.

I would also like to mention that Nilibar is an actual fabric and tailoring shop in Ludhiana. The original owners were refugees like my grandparents. The shop is still there, thriving, offering everything from daily wear to wedding trousseaus.

1

THE PEOPLE, THE SMELLS, THE VOICES, THE YEARNING, the hands clutching bellies – for that's where their few precious belongings were – the odour of fear, the taste of dislocation, the sounds of desperation: that is what Gurdev sensed all around him when they reached Lahore station. He was pushed aside, stepped on, even shoved a few times but he went on, pushing and stepping on and shoving humanity out of his way. His wife, Simrat, followed close behind him, her hand holding on to a corner of his kurta, their two children tied to her waist with two dupattas. They stood on the platform, a metal trunk on his head, all other belongings left behind in their home of ten years. They watched as the Lahore train chugged in. They stared like everybody else, to see who was hanging at the door of each compartment as bogey after bogey moved slowly past them. They saw no one standing in the doorways because all the doors were shut. All the doors were closed because what was inside had to stay inside. They saw blood dripping out of some doors. They saw what looked like heaps of crumpled clothing lying on seats and on the floor as the train suddenly picked up speed and then they saw nothing but a blur. This was not part of the plan. Some skirmishes, loud voices, a few deaths in the heat of passion, those were possible. But large-scale massacres, butcheries, annihilation of entire clans, that was beyond Gurdev's imagination – but it happened and he participated like everyone else.

Gurdev liked to think and plan on his own. Well before Partition, but soon after the Hindu-Muslim riots began in Calcutta in August 1946 and unrest was moving westward, Gurdev had begun to wonder how this would all end. Even as early as February 1947, after British Prime Minister Clement Atlee's address on the radio, in which he had said that the British would leave India by June 1948, Gurdev had known there would be a partition. There was regular talk about dividing India in two, a Muslim state for Jinnah and the Muslim League and a secular state for Gandhi, Nehru and the other Congress wallas – more likely a Hindu state, but no one ever admitted that. He knew the League had grown while Congress leaders sweated in jail through the Second World War. It had reached a point that it couldn't stay within one India. He wanted to be ready when his village fell to the other side of the border, as he knew it would. He had made his plan. It involved a brief visit to Delhi, followed by a final migration.

Gurdev left for Delhi on 3 March 1947 from his village, Sukho. He travelled by bus to Rawalpindi and then by train from Rawalpindi to Lahore, arriving in Lahore mid-morning. His train from Lahore to Delhi left that evening. At the Lahore station, as he got off on a crowded platform, he had to push people out of the way to get off the train. He nudged a coolie and moved his head up and down, his eyes and brows following his head. 'The Sikhs, your people, they will get us all killed,' was all that the coolie said. Gurdev went out of the station and followed the noise down Empress Road and over to Egerton Road. He skirted the Punjab Assembly Building, and joined the crowds gathered there to watch Master Tara Singh brandish his unsheathed kirpan in the air and shout for the rights of Sikhs. He saw and heard the Sikhs chant after their leader – 'Pakistan Murdabad, Pakistan Murdabad, Death to Pakistan'. He heard the raspy voice of a man standing close to him – 'They can kill us all but we will never leave Pakistan, never leave the birthplace of our gurus.'

Gurdev was a Sikh. He wore a turban over long hair that he had cut once before but never since. He respected his religion. What these people were saying and doing made him afraid – not for himself, because he had his plan, but for his parents who had never agreed with him on anything. Without thinking too much about what he was doing, he left the crowd and made his way to his childhood home in Model Town, a part of the city that had been built by a group of Indians as a special enclave for the rich. In 1902, two hundred rich traders, landowners, doctors and retired judges had gone to the British government and asked for 2,000 acres of land outside Lahore to build a modern community, away from the congestion and grime of the walled city, and got it. Their request didn't interfere with the homes on Queens Road and Empress Road, where the British themselves preferred to live. Model Town was ten kilometres away, easy in a car but now Gurdev wondered how he should go. The streets in town were deserted, the shops shuttered. He could still hear guttural war cries following him as he hurried towards Firozepur Road. Nobody would be out now to challenge the Sikhs; they were too afraid of a face-to-face confrontation. The Sikhs had perfected that art. With their kirpans by their side, they were not afraid, but Gurdev was. He knew that there would be retaliation and it wouldn't be against those who could fight back. There would be attacks in people's homes while they ate or while they slept. People like his parents. Gurdev stopped a rickety, overloaded bus and got on. He looked around for other Sikhs and seeing several villagers in soft turbans like his own, he sat down, wary each time the bus stopped. He got off near the entry gate of Model Town, and as expected, the guard stopped him – not for his turban but for his shabby clothes. He gave his parents' address and went through, the number A-8 rolling off his tongue like it had ten years ago.

When he reached his old home, he hesitated before he opened the big metal gate, not because he was nervous but because this had not been part of his plan. He had left home ten years ago and that was the past. He thought little of it but as he lifted the latch off the top and pushed the recently painted black gate, solid metal, no chinks, he felt the warmth of elaichi-flavoured tea in his mouth, he tasted the tea-soaked butter biscuit melt on his tongue, he heard voices of all timbres and pitches bouncing off the high ceilings and plastered walls, and he smelled eggplant roasting on an open flame. This last memory made him gag – burnt eggplant smelt like singed hair. As he entered, he heard only quiet voices as if deliberately trying to keep from being heard and smelt only smoke from the city, or maybe from his own clothes.

'Raheem, Sitara,' he called out for his parents' helpers, an old couple who had brought him up. No one came. He called again, louder this time, his voice more urgent. He went back to the gate to look for a bell. There wasn't one. There had never been one. His parents had had a guard at the gate. Now, there was no one, not even the narrow guard booth that smelt of dirty socks and pickles. He wondered why his parents had done away with the guard. He went up the steps to the verandah and knocked on the sky-blue wood door. When he was younger, the wood door was always open and the screen door latched. Now, both were closed. He knocked again. This time, he heard footsteps rushing towards him. The door opened in a flurry, and old Raheem, shorter than he remembered, his quivering yellow-white beard that swept the top of a yellowy white Pathan suit, stood before him. Gurdev said nothing, just hugged the old man close.

'Puttar, how are you? So many years. How could you forget about us? I know, I know. You do what you want to do, what you have to do. And who can blame you?' The old man went on as he pulled Gurdev into his parents' sitting room. He didn't say anything as he opened the door and ushered the tall man in.

'Raheem, what is that racket? Who's at the door? Say something, old man,' Gurdev heard his mother say as she counted stitches on a cross-stitch wall hanging. She dropped the fabric on the floor and stood up when she saw him, her face happy yet drawn, her smile wide yet her eyes narrow.

'Why are you here, puttar? Your father, I don't know what he will say. Is everything okay? Who do you have now? A wife? Children? I hear they are sparing no one. Are your people okay, puttar?'

'I am okay but I have come to check if others who are also my people are okay, Biji. You have to leave this place...'

There was the sound of a throat clearing behind him, a familiar sound. Gurdev turned around to see his father, aged but still tall, his back erect. He walked up to him and tried an awkward hug but the old man stepped back and put out his hand. Gurdev took it in his and shook it.

'We will stay right where we are. No one is going anywhere. You can do what you want. You always have.'

Gurdev flinched and backed up, moving closer to his mother, who had sat back down with her embroidery.

His father went on. 'They are our friends, son, these British people. It's because of them that we live here in Model Town, away from that mishmash and mayhem. But what would you know about friends? You left all yours here and disappeared. And look at you. You look like a peasant; you even talk like a peasant. Your turban is crooked and soft – do you know who wears soft turbans, son? Peasants! We aristocrats wear starched turbans, sharp and firm like us. We won't sit back and let these people take what is ours. It is our land. We have cultivated it for five generations. You watch – the Chenab will be the boundary line – nothing less. We will be a part of India but with everything that is ours today. We will give up nothing.'

Gurdev listened quietly, then straightened his soft turban and got up to leave. He walked to his mother's writing desk and wrote something on a piece of paper.

'As you wish, Papaji. I can't force you but I would advise you to leave now. If things happen as you say, you can come back. If you had seen Master Tara Singh in action, you would know that this has become about religion. Please be careful. If you need me, you can write to me at this address in Sukho or send a telegram. I don't know how long we'll stay but I am going to Delhi now – to make some preparations. I have a wife and two boys, by the way.'

'That Master Tara Singh should have remained a teacher. He's going to get us all killed,' his father said. Thankfully, he didn't say anything about Gurdev's wife being a peasant. Gurdev was not in the mood to fight with his father.

'Speaking of violence, why don't you have a security guard at the gate any more?' Gurdev asked his father.

'Son, you don't need to worry about us. We can take care of ourselves. If you were so concerned, you wouldn't have run away like you did. Anyway, Raheem's son Farid is taking care of security for us now. He doesn't need a dirty cabin. He moves around the whole house and takes care of things.'

Gurdev wanted to ask if Raheem's son was ex-Army or if he had any other qualifications as many good security guards did, but he stopped himself. As if on cue, his mother called him aside.

'Puttar, you come with me for one minute before you run away angry again.' Gurdev followed her into her bedroom. She pulled the latch closed behind them. His parents had always had separate bedrooms. He watched his mother step across the room over a Kashmiri carpet, one he had always been told to skirt around as a young boy with dirty feet, and open a cupboard, unlocking it with a key from an unwieldy bunch. He saw her fumble a little and look back to see if he was watching while she took out another set of keys. She looked smaller than before but still elegant, her hair dyed black and tied up in a bun, her clothes pressed and crisp, her face made up, lipstick bright – even though she had been sitting alone doing cross-stitch.

She walked back closer to where he was standing and motioned to him to move a large upholstered chair to one side, off the Kashmiri carpet. She sat on the chair and pushed up one end of the carpet. Gurdev saw a metal trapdoor below. He had never seen this before. He looked up at his mother, eyebrows raised, his face still expressionless. He took the one key she held out of the bunch and unlocked the trapdoor. The key turned sideways, serving as a handle to pull the door open. He peered inside, curious. Was this a secret tunnel that they could eventually escape through? Unfortunately, it was a shallow, metal-lined container filled with stacks of dollars, pounds and Indian rupees. He looked back up at his mother seated on the chair as he kneeled on the floor, as if in penance. This money, my God, it could change his life. He had worked so hard but saved so little. It was true what they said, money begot money. To get rich with nothing was impossible. It was probably her intention to give him some, but he wasn't going to ask for it. He wondered why the secret space was in her room and not in his father's. Probably because that is where a thief would not look.

'Biji, what is this? How did you get this money? What are you going to do with it? And these rupees will be worthless soon – once the British leave.'

'Puttar, I want to give you something. You took nothing when you left.'

Biji reached down and picked up four sheaves of dollars and put them in a velvet bag that she had picked up from her closet when she had got the second set of keys. She looked at Gurdev and put the bag back down. Was she changing her mind, he wondered? After all, he had left her and never turned back.

'Biji, I'm meeting you after ten years. Let's sit down for a few minutes. All this can wait, no?'

'No, Puttar. You don't know who's watching. I want to go from here but your father, he's more stubborn than a stuck pressure cooker. I want you to have this. It will always be worth something. I know things will change, after independence, whenever that happens – what are they saying now?'

'June 1948 is when Atlee says they'll be out – but I think it'll be sooner. They are tired, the British soldiers, or so my friends who returned from war tell me. They want to be home, not here in India. Great Britain has no money. So, it will happen sooner. Biji, but tell me, how did you collect so much money?'

'Puttar, all we have is land and cash. The rent keeps coming in and whenever there is a chance, your father converts the rupees to dollars and pounds, whatever the black market is running at that time, and puts it away. Had we bought that hotel … anyway. No point talking about the past. Take this, Puttar. This is for you and your family's future.' She picked up the velvet bag and put it in Gurdev's hand. He closed the trapdoor, locked it up and gave her the keys. As he stood up, he noticed a slight movement outside the curtained glass door, a shadow that moved quickly away. He watched as his mother put the keys back in her cupboard but before she locked the cupboard, she took out a small silk pouch.

'This is for your wife. I never got to give her anything either.' Without even looking inside, Gurdev took out a yellow handkerchief from his pocket, wrapped both pouches in it, tied the two diagonal ends into knots, and slipped the bundle into a pocket in the salwar bottom of his Pathan suit. He was certain that his mother had given a trinket for his wife. How would she give a woman she had never met, anything of any value?

When Gurdev left the house, his father had retired for his afternoon nap and Raheem had also disappeared. As he walked down the steps, he noticed a younger man in the back. He called out to him, but the man didn't hear him. Gurdev had to leave to catch his train so he patted his pocket instinctively, opened the gate and let himself out. He latched the gate behind him, peering over it to see if anyone had come to the other side. The young man was there, his ear to the gate, checking to see if Gurdev had left. Gurdev walked away with a deliberate step and headed back to the station to catch his train to Delhi.

Gurdev boarded the night train to Delhi from Lahore at 10 p.m., late by five hours. He slept fitfully sitting on his seat, his head leaning on the window, visions of Master Tara Singh's sword catching a sharp ray of sunlight crawled in his head. If that sword was coming down on your neck, you probably did want to be blinded by sunlight when it sliced your head off.

Later, he heard the raspy voice of the man in the crowd, 'Don't spare them, not a single one.' Gurdev jerked awake and looked around him. The second-class sleeper was full, but like him, no one had a berth to lie down and sleep. Everyone was sitting up, covered with a cotton khes from head to feet, knees drawn to chest, rolling side to side as the train made its way to Delhi.

As the train pulled in to Delhi, nine hours later, Gurdev saw that the station looked much like Lahore station, with more people standing than trying to get on or off a train. He walked to the door as the train chugged in, still moving slowly and heard wailing – loud funereal wailing from women on the platform. One old lady fell on her son as he got off the train; his bag fell to the ground as he tried to steady himself and his old mother. Gurdev held him by one arm as the man helped his mother.

'They killed them, they went on a shikaar and killed my son – your brother,' the old woman wailed. Gurdev left the two and many more teary people to look for someone who could tell him what happened. The stationmaster, a somewhat young Indian man, stood outside his office, his hands clasped behind his back. Gurdev went and stood next to him, observing the scene from his vantage point. Almost everyone who came off the train was met by a teary eyed relative. Some hugged, picked up their luggage and moved on; others wailed loud and long, then hugged and moved on; and still others said nothing, just fainted quietly toward the dirty platform floor, held up by helpful arms. Gurdev stood there, not rushing to help anyone, taking it all in. The stationmaster looked at him and shook his head, then walked back into his office. He gestured for Gurdev to sit and told him what happened. After Master Tara Singh's rally yesterday, Muslims attacked Sikhs where they could find them – in bazaars, on the streets, even in their Gurdwaras as they prayed. Hundreds were slaughtered. Gurdev sat on the chair across from the stationmaster, gazing at the sepia frames on the wall behind the man. There were photographs with lots of people, a turban or two visible in the crowd. He stared as if looking for familiar faces, as if looking for his parents' faces, thinking that if he found them in these old photos, they would be alive.

'They didn't go far past the city centre. But they burnt everything that had a Sikh name on it…' continued the stationmaster. Gurdev searched his memory for a sign outside his parents' house with his father's name on it, Pritam Singh, a decidedly Sikh first name if the last name wasn't a dead giveaway. He couldn't recall seeing one.

Walking out of the station, Gurdev found a rickshaw and went about finishing the business for which he had come to Delhi. He had a way of putting things away in his mind so he could tend to only one thing at a time. He felt about his middle to check if all the packages were there, especially the valuable ones from his mother. He had divided his own savings into small packets also wrapped in old handkerchiefs. He went to Jangpura first, a neighbourhood named 'Youngpura' by a Colonel Young, who had been asked to relocate the residents of Raisana village to make room for Rajpath and the government buildings from where this country is run.

Gurdev's first stop was a brick home in the front lane of the colony. Harnam Singh, a first cousin on his mother's side, welcomed him into the house with a big hug, Punjabi style, he said. They had freshly made tea and hot pakoras with sliced onions and green chillies, and a little pinch of ajwain, like his mother used to make. Harnam's wife brought everything out of the kitchen and then slunk back, but Gurdev could see her peering at them from behind the curtain. After a little while of talking about other cousins, older relatives, children, births and deaths, Gurdev thought for a moment about his own parents but pushed the thought out because he didn't want to think the next one. Instead, he turned away from the direction of the kitchen and lifted his kurta, feeling through his hidden pocket for one handkerchief-wrapped bundle of money. He handed it to Harnam.

'This, Harnam, I am leaving with you for safekeeping. I will take it from you when I come back with my family. Guru Nanak will keep us safe, I'm sure.'

'What if you don't have to leave at all? They are asking people to stay where they are. That is best, no? So many crowds will come to Delhi. Where will they all stay? Our life … we have no place in our house, other relatives will also come…'

'Harnam, our people are being killed in West Punjab, slaughtered like animals. We have to leave, then we'll see.'

Gurdev next went to his wife's brother's house. Sujjat Singh lived in the same locality but on an inside road, with bigger plots and larger homes. His house had a small garden in front, and his wife sat with them through the whole conversation. They didn't offer anything but water. Gurdev was full anyway, and he had never been impressed with Sujjat's wife's cooking – and Simrat thought she was a terrible cook, too educated with not enough sense about zaika. Conversation with Sujjat died quickly. He was a small-mouthed beardless man with a stiff turban larger than any Gurdev had seen. Sujjat's eyes shifted from Gurdev's middle section to his mouth but never met his eyes. His wife, Parveen, was a tall well-built Sikh woman who announced that she was a Sikh woman from as far as you could see her. She walked with purpose, had a long, sturdy neck on which sat a head that almost bent backwards with the weight of her long hair, oiled and braided, running past her knees. It wasn't a measly braid either, it was as thick as Gurdev's fist on top and tapered down into her parandi, a black threaded wrap that she braided into the last section of her hair and knotted at the bottom with coloured pom-poms that matched her well-fitted salwar kameez. She worked the braid, bringing it forward from one side then the other, as if she was using it as some kind of sign language with her husband. Gurdev stood up and went into a corner to retrieve the money again and handed it to Sujjat.

'Sujjat, this is money I will need to rebuild our lives. I don't want to risk carrying it with me when I'm travelling with Simrat and the boys. Please keep it safe for us.'

'Virji,' Parveen responded before Sujjat could say anything. 'We don't want to keep your money. What if something happens to it? What if robbers break into our house?' she said as Gurdev looked around at iron bars on all the windows.

'Gurdev, Parveen is right. We'll keep your money as long as we are not responsible for anything happening to it,' added Sujjat.

'Sujjat, I have faith in you. I'm sure you'll protect it as you would your own money.'

With that Gurdev left the couple, the woman swinging her braid and the man wringing his hands. He knew that money was tight with everyone these days. He also knew that the temptation of using his money to pay off debt or buy a refrigerator would be strong.

Gurdev walked out to the main road and hailed another cycle rickshaw. He was going back North into the beautiful wide roads of New Delhi. 'Akbar Road,' he told the rickshaw puller. He saw the man raise his eyebrows. He was going to see Satnam Singh, his childhood friend from Lahore, a rich man who lived in a haveli on the British side of town. He ran a shipping business – packaging and sending personal belongings across the country, at this time mostly back to Britain. They greeted each other as old friends do. Gurdev lifted the short chubby man off the ground in a big hug and Satnam, instead of fighting him, wrapped his legs around Gurdev's torso, and hugged him right back.

'I will not be able to do this much longer, Satnam. Either you've become wider or my arms have shrunk.'

But both men were sombre. Both had trouble on their minds. Satnam's parents were also still in Lahore. Neither said anything about what had happened the night before. Gurdev handed his last handkerchief without any comment. He didn't need to say anything. Satnam was not a relative.

The sums Gurdev had distributed were not large but they were everything he had other than the velvet pouch he had just got from his mother. This he kept with him, close to him. It meant more to him than the money. And after he was done with this job, he had to go back to see if his parents…

Gurdev had always thought his parents to be pompous and self-serving. He had left home because he couldn't live their life, and he'd been away without any contact for over ten years. So why was he feeling this warmth, this regard, and this concern for them now? Why were simple onion pakoras stirring emotions he thought he never had? He was an only child but had never been attached to his mother unlike most Indian men. He knew his mother had lost other children but all before him. He had been a miracle for them, and they had treated him like a little god, but he hadn't liked it then and he hadn't liked it now, when she was giving him money. He was glad for the money, but his mother hadn't even offered him a cup of tea or a butter biscuit. Yet, in these times, he was filled with both forgiveness and dread. Dread not for himself but for everyone around him, Simrat, his boys, his parents, the Sikhs who had been demonstrating with Master Tara Singh that day. He knew many Sikhs felt confident because they had fought wars for the British, with the British. They were killing Muslims, lying in wait in wheat fields by the hundreds, camouflaged until the train hit the tree limb they had put on the tracks and massacring everyone – women, children, young men, and old men – like they had back in Europe, in a war, against a real enemy. Here, they were killing their own people, people who looked like them, for no reason. And in turn, the Muslims who had themselves been to war, though not in numbers as large as the Sikhs, fought back and killed Sikh women, children, old men and young men.

Gurdev carried his dread back with him to Sukho, always awake, always looking around. He sat on the roof of the train, in case there was an attack by the Sikhs, so that he could be identified as one of them. He wondered what would happen on the journey back to Amritsar, when they were on the other side. He carried a bigger dread – what had become of his parents in the violence after the Sikh call to battle in Lahore. He didn't stop in Lahore on his way back; he carried on home to Rawalpindi and to Sukho. He had to make sure his own family was okay.

Gurdev reached home covered in blackness, of soot from the train and of what he had seen on his way – spires of smoke on the horizon, empty fields, dry irrigation drains, the colour of the landscape grim.

Simrat opened the door for him and immediately placed in his hand a salve for one of his dreads, a telegram from his parents. 'We are okay. Don't worry. Friends are everywhere.' He read but was not consoled for more than one minute – a minute to be grateful that they were alive but their words petrified him. Friends were not everywhere. He was sure of that.

2

SIMRAT SAT IN HER VERANDAH AS SHE WATCHED HER husband lock down for the night. She felt something for him, but it wasn't love. Obviously, women didn't marry for love. She knew that. Women married men who could take care of things. Many men in her village looked like they could take care of things, but when the time came, they did nothing. She had met Gurdev when he had come to work on her father's farm. She had noticed him because he was big and determined. She saw purpose in his stride and in his work. She liked people with purpose. Her father had suggested a match to save on dowry and because he too liked Gurdev, who looked like a drifter, a migrant worker but whose grime was only skin deep. Gurdev was not coarse in his language or messy while he ate. He didn't scratch his balls as he walked along or stand by the side of the road, in open view, to urinate.

Simrat was a tall woman with square shoulders, not gaunt but with edges. She didn't get her shape from her short and round mother. She was flat, front and back, like a narrow two-dimensional animated rectangle with a small head perched on top. Her face was typically Punjabi, symmetrical, and the only part of her body with curves. It was heart shaped, with a slightly upturned U-shaped nose and large round eyes. Her upper lip and lower lip were roughly the same size and perfectly centred. Despite all that symmetry, it was not a pretty face. But it was a kind face, one that you would want to tell your story to. Her gait was brisk, her voice firm but not loud. She sounded like a patient schoolteacher and, when she was being nice, like a gentle buffalo whisperer. At heart, she was a good person, not selfish or self-absorbed but looking outside of herself to understand the world.

Simrat watched Gurdev tie up Ruby, the buffalo, in her stall and cluck to the chickens. Gurdev had named the buffalo. Fortunately, he hadn't named the chickens because he would kill them when they stopped laying. When the time came, he chopped the bird's head off its neck and watched it run around headless, blood dribbling out of the cavity, not like a fountain, more like a faucet turned on a little. Simrat had always thought it was a story, that a chicken runs around without its head, but she had seen it so many times now that she had to believe it. The Muslim butcher in town did it differently. He made a small slit in the chicken's neck and hung it upside down to let the blood drain out. She had seen the chickens hanging this way outside the shop. She bought those chickens when none of their own was ready for slaughter. The meat from home chickens was tough and old, but the butcher's spring chickens were what her boys liked.

Simrat liked that Gurdev took care of things. She depended on him, maybe too much. She knew he didn't think much more of her than a woman whose job it was to birth children, cook and clean, and do as he said. It made her angry, but she kept her anger to herself. She had a problem with her temper from when she was a child but she had learnt to suppress her impetuous streak and go along. She had learnt to grind her teeth and go along. She had learnt to clench her insides and go along. And after her marriage to Gurdev, all she did was go along. He didn't like disagreements, and he didn't like it if she had an opinion.

It was 3 June 1947. They had both heard the news on the radio earlier that evening. The whole village was talking about it. The British were dividing up their country. Sukho was a revolutionary village. It had sent many young men to fight for India's independence – Muslims, Sikhs, Hindus. They had all gone, together. It was mostly a Sikh village but with a lot of Muslims and few Hindus. The villagers had never before considered these fractions but now they were speaking in factions. The Muslims gathered under the banyan tree, the Hindus sat by the Tulsi plant outside the temple, and the Sikhs gathered in the fields, amid tall stalks of sugarcane. Everyone wanted to know how the lines would be drawn. Everyone wanted to know what would happen to them.

Simrat had a knitting group, they met every now and then, depending on whose husband was travelling out of town and whose mother-in-law was too sick to care. It was a mixed group, all religions, because everyone was always knitting something – sweater vests for their husbands or booties for newborn babies, warm inner banians for young children or mufflers for fathers-in-law. They exchanged patterns and helped each other with the complex ankle curve on baby booties and on cable patterns that twisted and turned on the fronts of grown men's sweaters. Mostly they drank tea, gossiped about everyone who wasn't there and, nowadays, about what was going to happen to them all.

'I'll tell you all what I know if you tell me what you've heard. First of all, Ashfaque Bhai has doubled his usual requirement of flour and oil. Saba, you tell me. You are his neighbour. Does he have guests?' said Simrat.

'Didi, I don't want to get anyone in trouble but there are many new people in Ashfaque Bhai's house. All men. It worries me too. My daughters, they don't cover their heads or anything,' said Saba.

'And the vegetable seller, that Ramu, he had no vegetables left to sell yesterday. Usually, he keeps trying to put some rotting tomatoes and fully blackened dhania into my bag. Yesterday, he didn't even have that,' said Parminder, a sweet young newly married woman.

'What about the butcher? He is usually sitting outside his shop, snoring loudly, jerking awake as someone passes by. Some days, I have to poke him to wake him up and I don't like doing that. But this morning he was in his shop working away, measuring and chopping. I had to wait in line,' said Shahsultan Bibi, the oldest in the group, the one who knew the most about knitting and almost everything else.'

The leaders, Jawaharlal Nehru and others, were all saying that there would be no need for people to move. Everyone would stay where they were and each country would manage their majorities and their minorities. But the women knew what their men were saying. The Muslims, were heard mumbling that they couldn't live under Hindus and the Hindus and Sikhs were heard mumbling that the Muslims would convert them all to Islam. There was going to be trouble in the village; they just didn't know when.

Simrat went home and told Gurdev what the women were saying. Gurdev was initially dismissive, as he was to almost everything she said. But then he said that he knew that the population of the village was rising. New people had come in, and they were not anyone Gurdev knew. They were Muslims, trying to ensure that the village went to Pakistan because word was out that the British were using population distribution by religion to decide which way a village went.

Gurdev spoke to Simrat that night. 'Things are not good. We will leave for India soon. It may be a few days or it may be several weeks. Be ready, but don't say anything to those knitting friends of yours. When the wind changes, you don't know who's still your friend and who becomes your enemy.'

'Can I at least tell the Sikh women?' she asked. 'They will need to make preparations too, no?'

'I've tried to tell everyone I know, all the Sikhs. Like my parents, nobody is listening. Like my parents, everybody thinks they have friends. Don't say anything else. They will either say you're crazy to leave everything you've made here and try to dissuade you, or they will let the word out and someone will come and kill us while we sleep, set our house on fire or something. Stay quiet and get ready. That's all.'

Simrat knew not to argue but prepared her two sons, Ravi and Angad. They were ready, night and day, a few favourite things wrapped up in a piece of cloth tied to their waists. Schools were closed. Summer burnt through their brick roof and into the rooms below. And Simrat had a problem. Her stomach was cramping painfully after every meal. She got bloated with gas, forcing her to run out into the verandah frequently to avoid embarrassing trumpet-like farts in public. She didn't know what to do. She couldn't tell Gurdev. He was too preoccupied. She didn't know what to say anyway, and his response would be to take some home remedy – ajwain or churan or something. She couldn't go to the vaid because he would surely tell Gurdev or recommend some bitter ayurvedic herbs. She started watching closely to see what made her feel worse. The fresh buffalo milk, which she drank morning and evening and in her tea and in steaming rice pudding and in thick homemade yoghurt, was the first to go. Each time she had some, she felt the cramps rise, almost as the dairy product entered her stomach. Nobody noticed anything because she was the one who took care of everyone; no one ever served her or even knew what she ate. Next, she stopped the lentils and wheat till she was down to some steamed vegetables, boiled rice and a banana or two. But the cramping stopped and she was ready.

On 1 September, Gurdev announced that he was going to Lahore to check up on his parents. There had been telegrams from them, always saying they were fine, they had friends. But after 15 August, Independence Day for India – 14 August for Pakistan – when the lines had finally been drawn and Lahore had gone to Pakistan, it was time for all of them to leave. Simrat wondered why Gurdev wasn't taking care of his own family first, why he was going to his parents who had already refused his help. She was afraid but she didn't say anything, only listened to him talk.

'I must go. They can't stay there. No way that Lahore was going to be ours. I had told them that. But my father was sure. Chenab would be the line, he had said. Lahore would be ours he had said. Where? Lahore is gone. Now their lives are going to go. I have to get them out of that house and someplace safe. We'll take them with us on our way to Amritsar. I'll be back soon. If anything happens, take the boys to the Gurudwara and stay there. Wahe Guru will keep you safe.'

Gurdev had said he was going to be gone only two days but Simrat was worried. She was concerned about her health and she wondered what the Gurudwara could do to help them, but she went on and even went to the mill to see what was happening there. Two young men worked for Gurdev at the mill, both Muslim. Things seemed in order but as she was leaving, one of the men walked out with her. 'Don't stay too long, baji. Bad times are coming.'

'Khurshid, what do you know? Is there going to be an attack? Is something being planned? Please tell me, I have to protect my boys.'

'Baji, go away from here as soon as Gurdev is back.'

Gurdev returned on 3 September in the middle of the night. Simrat quietly let him in while the boys slept on cots out in the courtyard. They hadn't made up a cot for him so he went inside and slept in the sweltering room. In the early morning, there was a knock at the outside gate. Simrat knew Gurdev would sleep late because he looked exhausted when he had come in. She went to open the door without thinking but her sons stopped her. They asked her to find out who it was. A woman she didn't know called out to her from outside. She said Saba from the knitting group had sent her with some freshly made barfi. The thought of the milky barfi made her gag but she reached up to open the door anyway. Her younger son stopped her. He put his finger on his lips and pointed to the older one, who had run up to the roof to see who was there. He shook his head, indicating not to open the door. Simrat ran to the toilet, her belly exploding with fear, and sat there till the cramps passed. Just like Khurshid had said, they had thought Gurdev was out and come to get her.

For the next several days, till they finally left Sukho, Simrat slept with a big cleaver in her hand, the one Gurdev used to kill chickens. Gurdev wouldn't tell her when they would leave and she didn't want to ask. She didn't want to ask him anything. She had asked for his dirty clothes to wash and he had snapped at her: 'Is that all you can think of, my dirty clothes? Is there nothing else you can put your mind on? I will not change my clothes till we are safe. Now go find something else to do.'

On 7 September, after hearing news of a Sikh massacre in a town less than two hundred kilometres from theirs, Gurdev took the boys out into town to collect his property papers. When they came back, Simrat heard wailing outside the door. Both her boys stood on the doorstep, refusing to enter. Tears, snot and dirt covered their little faces. Both boys held the tops of their heads as if they could hide what wasn't there – their long hair. Simrat looked at Gurdev, who shrugged and pursed his lips. She knew he had thought of this while they were out. Not wearing long hair under patkas would keep the boys safer, she knew. She said nothing. Simrat's own hair was coarse and curly. It grew sideways instead of down. She had an unruly mop forced into a thick braid, not the long, graceful plait that moved with her hips that she dreamt about. That's why she liked her parandis. They made her feel like she had a long plait. Simrat didn't mind that Gurdev had cut the boys' hair. She believed in many things that the Sikh religion preached, but this not-cutting-hair part she didn't understand. Her boys' hair smelt in the summer and weekly washday was the most unwelcome day. Gurdev didn't help so Simrat had to chase, catch, hold, wash and later comb – the most unpleasant task. She had to follow all this activity with aloo paranthas. She smiled and hugged both the wailing boys, wiping their dirty faces with the end of her dupatta.

Simrat looked around at her home; she went and peeked into all the corners. She swept and mopped continuously. She didn't want to leave a dirty house. She touched her frugal belongings, her red and gold wedding clothes, her three silk suits and dupattas with resham embroidery, her grandmother's phulkari. She stroked the fabric, the silken strands as they wound one way then the other. She touched the silk to her face and kissed it gently. Then she lay it back down in her own steel trunk, the one they would not take with them. He had already made that clear. She could not understand why they were taking his trunk and not hers. Why couldn't they take her things, her hair parandas and her wedding bangles, her jangling kaliras that hung off the bangles, all plastic and cheap metal – but they meant something to her. She liked her cooking utensils, well-worn and clean, her big brass flat dish that she used to knead flour in, the cast iron kadai that she fried pakoras in – why did she have to leave all this behind? But she didn't dare ask Gurdev anything. Instead, she walked about stroking everything, touching the cool metal with the back of her hand, making sure there wasn't a speck of black on the bottom. After every meal, she scrubbed everything with ashes from the stove. She did this every day for five days and on the sixth day, Gurdev announced in the morning, after breakfast, that they were leaving – that day.

On 12 September 1947, Simrat and her family packed up the bullock cart with nothing but one trunk and the few precious things everyone strapped on to their bellies. As planned, it was Gurdev's trunk that they took with them, with two extra sets of clothing each and a few photos and documents that Gurdev had decided on. Simrat had put in an old bed sheet, to be ripped into strips and used during her period, but only after explaining to Gurdev that it was essential. Gurdev had earlier taken the silver trunk away and had the whole thing painted black, covering his name and his father's name, making sure that there was nothing indicating they were Sikhs except the turban on his head. That too he knew how to turn into a Pashtun turban by turning the Sikh one sideways in an emergency but also tying a proper one if needed.

Simrat kneaded flour in her brass dish for the last time. She used up the last of her ghee, gur and flour and made as many rotis as she could. She wrapped them up in muslin cloth, the one she used to make thick buffalo cheese, and wrapped them again in a cloth flour sack. Then she packed up the vegetables – capsicum, carrots and cauliflower, which she had been drying in the sun to keep from spoiling, along with some boiled rice. Both packages, along with four empty steel glasses, four spoons and two sharp knives, she put into a satchel that she slung across her shoulder. Once she left her home, exited from the front door, she stopped thinking and followed. She saw nothing but Gurdev's broad back and the tops of her two boys' heads, their short hair still prickly. Both boys wore salwar kameez in the village style, like their father. Simrat's eyes didn't waver from these three to look at anything that went on around her. She had no time to be scared, no will to look at others around her, no empathy to spare.

3

GURDEV RETURNED FROM LAHORE TO SUKHO SHAKEN, disoriented and wobbly. Simrat had asked him if everything was okay and all he could say was that they wouldn't leave – his parents. He couldn't convince them to come to India with them or even to move out of their house. How could he tell her what he had seen, what he had done. How could he tell her that his parents were dead – burnt alive in their mansion? How could he tell her what he had done to their murderers? She would never agree to come with him to the other side; she wouldn't even want to be with him, he was sure. But she was preoccupied herself and didn't ask any more questions. She couldn't see that he was blanketed by a quiet rage, one that had turned him into a stealthy, heartless murderer. Gurdev was a man with a temper, he knew that, and he was a man who bore grudges, carried them around on his turbaned head till they either slipped off without his knowledge or he finally shrugged them off, usually because the person he held a grudge against was dead. This time he left the grudge behind but brought back a large measure of guilt that slumped his shoulders as he tried to straighten them with justifications. He knew he would have to go back someday, to relive that fiery night.

In the meantime, the same neighbour-kill-neighbour disease had spread from large cities into the countryside. The Muslim League sent runners, young men who went from village to village spreading news that Sikhs were arming themselves and would soon raze Muslim villages to the ground – all Mussalmans had to be prepared: take first action or die. At the same time, Sikhs were gathering together and planning their defence. Recently, there was news of two Muslim butchers Sadiq and Taj, who had dressed up as Nihang Sikhs, with fake beards and moustaches, deep blue clothing and long spears and killed a prominent Muslim landowner. They were caught and when the fake beards, moustaches and clothing were found, they confessed. If they hadn't been caught, Sikhs would have been killed across the district indiscriminately.

Gurdev and his family lived in the village of Sukho, over two hundred and fifty kilometres from Lahore. They lived in a brick house on a narrow road outside the village. Gurdev had built a walled compound, not different from other homes in the village. His buffalo, Ruby, lived in the compound and so did his chickens. People knew each other, they trusted each other but still no one left their animals outside their house. That was because several years ago, Sumer Singh's buffalo was stolen. She had begun vomiting after a visit to the local pond. Sumer had tied her outside the front door while he went to get the hakim. When he came back, the buffalo was gone. She wasn't in the village either. No one had seen her. A stranger had walked past the front of his house, untied the buffalo and walked off. The front door had been open while Sumer's wife scrubbed the grassy vomit off the dirt floor.

Simrat used an area of the compound for washing clothes and utensils, and during the summer, the family slept outside on narrow wood and jute manjas covered with cotton dhurries. The house was secure, only one entrance, and the walls were high but not high enough to prevent someone from throwing over a burning rag or a crude bomb, a common occurrence but more common was what happened to Simrat while Gurdev was sleeping after his return from Lahore. He had come back late in the night, quietly slipping into bed inside while the rest of the family slept on cots outside. His elder son, Angad, had told him the whole story.

As Simrat sat milking the buffalo early in the morning and the boys fed the chickens, there was a knock on the door. She got up to open the door, not suspecting anything. But Gurdev had taught his boys well. Angad ran up to the roof to see who was at the door – there was no other way to tell without opening the door. Ravi ran to his mother and pulled at her dupatta with a finger on his young lips. He pointed to Angad, hiding behind the water tank on the roof, looking around. Angad shook his head at his mother and brother – don't open the door. He slowly came back down the stairs and indicated to his family to come inside.

'There is only a woman at the door, but I saw two men hiding behind a tree, Biji. Papaji told us about this. He said not to open the door unless we checked. The woman will make you open the door, then the men will attack.'

When Gurdev found out what had happened, he gave himself a few more days to take care of his business and buy train tickets. The thing was, there was never a good time to leave. He preached to everyone to go, but it was difficult for him too. He hoped that as more time passed after the lines being drawn, the violence would die down and people would come to their senses. But he knew that was not the case. He had lost his senses and all around him were senseless men like him, crazed with fear, hatred and insecurities that seemed insurmountable. And it was men, only men. The women were silent amid the violence. They remained hidden.

On 7 September, there was news of over a hundred Sikh men, women and children being massacred in the nearby village of Vanike Tarar, only two hundred kilometres from Sukho. Gurdev found out that the killings were carried out under orders of the local sub-inspector, a Muslim.

On 12 September, the family finally began its journey, making their way first from Sukho to Rawalpindi, fifty-one kilometres apart, and then on the longer stretch, from Rawalpindi to Lahore. They rode in Gurdev's mill bullock cart from Sukho to Rawalpindi. He patted the bullock on its head as they got off, certain that the cart would vanish minutes after they entered the station. They waited for hours for a train that was scheduled to arrive at noon.

At 6.30 p.m., they boarded their train to Lahore. The train was filled with Hindu and Sikh refugees, over one hundred humans in a bogey meant for thirty-six. No one paid any attention to male-female proprieties. Most young-old courtesies were forgotten – if you could push and sidle, you got in. If not, you had to wait for the next train. Gurdev got his two boys and wife up on the train, physically pushing them in with his broad back, right into a large, soft mattress of humanity. He pushed the trunk in close to the floor; between trouser- and salwar-clad legs. He slid the trunk to the left, against the metal wall of the compartment, and pushed his two boys down on the two ends and Simrat in the middle. There was no time for words or directions. The noise in the compartment was voices, mostly Punjabi, shrill and high-pitched from fear. He watched as his family disappeared behind those standing up, the boys reaching their heads upward between buttocks to breathe. He caught one boy's eyes and pointed his finger up at the roof. He saw confusion in his son's eyes but ignored it and jumped off the train.

Gurdev joined a group of men on the roof of the train, keeping a close watch for attackers. Their train slowed down a few times during the four-hour journey but never stopped. It was the night train, a normally scheduled train, not one of the special refugee trains that had been organized by the government. The timings for those were a poorly kept secret – railway officials gave them to anyone who asked. He had paid for his family. But no one checked tickets. When they arrived in Lahore, they heard that the refugee trains going from Lahore to Amritsar were attacked several times by placing trees across the track, forcing the train to grind to a halt. Attackers boarded the trains with swords and spears, slashed and ripped through cloth, skin, bones and flesh, and sent what looked like a teetering pile of dirty laundry on its way to the dhobi ghat.

Gurdev was certain they couldn't take the train for the last stage of their journey, from Lahore to Amritsar. The only trains running that last part of their journey were Refugee Specials. People were still getting on those; Gurdev wondered if they knew what could happen, what was likely to happen. What drove such suicidal behaviour in people? They were willing to take such a chance with their lives when there was still so much to live for – or maybe they felt they had nothing to live for any more so it didn't matter. Gurdev had heard people, including his father, God rest his soul, say that they would rather be dead than leave their land, their homeland. He wondered if these same people held humans as dear to them as they did their land. Or maybe they were in that state of physical stupor – push them this way and they went, push them another way and they went.

As they approached Lahore station, he could see the throngs on the platform from the top of the train where he sat with a group of Sikhs, all with their backs against each other, eyes searching for attackers. He saw people clutching meagre belongings that they would hold to their chests as they were pushed on to the next Refugee Special and maybe survive the thirty-nine-kilometre journey to Amritsar.

The only alternative to the death trains was walking, but Gurdev wasn't sure if his young family could walk this last stretch. They would have to join a kafila, a foot brigade. But kafilas were also being attacked. Wells all along the road to Amritsar had been poisoned so drinking water was scarce. And trudging along slowly made them an even easier target. He worked out the odds and decided that they were better in the kafila. In a train, they were meat on its way to the grinder, no way out. In the kafila, they could hide from attackers in the bushes, he could fight back or they could get lost in the crowd. His children were old enough to walk, he decided. Especially if they were right in the front. He would lead them, he decided. He would lead everyone.

At Lahore station, Gurdev followed the crowd to where the kafila to Amritsar was assembling. They had to fight their way out of the station, pushing and elbowing people who were pushing the other way, trying to make sure they could get on the next train. He walked to the front of the multitudes assembled on the narrow dirt road that wound its way between Lahore and Amritsar, his black trunk on his turbaned head, his wife next to him, the two boys tied to her with her dupatta. They walked nearly two kilometres, passing thousands of villagers, some on bullock carts, others walking like them, some on horseback and a few on piggyback, to get to the front.

They sat down at the very front to wait for morning. At daybreak, there was a buzz in the air, an electric current that lifted everything and placed it up against the orange sky. Bullocks silhouetted against the light stood placidly, waiting to be hitched to their carts for yet another ride, tall men with turbans mounted proudly on their heads walked about purposefully, filling up water skins from water trucks that came around every few minutes, spilling on to the dry earth saturating the air with the sweet smell of wet mud. A few soldiers milled about on horseback, keeping an eye on the horizon.

As the sun rose up slowly from the edge of the horizon, Gurdev stood instinctively, startled by the sounds around him. The bullocks were snorting as they were hitched, children were crying, crows were cawing, there was a shifting of air, a stir that began from the ground and wound its way through the kafila and then back again, a soundless call to begin moving. Everyone was ready. Gurdev hauled the trunk on his head, Simrat tied the two children to her dupatta and they began walking, followed by miles and miles of humanity, all clutching their belongings, many things looted along the way or sold for food and water or simply thrown by the wayside, too heavy and cumbersome to carry – photo frames of dead elders, wedding ghagras and various knick-knacks littered the side of the road

Once they began walking, early in the morning, he realized there was no leading. There was a wave; if you caught it, you went. Some didn't. He saw old people sit down by the side of the road, waving their families goodbye. He saw young women carefully place their young babies, wrapped in swaddling, behind bushes – the choices were difficult, yet everyone was making them. At one point, Simrat picked up a baby left by the side of the road, swaddled in blankets, and held the child to her chest. The baby was silent, the mother wept silently. All around them, the kafila moved on, widening and then narrowing again. She looked at Gurdev, who shook his head. He heard the young woman say, 'Let it be Bibi, it's a girl. She has no life before her anyway.' Simrat placed the baby back down but sheltered by a bush.

The kafila went on for miles. Gurdev heard some skirmishes, screams, guttural cries of Allah Ho Akbar, but he didn't turn back and he didn't stop. He had guessed that the column would be attacked in the middle, not in the front and in the back – for people with the most to lose thought they could hide in the throng. The attackers knew that. The loot was always the best from the middle. The stragglers had nothing. The leaders had something to prove and would fight back. The middle was soft; they gave up everything so their lives would be spared. They didn't know that the attackers wanted to kill them more than they wanted their jewellery and their money. They soon found out and Gurdev heard the howls of the dying, the wails of the ones left alive, the sounds of scraping feet as the attackers dragged young women away.

But he did nothing. He kept going. It was the only way he could save himself and the people around him. After a whole day of marching, the kafila reached the border and mounted Indian soldiers began trotting alongside, providing a sense of comfort that Gurdev hadn't felt since the British had announced that they were partitioning India, back in June. What was it that his father had said about his homeland – that he would never leave it? As soon as they crossed the border into India, Gurdev felt he was home. He joined many others as they fell to the ground, kissing the dusty earth, their lips already dry and cracked, now filled with the dust of their new homeland.

Gurdev and his family reached Amritsar with the kafila at nightfall and followed a group of travellers to Khalsa College refugee transit centre. They hadn't eaten since the night before, when Simrat had given the last gur roti to her boys to share. The gates of the college were wide open, no signs or welcome banners, but Gurdev could sense the warmth and the welcome. They sat down on the ground in neat rows as volunteers brought plates made of peepul leaves and laid them down before each exhausted traveller. Daal, vegetables, pickles, raw onions and rotis called parshadas were brought around by men and boys as young as six or seven. As they ate, Gurdev looked around for familiar faces and listened to conversations around him. He looked at his family: Simrat looked grey like the clouds that were building up outside. His boys looked robust, farm grown, like the sturdy stalks of wheat they had grown up around. He smiled at them, a smile that didn't go further than his lips because his ears, his eyes and his mind were absorbing what he was hearing around him.

'Delhi is burning. Our people are killing the Mussalmans wherever they can find them.'

'Serves them right. Their kin didn't spare us.'

'Drive them all out. Send them to Pakistan like they've sent us to India.'

'The Mussalmans are all in refugee camps – in Purana Qila and Humayun's Tomb. Everyone, rich and poor, I'm hearing. And the Pakistani government is sending special trains for them.'

'They are killing us, we should kill them. Let's go to Delhi and join our friends.'

'The old Delhi Hindus and Sikhs are protecting some of them – have you heard?'

'Let's kill those traitors too.'

Gurdev listened to the conversation getting rowdier and violent as more people finished eating and stood up. He didn't join in. He didn't agree with them. There were a lot more Muslims in India than Sikhs and Hindus in Pakistan. They couldn't all be sent across the border. And what if some didn't want to go? Nehru and Gandhi had said that those who wanted to stay could but those who couldn't give up their attachment to the Muslim League and Jinnah should go.

The thought of killing and bloodshed made him physically ill. He stood up and gagged, holding his head in his hands. Slowly, he sat down again, head still in his hands, hanging into his lap. He felt Simrat's hand on his back. He looked up at her and stood up. 'We'll stay here for some time. Things are not good in Delhi at the moment,' he announced.

'But my brother is there. He'll take care of us.'

'I know he's there. All my money is there. We have to go, but I will decide when to go and who to stay with,' said Gurdev.

'I was also listening to the conversation around us. Nobody is coming for us. It's those Mussalmans they are after.'

'Simrat, there is unrest. We don't have a place to stay. The Muslims of Delhi have become refugees. I don't know where they'll put people like us – the real refugees. We are the ones who've lost everything, including our ability to hate, or do you hate them? Do you? Do you want us to go and do the same thing to them that they've done to us? I can't do that. But if I go to Delhi, I may not be able to stop myself.'

'We have a place to stay, Gurdev. With my brother. He'll welcome us,' said Simrat, ignoring the rest of Gurdev's tirade.

'We won't stay with your brother. He is a good for nothing, useless fellow. As it is he owes me my money – he'll want some of it as compensation for letting us stay with him – that's how he is. I need that money to rebuild our lives.'

'He's not like that. He won't keep your money. He's my real brother...'

'We'll go when I think it's time to go, not before that. Anyway, what is the difference? This refugee camp or another one in Delhi.'

'Why do we need to stay in refugee camps, Gurdev, when my brother's house is there for us? Why are you making us suffer like this if we don't need to? Only those who have no one on this side are staying in these camps. We have people. We have money. You said so yourself.'

Gurdev stayed silent. He knew Sujjat Singh. He hadn't known him long, but long enough to know that he was a man who lived on the edges of somebody else's life. He copied, stole, misrepresented that other person's life in order to create his own. He could not imagine moving in with Sujjat and Parveen. Simrat wanted to, but Gurdev knew what it would be like. The impoverished relatives from across the border – traumatized and scarred by everything they had seen. At first, they would be a spectacle for their friends. Everyone wanted to hear stories about the crossing. Then, they would put Simrat to work – the mutton recipes from back home that no one remembers, the pickles that only she knows how to make, the thickened milk desserts that take hours of standing and stirring – Gurdev could see it coming. Sujjat would interfere in everything he did, hoping to steal or copy something. He would want to be his business partner because he was not capable of doing anything himself. He knew they lived off rent from land that Parveen had inherited from her grandparents. Soon, they would ask Gurdev to pay rent, they would deduct from the amount they owed him.

Gurdev shook his head as Simrat looked on defiantly – the most defiant he had ever seen her but he said nothing more, turned around and walked away to join a group of men discussing how and when to leave Amritsar. Most, like Gurdev, didn't want to stay on and find work here, it was too close to the home they had left. The border didn't feel real enough till more distance had been put between them. Some talked about going further into Punjab, others about heading South but most wanted to go to Delhi, the place they knew they would find others like themselves.

Gurdev and his family stayed in Amritsar for six weeks, right there in the Khalsa College building. The college had been established in the late 1800s by a group of Sikhs assisted by the Sikh maharajahs of the time. It was an ornate structure designed by Bhai Ram Singh, a celebrated architect in pre-Partition Punjab, with red minarets and palanquins lining the length of the structure. Gurdev's father had studied there and he had seen it before on a visit to Amritsar as a child. He had come with his parents to the Golden Temple. His eyes dimmed at the thought of his parents. He should have insisted. He should have physically lifted the both of them and brought them away from Lahore.

Their small group got a corner of a verandah and four rough blankets. They ate food cooked and served langar style in the college canteen, like when they had arrived. There were common bathrooms being used by hundreds more than they were meant for. Simrat managed to get one bucket of hot water for the four of them. They took turns bathing, two per day, half a bucket per person.

Every day, dozens more like them were arriving, all with stories, all filled with dread and visions of gore, all holding on to what little they had. One afternoon, Gurdev stepped away to talk to some people about what was going on in Delhi. Simrat was working in the kitchen, helping cook food for the next langar. Gurdev had told his two boys to sit on the metal trunk and not move, for anything. Both boys sat on the metal trunk, playing '*akar bakar bambe bo*' with their fingers until they grew weary of the repetitive game. Then Ravi stood up, clutching his crotch.

'It's coming. I am going.'

Angad held his arm. 'No. Papaji told us not to move till he got back.' Then he stood up also clutching his crotch. 'Mine is also coming.'

'Let's both go. We'll run to the toilet and run back. We won't even wash our hands. Don't tell Biji.' The two young boys left their post and ran. When they ran back, they found the lock on the trunk broken but placed back in the latch. Angad gingerly took the lock out and opened the trunk. It had been rifled through; all the clothes were upside down. He quietly shut it. He didn't know what had been inside so he couldn't tell what was missing.

Gurdev returned a short while later to find the two boys sitting on the trunk, tears streaming down both faces, noses red, short gushes of air going in and out of both sets of nostrils, almost in harmony. He looked around to see if anyone was watching. He turned to the two boys, his big face soft, his arms outstretched. He pulled both boys to him and hugged them till their sobs softened.

'What happened, boys? Did someone hurt you?'

Both boys began crying again, this time louder, for greater effect, hoping their mother would hear them and come and rescue them. 'I—I … had to go … and he also had to go … so we went.' Angad held up the broken lock. Gurdev looked at it, only slightly perturbed, and hugged the boys again.

'Don't worry boys. We have two things worth stealing and I carry them with me. Now, let's see what the thief did manage to take in the time you ran to the bathroom and back. And go there and wash your hands now.'

Gurdev smiled as he searched through the trunk. There was nothing there but old clothes for the family, some documents and two photographs in frames. One was a photograph of his parents and the other of Simrat's parents. He felt himself stumble as he realized that both photographs were gone. He held the sides of the open trunk to steady himself, the edges wedging into the palm of his hand. They were gone and now the one piece of them he had kept was also gone. He pressed his hand on the sides of his legs, the upper part that was always covered by his kurta. The bulges were there, two extra pockets that Simrat had sewn into his salwar pants before he had gone to Delhi, what now seemed like a lifetime ago. Now they held his mother's last gift to him. He couldn't leave that anywhere, or even touch it. People these days could smell money on your fingers.

Gurdev closed the trunk and went out to buy another lock. It was time to go to Delhi and restart their lives. He couldn't help wondering when he could go back to Lahore. He had no longing for his village, but he wanted to see his childhood home again, a burnt-down shell as it probably was now and would probably remain, for who had the money to rebuild in these times?

4

GURDEV, SIMRAT, RAVI AND ANGAD WENT FROM Amritsar to Delhi by train. They had not seen Amritsar Junction station before because they had walked from Lahore to Amritsar. The station was more a dharamshala than a station where people come and go. Here people stayed. They either had nowhere to go or were so disturbed by everything they had seen that they had forgotten what was to happen next. There were also some who were waiting for a train and had managed to get to the right platform by walking over sleeping bundles clinging to rolled up bags with metal trunks wedged between their legs. Gurdev and his family were among this group as they walked up the footbridge that ran over the tracks and down the other side to platform number four, where the Delhi train was due to arrive.

Platform one saw all the trains coming in from Lahore, some untouched, but many carrying bodies of people who had been killed on the way. Gurdev rushed his family to the other side as one such train chugged in but sped through the station instead of slowing down.

Their train arrived from Delhi one hour late. Passengers got off slowly, gathering their luggage and their matkas of water. Coolies ran around with big canvas hold-alls and steel trunks on their heads, hoping to come back a second time when passengers for Delhi boarded. After two more hours of waiting while the train was shunted away for cleaning, it was finally time to board. They were in the three-tier bogey, third class. People pushed their way in, grabbing any seat they could, putting numerous cloth-tied bundles wherever they could. Gurdev was no slacker when it came to pushing and neither were his boys. It was an essential skill to master to live in India, to push and settle and adjust and shove. Simrat couldn't do it. She would rather stand in a corner all night than fight with anyone for a place to rest her tired body. Gurdev managed to grab four sleepers, two middle berths and two upper berths. He put their trunk on one upper berth. He placed one boy on the second upper berth and the other on a middle berth and sat down himself, shoulders hunched, legs dangling, on the other middle berth. Simrat looked at them from the entrance of the cabin, quiet, pale, eyes ringed with darkness but a smile on her lips. Eventually, they had to fold the two middle berths and sit on the lower berth till everybody ate their dinner and only when the lower berth people, two Sikh men, decided to sleep could they unfold the middle berths and sleep too.

Gurdev settled the two boys on the upper berths, hardwood slats with nothing but a bunched-up shirt to use as a pillow. He unfolded one middle berth for Simrat and helped her up. She lay down on her side, back rounded, head tucked into herself, and closed her eyes. Gurdev lowered his own bunk and climbed into it. But as he removed his turban and placed it gently next to him and lay down on the hard surface, he saw the man in the berth below him on the opposite side looking up at him. He was an older man, about fifty-five, a grey soft turban on his head, mussed but still distinguished. His beard and moustache entirely grey, no signs of faded black dye that many have their wives touch up when they dye their own hair. His beard was rolled up tight under his chin, secured by a small bobby pin. The other man was younger, no more than forty. He wore a stiff turban and his beard was neatly wrapped in a net, an old-fashioned look that took longer to groom. Sikhs in the army usually wore it this way. Gurdev peered down below at the younger man, wondering if he was also looking his way.

'Where are you coming from, Puttar? Punjab or the North West Frontier Provinces? Your accent sounds like you are from Lahore,' asked the older man.

'Prahji, I was born in Lahore as you rightly guessed, but I've been living in Sukho for the last many years. We came from Sukho, but it has been some time we've been in Amritsar now.'

'So you don't know what has been happening in West Punjab, I suppose?'

Gurdev pointed his chin at his wife and put a finger on his lips. Her parents were still there, also not ready to move. He gestured for them to accompany him to the end of the train.

The three men got up from their berths. Gurdev whispered an 'I'll be right back' in the general direction of his family and followed the men towards the lavatory end of the train.

'Prahji, the Mussalmans have been taking away our women, the older ones they kill, the younger ones they keep and God knows what they do with them and for how long.

They are taking married women and single women, sparing only young girls less than twelve. How do you take revenge for this, Puttar, how? We will get them, eventually, but till then what?' said the younger man.

'So, what have our people been doing? They had to do something. Many in my village didn't want to leave even,' said Gurdev.

'Everyone is leaving now. If they don't leave, they are beheaded ... or worse. Men are poisoning their wives and daughters, their own ... wives so that they don't fall into the hands of those monsters. Women are willingly taking the poison or jumping into wells...' The older man stopped for a minute and looked up at the layers of paint on the ceiling, his eyes watery, slightly opaque with a rapidly spreading cataract. My wife died some years ago but my brother's wife...' He pointed his chin at the other man who had bent down to look out of the barred open window at the dark countryside racing off by the side of the train.

'She killed herself along with four other women, including his teenaged daughter. They cooked rat poison into their rotis and ate them. She left him a note. Save yourself, it said.' At this the other man turned around, his eyes filled to the brim, but not a drip on to his perfectly netted beard. 'I would have taken care of them. Who told her to take matters into her own hands? She never did before. She couldn't eat a third roti without asking me first but this she could do.' He turned towards the open window again.

Gurdev put his hand on both men's shoulders but said nothing. What could he say? That old dread returned for a minute but then he realized that everyone was safe. Almost everyone.

Gurdev learnt that the younger man's name was Colonel Hardit Singh and the older one was Harjit Singh. Both men lived in the village of Harial, a mere fifteen kilometres from Sukho. Gurdev had been there. Many of his customers came from that village and other surrounding villages. They told him that many people from their region had already gone to Delhi and were staying in Kingsway Camp. That is where they should all go. Gurdev agreed.

Quietly, the three men made their way back to their berths, removed their turbans and set them down by their heads, their long hair covered by patkas. They lay down. Gurdev's eyes moved sideways to where Simrat lay asleep, her rounded back towards him.

They arrived at Delhi Junction mid-morning. The October sun was rising, warm but not blistering, poking its elongated fingers into the compartment, raising dust particles that swam this way and that. Gurdev got the boys down and ready. Simrat had already been up for some time. She sat next to Harjit Singh on the lower berth, chatting amiably. He overheard something about langar and the communal kitchen but didn't get involved. He was more concerned about his money. He patted his waist instinctively but this was not the money he needed now. He needed his rupees back from the people he had left them with.

Kingsway Camp was an army barracks converted into a refugee camp by the Government of India. Gandhi had been begging people to stay where they were till the end. Neither Nehru nor Jinnah had expected this mass movement of people in such a short period of time. Neither side was prepared. The Kingsway Camp was somewhat organized and clean. Word was that supplies intended for the Purana

Qila and Humayun's Tomb camps, where the Muslims were housed, were all being rerouted to Kingsway.

Gurdev and his family followed Colonel Hardit Singh and Harjit Singh out of the station. None of them had much luggage, but that didn't help them move between the people who were still collecting their various cloth-wrapped potlis and clay pots of water. Nothing could be left behind. The Colonel got one rickshaw, then grabbed hold of another one from the back, keeping the man from pedalling away. Gurdev got one more. He put Simrat and one boy in one and got into the other with his metal trunk and the younger boy. The Colonel shouted instructions. The camp was eight kilometres away. The rickshaw puller was right to try to pull away. But almost everyone who came off the trains was going to the camps. Some were going to the government centre for ration cards because that is what the notices in the newspapers had been announcing. Everyone who was leaving India or Pakistan had to submit their ration card at the centre and everyone coming into Delhi had to get a new one – to ensure an uninterrupted supply of rations. Simrat had cut out the notice from a newspaper, but Gurdev had laughed.

'These people … the colonists have gone but the colonial bureaucracy lives on. People's lives are ending, their entire worth stamped out of existence and these people are worried about ration cards. Don't worry, Simrat. I'll make sure that you and the children never go hungry. The black market is alive and well.'

Simrat had coughed and swallowed. She was never a rule breaker. 'The black market – the grain is all spoilt there is red brick in the chilli powder, the oil is stale. Everything is second rate – don't you read the papers, the government warnings?' she said.

'It's the government shops that supply to the black marketers, didn't you know? That's the whole racket. This whole ration-card business was a way for the British to keep track of us, make sure we don't eat too much, get too strong to fight, you know.'

Simrat went red in the face. She had so diligently taken her ration card each time and gone to the government-certified ration shops only. She had got her allocated quantities of rice, daals, atta, etc. and never questioned where Gurdev found more when they had guests or ran short.

At the camp, Gurdev stood in line with the two men from Harial, his new friends. They looked much better in their western-style pants and shirts than he did in his bedraggled Pathan suit that Simrat had washed in Amritsar. It was the sort of fabric that always looked grimy so it wouldn't show the dirt from the oil press and the fields. Gurdev's beard was scraggly, unkempt, bound neither by a hairpin nor the neat net that held the Colonel's face together. It hung long, almost to his chest, black and lightly spotted with bits of silver. His face was dark from walking in the sun from Lahore to Amritsar, burnt the way Indian skin burns, not turning red and blistery but dark, thick and blotchy. His dry lips had recovered but were covered by his whiskers, untamed and untrimmed. His turban sat on his head as if by compulsion, soft and untidy, barely keeping his unruly hair in. Like his father had said, he looked like a peasant.

They got to the desk at the end of the line, the two brothers first. They spoke softly to the man sitting at the metal desk with a large hand-drawn map of the camp laid out before him. Gurdev peered over their shoulders looking for spots that were available, proximity to the bathrooms, proximity to the exits, etc. The brothers were given a tiny space to share in a distant barrack. The man had looked at their neat appearance and decided they wouldn't be there long. Gurdev's studied shabbiness earned him a larger barrack; still only one room, but they could divide it into a space for the children and for the adults. The man in charge didn't know that they wouldn't be there even as long as Hardit and Harjit.

Next, they went into a tent to collect quilts, pots and pans, and rations. The space was well organized, army style, with a section for each item. Each family member got their own allotment and had to sign their name or put a thumb stamp in a register. Gurdev's mouth was a straight line, his forehead was creased like crumpled brown paper, his nose flattened with each exhalation. They didn't need to go through all this, he knew, as he patted his middle instinctively, but he also knew that this was his destiny, the life he had chosen. His wife and sons knew nothing about his wealthy past and what that kind of money could do for them. His boys knew nothing of indoor plumbing and English toilets and an education in London. They knew nothing but the simple life of the village, their school and some English classics that he had introduced them to.

The family bid farewell to Harjit and the Colonel. The brothers were off to a remote corner of the camp, the walk to the common toilets at least ten minutes. Their own space was dirty. There were squatters in it, who began gathering up their things as soon as they saw Gurdev with his trunk on his head. There were six people lying about on dirty blankets, nothing like the quilts and sheets that Gurdev and his family had received a few minutes ago. They had been given a smaller space close to Hardit and Harjit's, but they were a family of sixteen people from the North West Frontier Provinces, where most people were Muslim – there were some Hindus and Sikhs and almost all had come across. Their language was Pashto, not Punjabi, as much as Gurdev could tell. People who spoke Punjabi were more accepted by the locals of Delhi, at least initially. Later, when Gurdev moved out of the camp, he realized that the people of Delhi wanted refugees from Pakistan to stay in refugee camps forever. They didn't want them amid themselves, co-mingling, children marrying each other and wives attending kitty parties. The refugees were the refugees and would remain so for generations. It was at times like this that Gurdev felt that sharp pain in the middle of his chest – he was an outsider, like the Pashtus – it was only a matter of degrees.

Gurdev stared at the bedraggled family as they shuffled out from the barrack and down the courtyard, their belongings dragging in the dust behind them, children scampering to keep up with the adults while Simrat began cleaning. Gurdev stood there for a few minutes then walked briskly behind the squatter family. He turned into a row of barracks that looked well settled, with partitions and privacy curtains already in place. Some even had nameplates nailed to their sections. Most were handmade but many looked old and worn, carried over from the homes they had hung outside, homes that had to be abandoned. He saw wooden charpoys covered with colourful mattresses in one of the barracks. There were hooks on the walls for clothing and overturned wooden crates covered with cushions for seating. He peered in to see if anyone was home, spoke to a double-chinned, middle-aged woman and went off outside the camp, walking purposefully in the direction she had pointed.

Simrat had swept and mopped, dusted and scrubbed till you could see the old marble-chip floor, a sound base that covered most Indian floors. But all she had was the quilts and sheets that had been allotted to them earlier that day. She kept them piled up on the trunk and sat on top wondering what to do. That's where Gurdev found her when he returned, sitting on top of a high pile, legs dangling a least a foot off the ground, a smile on her face like she had when she had accomplished something important.

Gurdev walked in carrying two charpoys, one under each arm, followed by two men, one carrying two more charpoys and one carrying four rolled-up cotton mattresses and a pile of cotton fabric on his head. Simrat jumped off her perch and grabbed one of the charpoys from Gurdev flipping it to its side. She took one of the mattresses from the man and laid it down flat. She fluttered one of the coarse white sheets in the air and spread it over the mattress that smelt like fresh cotton and looked like an English garden. She placed the new quilt on top of the sheet and one bed was ready. She pulled two charpoys close together on one side of the room and two close together on the other side.

With the beds made, and the trunk pushed safely under the bed, Simrat lay down in a foetal position like she had in the train. It was a protective stance, a way to console her body, to hold it like one holds a crying baby. Gurdev turned away. He couldn't ask. He had much to do before he would ask.

5

THEY SETTLED IN – GURDEV, HIS TWO YOUNG BOYS, AND Simrat – at the refugee camp, amid thousands of others like them, people of all types, all clinging to the little they had brought with them, trying to find a way out, clamouring for the food that was available, squabbling over the flap of one tent swinging over the neighbour's tent. The screams of children being beaten by their mothers, wives by their husbands rent the air night after night.

Simrat, despite the cramping in her stomach, took charge. She organized a communal kitchen, where a group of families put together their rations and made a cooking group, a cleaning group and a shopping group. At first it was only a few but soon others realized that maintaining a separate kitchen was not easy. A chulha, along with everything else in the barrack, took up so much space, and the smoke and smell got into everything. Women began coming to her for things – from how to dispose of sanitary napkins to what to use as sanitary napkin, from when to have a bath and when to wash their long hair to treatments for coughs and colds. She

52

also tried to teach the frontier and farmer women how to stay clean. Many had never used toilets. One woman told her that they went in the fields to defecate before the men woke up, and the men woke up early. They had to be back in the house or they were raped in the fields. They couldn't tell anyone. They had to go on with their day.

Simrat had also grown up in the village. She had also gone for her morning business to the fields when she was young. She went with her mother and a few more women. They had their spot, not far from the tree but not too close because the men ate their lunch under it. They covered up their business with dirt using the same steel utensil they carried water in to wash. She sat right next to her mother at first but as she got older, she sat not too far away but facing the other direction. Her mother had also told her to never eat or drink anything outside the house. Nobody wanted unpredictable bowel movements – there was nowhere to go. Simrat and her relatives didn't have to go before the men because men in their village had their own area. There were a few families that kept black pigs and let them run around the fields to clean the mess. It was only after she met Gurdev that Simrat learnt about toilets that could be made inside the house. She found it dirty at first, to have all that her body rejected so close to where they were cooking and washing. But Gurdev wouldn't have it any other way. There was no sewage system in the village when Gurdev built his house, only open drainage. So, he built a small toilet in the corner of the plot closest to the road, a ceramic bowl shaped like a rajma with a water-filled hole on one end. There were two white bricks on either side of the bowl to put your feet on. The hole in the ground connected to the drain outside with a pipe that Gurdev had buried below the surface. During monsoons, the water sometimes came backwards but most of the time, throwing a few mugs of water into the hole took care of things.

Simrat knew that Gurdev had come from Lahore. She also knew he was educated, much more than her, like those English people, actually. She had heard him talking on the phone in the post office once. He sounded like them. He spoke to her in Punjabi, city version but now after so many years in the village, he had learnt the Gujarkhani dialect. He read English books to the boys but not how he was talking on the phone. He talked like they talk, like an Indian. She had married a complicated man. He had so many ways to speak, which he didn't do much imagine the number of thoughts he had.

Simrat didn't like to think too much. Too much thinking made her worry and she had learnt that with Gurdev, she didn't have to worry. So, she didn't think while she doubled over every now and then, face plain and expressionless but eyes narrowed with pain, then straightened up, smiled a short smile at whoever was around and carried on with her work – washing clothes, cooking in the communal kitchen, or sweeping and swapping their space. And she didn't think while she ran to the bathroom, more and more frequently. She didn't think when she ate her meagre diet – no milk, no lentils and no wheat. Now, even some vegetables like, cabbage and cauliflower were affecting her. They were cooking rice in the community kitchen every day. Most days, she ate rice and potatoes but she didn't think; she went on and waited for Gurdev to worry. Colonel Hardit worried, though. He was there with Simrat in the kitchen and when she cleaned, he helped get everything out of the way. He didn't let her lift heavy things and washed the biggest utensils himself. But he was one of many and Simrat paid little mind to him.

Meanwhile, more and more people were coming to Kingsway every day. The government was setting up tents in the space outside the barracks, rows of tents, almost one on top of the other. The number of toilets remained the same. Water was scarce, still only coming for two hours in the morning. The common toilets were far away and Simrat often had to stop along the way, holding her stomach, then standing still to take deep breaths and then walking the rest of the way. But now, she had to wait because they were always full. She had to say something to Gurdev, but he was always out. He would come back and mumble things to her, but she was tired by then. She felt she couldn't understand anything that was even a little more complex than what she already knew – her mind was fuzzy, her eyes always droopy.

6

WHILE SIMRAT WAITED FOR GURDEV TO START worrying about her, he ran about doing what was more important for him. He went to collect the money he had left with people just a few months earlier. Harnam Singh, Sujjat Singh and Satnam Singh. Harnam Singh, his first cousin, gave the money right back, still wrapped in the same white handkerchief that Gurdev had given him. It didn't look like he had even untied the knot. Gurdev thanked him, hugged him and was on his way to his wife's brother's house. Once he got there, he waited under a tree till he saw Sujjat come back on a rickshaw and enter the house.

Sujjat Singh's wife, Parveen, came to the door when Gurdev rang the bell. She opened the wood door but kept the screen door closed. 'He's not at home right now, Gurdev Paaji. Maybe you should come back another time.'

'Bhabiji, I saw him come in five minutes ago. I wanted to give him time to wash his hands and face before he brought me my money. Can you please call him? I don't mind, I'll stand outside and wait.'

Parveen shut the wood door and bolted it. Gurdev heard her footsteps recede, and it was only a whole five minutes later that he heard another set of shuffling steps, Sujjat's favoured gait, and the door unlocking.

'Gurdev Prahji. Come inside, why are you standing outside?'

'Sujjat, I am here to collect my money. I've found a plot. I'm going to buy it, but I need my money.'

'But Prahji, you will get money from the Rehabilitation Commission. You might even get a shop for your mill, plus a house. Why don't you wait for that? Better no? And it won't even cost you anything.'

'Sujjat, I WANT MY MONEY. That's it. No more discussion.'

Parveen came out from the back room, her long braid swung to the front. 'Prahji, I had told you then only, don't leave your money with us. Now, we don't have it.'

'Where is it? Sujjat, what did you do with my money?' Gurdev looked at Sujjat's eyes darting from him to his wife and then down to his rubber-chappal-clad feet. How dirty his feet were, he noticed, and he lived in a nice house, not in a refugee camp where they shared a bathing space with dozens of people, bathing every other day if they could. He knew Sujjat was lying, and he had married a woman who lied even better than him. He grabbed the man by his shirt collar while Parveen tugged at his arm to let him go. He was not about to till he got his money. He lifted the man off the floor, his chappals falling off his feet. 'Now, go and get my money before I show you everything I had to learn to make it here.

'Prahji, we had not heard from you in so many weeks. And so many stories were coming in, we thought, for sure.

Parveen you – you said … give me two days, Prahji. I'll get your money.'

Sujjat looked at his wife who flung her braid back, swinging it long and hard, and stomped out.

Gurdev knew that if he left, he would never get his money back. It was here, he knew. Maybe not in the same handkerchief that he had left it in, but it was here. He sat down on the velveteen sofa and put his feet up on the smoked glass-top coffee table.

'I'll wait here till you get my money. Remember where I'm coming from, Sujjat. I have lost everything. I know how to deal with people like you. Now, go and get me my money.'

Sujjat left, rubber chappals flapping. He was gone almost thirty minutes. Gurdev put his head back and closed his eyes. Once he got all the money, he would go to an estate agent. He wanted a plot not in the first lane but in the second. The front plots were more expensive. He could picture his house – like his parents' house in Lahore … He opened his eyes, then closed them again. For a moment, he had felt like the whole thing had been a dream, the house on fire, the cement walls untouched but the wood window and door frames on fire, the curtains inside curling up and transforming into feathery embers, the outer brick walls turning black from the heat within but still standing. The fire had remained inside; he hadn't waited for it to shatter the glass windows and envelop the house from the outside – neither had they, the arsonists, the murderers. They had left and so had he.

Gurdev heard the flapping shuffle of the chappals moving towards him and opened his eyes. He kept his head propped on the backrest. Sujjat came in and handed him a bundle of notes, clumsily assembled, not in order of denomination, a jumble gathered up from various hiding places. Gurdev organized the bills and counted them. There were a few rupees missing but he wrapped up the neater bundle in a clean handkerchief he always carried and tucked it into his secret pocket, close to his mother's pouch. He never left that silk pouch anywhere. They had barely a curtain to contain their modesty, and he knew how well a lock on the trunk held.

His next stop was his friend Satnam Singh's home. It was a large, white-washed house with a big green lawn: cars of all manners stood in the gravel driveway and men of all colours flitted in and out of the arched doorway. People were still leaving India, still looking for ways to ship their cars and containers, filled with colonial furniture, back home. Gurdev found Satnam at the front of his house, the office, busily writing details of a shipment in a large brown-paper-covered register. To turn the page, he had to first place four carbon papers between four sheets of paper and then continue his rapid scribbling. Satnam was a burly man. You wouldn't know that he was short unless you knew him because he rarely stood up. He had a curly, unruly beard and an unkempt moustache that he placed his fingers on every now and then – not to twirl; more to make sure it was still there. Gurdev had known him as a child, a portly boy with a handkerchief over his tied-up long hair, always waddling at the end of the line but always the first one out for lunch. His mother sent hot tiffin every day, a houseboy brought it to school in a tall tiffin carrier – multiple layers of mutton and paneer and paranthas. Gurdev gave his own cold lunch to the chaprasi and ate as much of Satnam's as he could.

'You'll thank me later,' he would say when Satnam protested as he tried to fish out a morsel before Gurdev finished it all.

Satnam finally looked up from his register and got off his chair to hug his old friend. He reached Gurdev's chest.

'Still haven't grown any taller, have you?' Gurdev said. 'Looks like business is still brisk. Everyone making a run for it, huh?'

'Gurdev, my friend. I read about what's happening there and only think about you. Where are your parents? Did they come with you? I finally convinced my parents to come. They are staying with me till they manage something else.'

Gurdev shook his head. He couldn't say the words out loud, that his parents were dead. 'I've lost contact with them. I couldn't convince them to come with me. They said they would come when they were ready. You know how they are, Satnam.'

'Here is your money, my friend, kept safe and sound in my desk drawer. I lock it when I leave, even to go to the toilet, which itself is rare.'

Gurdev took the money, shook his friend's hand over the desk: the man had gone back to his seat as quickly as he had sprung up from it.

Gurdev had turned to leave when he heard Satnam call him back. 'This job will be over soon. Everyone has almost left now. I have found another job – with the government. I'll tell you more soon.'

Gurdev had met many property agents. Everyone in the camp knew one. People outside the camp wanted a percentage for referring one as if they, and not the agent, were going to find him a property. Satnam had introduced Gurdev to the property agent he was working with. The man knew of property that the government had released and property that could only be obtained through allocation from the Rehabilitation Commission. He took Gurdev to look at the released property, where he could pay cash and register it in his name. The agent's name was Mool Chand, an old Delhi resident; his family had lived in the city for six generations. He was sympathetic to refugees and knew his way around. He had managed many property swaps between wealthy Hindus of Lahore and wealthy Muslims of Delhi. Mool Chand wore a white turban above his clean-shaven, sun-darkened face. His turban was soft but nothing like a soft Sikh turban. His was more like a sun hat, wrapped round and large around his head, the rolls casting a shadow across most of his face, his gently sloping chin exposed but only when his head was at certain angles. Gurdev looked up at the October sun, still hot, still bearing down on his own exposed face – his turban covered his head sitting straight up and providing no shade – as they went from plot to plot in a cycle rickshaw. The rickshaw puller had offered to put up the screen but then even a light breeze pushed at it, pulling the rickshaw backwards as the thin man struggled to pull his large clients along. Gurdev had stopped him and put the screen back down. The rickshaw continued to move at the same pace but at least the puller's sinewy legs didn't look like stretched out rubber bands.

Gurdev didn't take long to decide. Options were limited. Land sharks were everywhere. Mool Chand told him that even in these difficult times, the latter would rather peel the skin off their bellies with their fingernails than offer a fair price.

'It isn't in them to not trap a rat that has slunk into their house to eat their crumbs, goes against their moral fibre,' Mool Chand continued in his colourful language.

'But we lost everything, we almost died. We are their kin – somehow, I'm sure,' protested Gurdev.

'Paaji, you are nothing. You are a refugee in their land, you will be nothing for generations, mark my words. Fifty years from now, your children will still be referred to as refugees, lacking class, crass, foreign and loud – all those things. You will work hard and make money. You will throw it in the faces of these genteel people, and all they will be able to say is – Punjabi refugees, what else can you expect? But we have no choice. We have to buy from the land sharks. Trying to buy from the government means paying bribes, which I know how to do, like I know how to use the toilet every day, but the trouble is that these days you don't know the terms. They look at the buyer and decide. Now, looking at you the bribe amount may be low but you never know. They may see something that is not visible to everyone else.' Mool Chand looked directly at Gurdev's mid-section and looked away.

The plot that Mool Chand had decided on for Gurdev was on Block Fifteen, a short walk from the main East Patel Nagar Road. It was a large plot, almost six hundred square metres; six times the size of plots being allotted to most refugees. Mool Chand was pleased with his discovery. It was a gem, away from the noise of the main road, two similarly large plots on either side. Neither had been sold and probably wouldn't for some time. Gurdev was ready. He didn't even think to ask Simrat. He had always made all the decisions and told her what he had done, sometimes not even that. He and Mool Chand rode to the land shark's office in another rickshaw. They pulled up to one of the other plots they had seen. They made their way into a tin shed with a metal desk surrounded by metal cupboards jammed into every corner. Business looked to be good. Roshan, the land shark, pulled out a cloth-covered binder, the land documents, an official drawing of the property perimeter, the measurements and current ownership. Mool Chand took out his reading glasses from a yellow plastic case he carried in a small leather satchel. He looked through everything.

'Where are the owners? Will they be present to sign or have they given someone their power of attorney?' he asked.

'The owners are here, don't worry. Once they know you have the money, they'll come and sign.'

'And how do we know that these owners are genuine and that you haven't sold the plot to anyone else. Let me tell you, I have daal-rice every day, and every day, I find at least one stone in the daal. This is after my wife cleans the daal, seed by seed. These are trusting people – they are not like us. They come from a land where houses have no outside walls and neighbours are like brothers. Can you look me in the eye and tell me that there is no elephant turning under that land, there is no herd of wild buffalo that'll come trampling over all that this poor man will build, that there will be no monkeys sitting on a tree next door destroying his peace, that there will be…'

As Mool Chand went on with his drama, Gurdev went behind one of the metal cupboards at the land shark's office. He carefully removed the handkerchiefs from his hidden pocket, tucking the thickest one back under his waistband. He counted out the money from all three handkerchiefs and placed it on the table.

'Here's the money. Now, get the owner.'

7

With Mool Chand's help, Gurdev got the property documents registered in his name. It took several days of standing in line, but he got it done. He had seen a painter painting road names on corner properties as he had roamed around the area with Mool Chand. With his property documents still in a cardboard folder clenched in his hand, he walked around looking for wet paint till he found the man. He dragged him to his new property and asked him to write 'Gurdev Singh' at the entrance, right on the low brick wall that the previous owners had built to mark the property.

The man looked at him, not perturbed a bit, and asked, 'Surname?'

'Write "Lahori", Gurdev told him, 'because that is where I am from.'

With the name written in white block letters, printed much better than the unreadable scribbles that the painter had left on wall after wall all around the neighbourhood, Gurdev felt solid ground beneath his large feet again.

'If you can print so well, why aren't you doing it everywhere? No one can find their way anywhere, thanks to you,' Gurdev said as he fished out a handful of coins from his pocket.

'You paid, Maharaj.' The man shrugged and walked off, to lead more people down roads they didn't want to go.

In all the four days that Gurdev was waiting in line to register his plot with the municipal authorities, each night he went home to Kingsway Camp and sat with his wife and children, talking about their day but not saying anything about his. Simrat didn't say much, nor did she ask where he had been or what he had been doing. His boys chattered like a loose bicycle chain clanging against its mudguard – annoying, yet indicating something of some importance. He heard the words 'school' and 'books' and stopped them.

'Simrat, it's time to find a school for these lafangas. All they do all day is run around in their shorts and banyans like dancing bandars. What are the other children doing? Have they started their studies?'

'Papaji, no one is studying. How to study even? It's not like anyone was allowed to bring books.'

Gurdev walked over to his trunk, pulled it out from under the bed and took out two paperbacks – *Oliver Twist* and *Treasure Island*. He handed one to each boy. 'I want a report on both books in three days. You have to read both books, and I don't want to hear the same thing from both of you, understand?'

They said, 'Yes, Papaji' in chorus and stood up. Gurdev looked at Simrat, who sat on the bed, moving around like those bobble-head dolls – her head rolled side to side, then back and front. He didn't say anything. He wasn't ready. And Simrat didn't speak either.

After Gurdev had his name painted on his plot, he came back to the camp with a smile on his face. People he passed looked at him and turned away. They were all scared of this large Sikh man who always had a grumpy face. His smile didn't reassure them because they knew that anger lay curled up below his twirled moustache. But Gurdev's smile grew wider as he approached their section of the barracks.

He called out to the woman next door, 'Mrs Sharma, we are moving out, you can expand now.'

Mrs Sharma peered out from behind her floral curtain and raised her hand at him, not at all sure what he had said.

Gurdev walked right past Simrat, who had come outside when she had heard his voice and he had held up his hand to say, wait, I'll be back. He walked to the end of the barracks where his friends Col Hardit Singh and Harjit Singh had been allotted space. Both men lay on manjas covered with colourful mattresses, like the ones in Gurdev's space. But unlike Gurdev's space, this one was open in the front, better to let out that man smell that filled his head when he entered. Both men were bare headed, their scant grey hair tied up in tiny buns atop their heads, kept in place with neon-green and pink rubber bands that looked as out of place on those grizzled faces as a cigarette would in the mouth of a little girl. Their turbans lay beside them on makeshift tables, perfectly tied with the back tail loose, to be pulled at and tucked in after all the hair had been safely corralled with the back of a knitting needle that they each used one by one. Gurdev saw this happen as both reached for their turbans when they saw him and went through the motions.

'I've done it, gents. I have bought my plot. All my savings are mostly gone but now I'm happy.' Gurdev hugged each man closely. He felt a kinship with them. After all, they had lived on land that he could have thrown a stone at – if he had thrown well and long. The two older men watched him walk back towards his own area, proud of this man from their world and jealous.

'That man is something. Where does he get all the confidence? He is a farmer like us, after all. I would never have the courage to buy a plot of land with all the money in my pocket. I'll wait here till the government gets to my application and allot me a property,' said Colonel Hardit Singh, his right hand on his still flat stomach, his left shifting the hastily placed turban on his head so he could remove it again.

'I think he's doing the right thing. Who knows what we'll get and when?' said Harjit Singh, the older of the two.

Gurdev walked over to his wife, who was still standing in the curtained doorway, stooped and wan, her clothes hanging on her like she had worn fat Mrs Sharma's by mistake. Gurdev hugged her.

She stood limp as he put his arms around her and whispered into her ear, 'Things will be better now, I promise. Wait till you see what I've done … for us.' The 'for us' was an afterthought. Gurdev thought himself a family man, and he told everyone he was, but he wasn't. He thought well of his wife but she was a simple woman with few demands. She said nothing, nodded and wiped her dry brow with the end of her dupatta.

'Give me a little more time and I'll get you out of this place, a few more months, that's all.'

—

'But how will you build a house in a few months?' Simrat asked. She knew about his surprise. There was not much she didn't know that went on in the camp. She knew that Mrs Sharma's husband next door begged for sex every night and didn't get it. She also knew that Mr Sharma was an expert in gemstones – he believed the right stone, worn at the right place could solve most of life's problems. She knew that the brothers, Hardit and Harjit, had suffered a tragedy but she also knew that they were good men whose women got swept up in some misguided notion and acted without thinking. She knew about the special camp for widowed women, where they locked up at night and no men except male children were allowed inside. She knew about Nirmal Singh, the tailor from Lahore, whose cutting and stitching made even Mrs Sharma look like as slim and well-shaped as a soaring Ashoka tree. She also knew Sangat Singh, the businessman also from Lahore and both their wives, Amrit and Paramjit. She knew that Nirmal and Amrit had been trying to have a child but couldn't and she knew that Paramjit could sing but Sangat wouldn't let her because he said only whores sang in public.

'I'm not going to build a house, Simrat. Where will the money for that come from? I'm going to build a hut on the plot, and we'll move there and we'll buy a buffalo and some chickens and plant our vegetables. You wait and see. Everyone will be jealous of us.'

'And the toilet, and bathing?' Simrat asked as she gagged at the thought of the buffalo.

Gurdev had his answers ready. 'I've thought of everything. At first we'll have an outhouse. Later, I'll make a sewage line to connect to the street. You don't worry about these small things. I'm there, no?'

All Simrat could think of as he spoke was the gurgling in her stomach, the cramping in her back and the bile in her throat. But she still didn't say anything. When Gurdev was ready, so were Simrat and the boys. Gurdev hired two cycle rickshaws to take their belongings to the new plot in East Patel Nagar.

8

GURDEV LOOKED AT HIS WIFE, HAGGARD AT THIRTY, looking as pale as the milk she was carrying in from the buffalo. He had seen blood in the pit he had dug for a toilet and had assumed it was her period blood, but then he had correlated and calculated and realized that it was something else. He had to ask her about it now, but what would he do when she told him? He had no money for a major illness. One day, when she sat doubled over on her low stool in the midst of making rotis, he went around to her, sat on his haunches and held her loosely around her shoulders.

'I know there's something wrong,' he whispered.

'What's wrong?' Simrat was startled.

'I've seen the blood and it's not … you know.'

'Then what is it?'

'Simrat, I know you aren't well. I don't know what's wrong but you hardly eat and then there's the blood in the toilet. We have to talk to a doctor. I've found someone. He can help us diagnose. Then, we'll see what to do…'

'I'm sorry, Gurdev. I've been waiting … for you to be free, I mean, I tried to control it, to stop it. But now … the pain is there no matter what I eat. And the blood, it keeps coming … You have so much more to do … I want to help you, but…'

Gurdev hugged his wife but his head and eyes moved above and out beyond hers. He stared into his future, a sick wife and two young boys, no money – or none that he wanted to reveal at this time – no work and nothing in sight. He would have to invest to start something, but what would he invest with? Not the dollars, because then word would spread that he had money and people like that Sujjat Singh would be camped outside his house looking for handouts. He had to keep that money hidden till there was a real emergency.

The next morning, with the children in school, Gurdev took his wife to Dr Vinod Bhargava, a young man who had finished his training and joined the government clinic for refugees. He himself was a refugee, but when Gurdev asked him how he came over, which route – via Lahore by land or via Karachi by sea, one that had been treacherous in so many different ways and the other a straight five hundred and forty-nine kilometres by boat – he blushed, because he worked for the government and had flown out of Lahore on a BOAC plane. He had seen none of the bloodshed and the heartache of the crossing, and had been given government housing in Delhi.

Young Dr Bhargava examined Simrat, checked the inside of her eyes and her fingernails, pressed her belly till she winced and shook his head.

'What's wrong, doctor?' Gurdev asked.

'Your wife, I will speak in front of her, has a severe gastrointestinal problem that has been left untreated for too long. She has also lost a lot of blood. She'll probably need an operation, but a specialist is needed. You'll have to take care of this without waiting any longer, or...'

Gurdev took Simrat home in a rickshaw, they had walked to the clinic, Simrat lagging behind, Gurdev striding ahead, not sure where he should look. On the way back, he was silent, still unsure about where to look. He didn't want to look at his wife of ten years, a village girl, simple down to her scraggly hair, her stubby toes and plump fingers. He closed his eyes to see her because he couldn't bear to open them and look over at her sitting next to him, wobbly and white, nothing like the robust Punjabi farm girl that he had married. He had wanted simple, no frills and no expectations. He had been with women in Lahore, including the one his parents had wanted him to marry: her name was Balwinder Kaur, but she had asked everyone to call her Bella. Gurdev sat in the rickshaw, jostled from side to side as the puller tried to dodge gravel and small ditches, and shook his head. He hadn't wanted Bella and he hadn't wanted her family's hotel business and he hadn't wanted the blood money, some of which he still carried strapped to his stomach, but this fact he pushed out of his mind.

Gurdev helped Simrat off the rickshaw at their gate – his neatly painted name 'Gurdev Singh Lahori' shining white on the brick wall, mocking him for not having even considered putting his wife's name as well, but this thought too he put out of his mind. He watched as Simrat made her way back to the shack, her back stooped, her steps slow and he felt a little stir but not too much. He paid the rickshaw puller, latched the gate and followed her in. The boys were at their neighbour's house, another refugee family but one that had arrived almost a year before they had. They had built a small house, a proper house and not a shack, and they had come over and asked Gurdev what he was doing, building a jhopri in a respectable neighbourhood. He had responded first in English then in his posh Lahori Punjabi, and they had embraced him as their own.

Simrat was sitting on their bed as he entered the single but spacious room that was their home. Gurdev had divided the space into three sections, their sleeping area, the boys' sleeping area and the daytime area – the kitchen and a small sitting space with low mattresses right by it. The spaces were separated by thick curtains, drawn open during the day. Not that Gurdev and Simrat needed any privacy – they had not been intimate with each other since they had left Sukho.

'I don't think we should go to the specialist. I don't want to go. He'll charge a lot of money for nothing. I'll get better. I'll have only soup,' Simrat was mumbling more than talking, clenching and unclenching her fist as she sat on the bed.

'I don't know, Simrat, I don't know. How did this happen even? Someone in your family probably had it. Obviously the specialist will cost money and you know my situation. I spent most of my money on this plot thinking it will make life easier for you, but no. Instead, I have to manage more complications,' Gurdev said.

'Oh, easier. This is not easier, Gurdev. I have to milk the buffalo and feed the chickens and collect the eggs and take care of the garden and cook and clean and take care of the boys while you...' She stopped abruptly and put her hand on her mouth. Her eyes fluttered, pushing her gaze down to her feet. Gurdev had rarely heard her talk back like that. He wanted to raise his hand and slap her like he would his boys if they had misbehaved with him. But he held himself. He had never hit her before, but she had never given him reason to.

'We will go to the specialist. Nobody will ever say that I didn't take care of you. That is my final word.'

They did go to the specialist even though Simrat didn't want to go. As she was, she would either start getting better soon or die. She didn't want to die, but she also couldn't go on as she was, sometimes running to the toilet as many as thirty times in one day. She liked the private bathroom even though it was only a deep hole in the ground and Gurdev did cover everyone's work with sand before he left the house. She sprinkled a little too, after each bloody visit. Her mug, the one she used for washing herself, was her favourite companion. And after her outburst, Gurdev began milking the buffalo and feeding the chickens. She didn't think much about dying, didn't think it was her time yet. She had always felt she had known what was going to happen.

The specialist, a gastro-something, was a man in a hurry. He immediately diagnosed her problem as ulcerative colitis, words she had trouble even pronouncing. He gave pills and some plastic bottles with long nozzles that she had to put in that place. He called them back after ten days.

After ten days of taking the medicines and putting things in her anus, Simrat for the first time thought she was going to die. The medicines had no effect, the plastic bottles made her more sore, her toilet frequency was so high that she sat outside holding the mug filled with water, ready to go.

They went back to the doctor who was again in a hurry, but this time he sat down for a few minutes. 'Operation necessary. No other way. Medicines not working because too much ulceration – should have gone to doctor earlier.'

Simrat stood outside while Gurdev spoke to the doctor about the cost of the operation and his fees. She could hear his raised voice: 'But I can't afford to pay that much. Is there a cheaper hospital? Is all that necessary? Okay, then. We do it tomorrow.'

Gurdev came out scowling, held Simrat's elbow and pulled her towards the road. She shook her arm loose and walked slowly behind him, neither saying anything. Simrat got home and began cutting vegetables for dinner. She kneaded the dough for rotis and set it aside. She lit the kerosene stove, placed a small cast iron pan on it, poured in some oil and threw in the onions. While they sizzled, she thought she heard voices outside but didn't pay attention. She let the onions cook and cleaned the lentils. She added ginger and garlic to the onions and let them cook some more. She returned to the lentils and washed them in water three times. The fourth time, she left them in the water and put everything into a pressure cooker, along with salt, ginger and turmeric. She added chopped beans and potatoes to the sizzling onions and covered the dish. She cut some onions and sprinkled some salt on them. She sliced three whole green chillies and slid them in with the onions. She stirred the vegetables, added salt and spices and some water and covered the dish again. Then she stood by the window, looking at the expanse of the plot that would one day be a beautiful house, her house. In her mind, it looked like her house in Sukho, but bigger because there was so much land. The land pleased her – she was a Punjabi, after all. Land was the most important thing. Gurdev had done the right thing by buying land. She stopped her thoughts to go back to her vegetables till they were done, took the pan off and placed the pressure cooker on the stove. She made sure the lid was placed right and clicked it closed. Then she went back to the window, drawing out the lines of the house with her eyes, her head moving up and down as she drew. Once again, she heard voices outside but she kept to her dreams. The pressure cooker began whistling a few minutes later and whistled four times at irregular intervals. She counted the fifth and took the pressure cooker off the stove. She continued with her cooking, making rotis and putting them in a box and then went outside when she was done.

The buffalo's stall was empty. Gurdev sat on the milking stool, his head in his hands. Simrat went to him and put her hand on his shoulder. 'What did you do? Was that necessary? Couldn't you have taken a loan?'

'I don't like to depend on people. She's gone now but I have the money for tomorrow. Hope you are happy.'

Simrat got ready the next morning, her favourite plastic mug in its place outside, first in line with mugs for her boys and Gurdev. She had a bath, and then ran to the toilet again. The doctor had asked her not to eat or drink anything. Gurdev walked with the boys to school, spoke to the neighbours and came home with a rickshaw. She had been in the toilet when he had left.

Traffic was heavy in the early morning. A fog hung over the city even though winter hadn't come in.

'Make sure the boys wear their knitted vests when it gets colder, under their shirts, not over. I have knit two new sweaters for you – with designs like you asked. Wear them alternatingly, not the same one every day. If the boys get a cold, give them ginger tea with honey and lemon. It's for you also. I have knit one muffler for my brother. If you can, give it to him or give it to someone else,' Simrat went on with her instructions, pulling her shawl tight around her as the rickshaw picked up speed down a low hill. Gurdev looked straight ahead, sometimes to one side as they crossed a road. The rickshaw puller went on straight, not bothered by anyone.

When they reached the hospital, Gurdev pulled Simrat into one corner of the busy reception and pulled out a small velvet pouch. 'My mother gave this for you. I haven't opened it.'

Simrat looked at him as she pulled apart the string. Inside were two round diamonds. Big diamonds. She took one out and looked at it closely, one eye closed. She looked at the other one the same way. She looked at Gurdev, who shrugged.

'These are real, Gurdev, and they are good, very good. I may be from the village, but I know that so much could have been bought with these.' She shoved the bag into her salwar pocket, turned away from Gurdev and walked away towards the reception as fast as she could. He made to catch her but she brushed him away, sitting instead in a wheelchair that a nurse had brought for her. That was the last time Gurdev saw Simrat.

9

~

GURDEV SAT IN THE WAITING ROOM TILL THE OPERATION was done, then waited till the doctor came out. 'Your wife, she is okay. Some intestine part is gone, but she is okay. She told me before the anaesthesia that she does not want to see you. You have paid the hospital and my fees, so this is your business. But now, allow her at least one week recovery time and go.'

Gurdev came back to the hospital the next day and the day after, but he was not allowed to see his wife. He tried going up to Simrat's room to talk to her but the nurses wouldn't let him through. The orderlies told them that he was coming. Even the doctors seemed to know her. He couldn't make sense of what had happened. One day she was a docile and obedient wife, the next day she had left him. He didn't know what to do, what to tell his boys, his neighbours, relatives – her brother. She would come back for her children, though. He was certain of that.

Gurdev came to the hospital every day and tried to see Simrat. Each day he was sent away. On day nine, he tried one more time, but the sweeper at the hospital gate told him to go home. His wife had left the hospital. He walked back home, raging and puzzled. When he got back, he washed his hands and face and then went to the neighbours' house to pick up his boys.

'They went with your brother, Gurdev. He said he had come in from Ludhiana to help you out. The boys seemed to know him so I sent them,' Anandi said. She had started out confidently, sure she had done the right thing but her voice softened to a whisper as she saw Gurdev's eyes widen, his cheeks shake and his tongue move from side to side in his mouth as if searching for letters to form words.

'I have no brother,' is what he wanted to say but instead, quietly, he said, 'Which one? I have two brothers.'

'He said his name was Hardit. Smart-looking fellow. Ex-army?' the neighbour went on.

'Yes. Good of him to come and help me out, a surprise ... thank you,' Gurdev mumbled as he made his way out of the house.

Gurdev walked slowly back to his shack and sat on the bed, the same bed that Simrat had sat on the night before they went to the hospital. He had not seen what his mother had given for 'his wife', a peasant woman whom she had never met and had assumed it was something cheap. He had peeped inside, but hadn't bothered to look closely and had given it to Simrat as a gesture of goodwill, something to make her feel good before her operation. What was he going to do now? What kind of man lets his wife leave him and steal his children? And what did she know about diamonds? He had an embodiment, a persona. He was not the kind of man who got taken – she knew that.

The next morning, Gurdev got up and got ready. He didn't know where to go first – to Sujjat Singh, Simrat's brother, where she was most likely hiding or to Hardit Singh at the refugee camp to thrash him for doing her bidding when he was the one who had been a friend to him and his brother. He was angry from the top of his soft turban to the bottom of his leather-jutti covered toes. His angry feet carried him to the refugee camp, and as before, everyone got out of his way as he stomped through the barracks, past the Sharma's place, still occupied, past his own, now empty and forlorn and to the end where time seemed to stand still.

Both Hardit and Harjit lay on their beds, turbans off, in yellowy banyans and white pyjamas, the standard uniform for middle-class Sardars once they got home from work. Both scrambled and sat up as Gurdev stomped into their quarters.

'You bastard,' he said looking at Hardit, who had quickly pulled on a shirt and placed his starched turban on his head. The man looked startled as Gurdev stood over him waiting for him to speak.

Finally, the former Colonel stood up straight, his shirt untucked over his crumpled white pyjamas and his turban slightly askew. 'What, Sir, do you mean by that?'

Gurdev was perplexed. This man should have crumbled at the mere sight of him, after betraying him the way he did, but he was standing tall.

'Did you not come to my neighbour Anandi's house and take my boys? Did you not do that at the behest of my wife, did you not...' He stopped suddenly. Simrat – it was not possible. She couldn't be doing all this on her own. Somebody had to be helping her, and if it wasn't this man, it was someone else calling himself Hardit to send him here.

Gurdev walked away, his head swaying from side to side, doing calculations and mapping Simrat's brain, still appalled that she was able to humiliate him like this. He sat down outside his old quarter, his face in his hands, wondering what he had done for her to walk away like this. Where could she go? Those diamonds were worth something, he wasn't sure how much but not enough to last her long. But she was a hard worker and she wasn't afraid of any kind of work, and the thought of her making something of herself made him ache. He felt tears sting his eyes so he bent his head over his knees, which is when his former neighbour Mrs Sharma walked out from behind her curtain.

'Gurdevji, it's you. Something has happened, no? I could hear you shouting all the way till here. Terrible times we live in.'

'Nothing has happened Mrs Sharma. Everything is fine. Did Simrat come here, by the way? She said she was going to meet her friends here and was gone for a long time so I came looking. She is still weak after her operation and all.'

'She looked okay, Gurdevji, but that was yesterday. She came here yesterday, not today. She was walking a little slower than usual, but she was okay. She wanted to show my husband some stones. He's a gemologist, you see. He knows stones, the ones good for you and bad for you. For your bad times, he can give you a stone, Gurdevji. Wear it in a ring or on a chain – it touches your skin all the time … it will bring good times to you in no time.'

'Are you the gemmologist or your husband, Mrs Sharma? What did your husband say about the stones that Simrat showed him?'

'Gurdevji, that is between him and her, no? I don't know so much.'

'Mrs Sharma, you know everything. Now, please tell me what he said about the diamonds. That will help my good times come sooner.'

'Gurdevji, the diamonds are high quality, worth a lot. My husband sent your wife to a jeweller, an old friend. He will give her a fair price. Okay? Now, tell me, what shall I do for you? Do you want to meet some young girls, maybe married, maybe unmarried, whatever you choose?' she said.

'Mrs Sharma, I don't know what you know but there is nothing wrong with my marriage. My wife will be back. She's angry,' this he said so loudly that Mrs Sharma folded her hands before him in mock forgiveness and went behind her curtain again.

As Gurdev began to walk again, he noticed two people following him closely, not making any pretence at hiding. They were both rough-looking men dressed in dark Pathan suits, one man short, the other of average height but well below Gurdev's stature. Both men wore soft turbans with scruffy beards, rolled up and kept in place with bobby pins under the chin. Gurdev looked back twice and saw that they were scurrying to close the gap between them. Meanwhile, in the further distance, Mrs Sharma had parted the curtain and was peering out to see what was going on, as were most of the others in the quarters down the line.

'Excuse me, boss, Sir, excuse me…' he heard right behind him, the voice coming from down low so it must be the short man talking.

'Yes, Sat Sri Akal ji. How may I help you?'

The two men were Sangat Singh and Nirmal Singh, both originally from villages even further north than Gurdev's but both had been working in Lahore when they had to pack a few belongings and leave. Their quarters were close to Hardit and Harjit's, and they had heard of him and had wanted to talk to him for some time, but then he had left the camp. Now they had found their chance again.

'It's God's blessing that you are here and we can talk to you,' the shorter man, Nirmal Singh, told Gurdev once they had found a place to sit down. 'We want you to join us in business.'

'Business? What kind of business?' Gurdev was suspicious, but while there had been many episodes of petty theft at the camp, larger schemes were hatched only once people got outside. Moreover, these men, in his brief experience with them, weren't hatching anything.

'We want to start a women's clothing business and we need your help. We want someone with your … push, your gallantness, your height, your manner, your … push.'

'I'm honoured by your request. But women's clothing … why? I know so little about women, let alone their clothing.'

For a moment, the fact that Gurdev's wife had just left him was forgotten and all the men laughed loudly.

'It is a money business. Women are always needing new clothes. It is always something or the other. Then their sizes keep changing,' said Nirmal with a know-it-all flourish of his hand.

The other two men laughed again, blushing at the way Nirmal talked about sizes changing.

'So, you know how to stitch women's clothes? The blouses and all that?'

'Obviously. That is my training.'

'You know how to take measurements?'

'How old are you men? Both of you are fathers. You should be ashamed of yourselves. Come on, now. Let's talk about the business. Do you want to do it or not?' said Nirmal.

Gurdev wanted to go home and think about it a little. He remembered that there was no one at home. Not that he would have consulted Simrat – maybe that was the problem. Maybe she wanted to be consulted. Maybe he had only assumed she was uninterested. Maybe she could have offered some advice of her own sometimes. Maybe so many things but it was too late.

He told the two men that he was interested.

All three men put their hands atop each other's like they had done as boys. Gurdev was in with all his heart, much to his own surprise. They made their way back to his house, making plans as they walked. Nirmal and Sangat were still staying at the refugee camp, waiting for their allotment of land or a house that had been vacated by a Muslim family headed the other way. They were impressed with Gurdev's foresight.

'But I have no money left, you know. I hope you still want me,' Gurdev said quietly as they walked along.

'We know, Prahji. We know what you did. We still want you. You are going to lead us, help us make decisions.'

When Gurdev got home with his two new friends, he found Sujjat and his wife, Parveen, waiting for them at the gate – his painted name now yelling at him in all its neatness and symmetry.

'Where is she? Where is my sister, Gurdev? I knew you were no good from the beginning and thought so much of yourself. Now how are you feeling? Everyone knows your wife has run away and taken your children. Everyone. I made sure of that. A man who can't even control his own...' Parveen nudged him as he said this, but he continued. 'A man who can't even manage his own family – how will he manage anything else? Are you people his friends?' he said looking at Nirmal and Sangat. 'He is not a nice man – that is why his wife ran away.' Gurdev raised his hand but felt Sangat behind him, holding it and slowly bringing it down again.

'Paaji, why don't you go home now, and take your wife along? You don't want to lose her on the way, do you?' Sangat said to Sujjat quietly and gently pushed him out of the gate. He waited till they were on their way back to the main road before he turned around to Gurdev and Nirmal. 'Let's go and have some tea. I'll make it. Gurdev, do you have any biscuits or snacks? Probably not. Never mind, I'm not hungry but let's have tea.'

The three walked into Gurdev's hut and settled around the kitchen while Sangat made tea, with sugar but no milk.

10

NIRMAL, THE LADIES' TAILOR, AND HIS WIFE, AMRIT, were a little older than Gurdev. They had no children and had been married for a long time. Nirmal was short and wide. He covered his beefy body with shirts he stitched himself. They were a shorter version of the Pathan kurta, a loose-fitting garment usually worn long, well below the knees. But for Nirmal, the usual length dwarfed him further so he sewed his with special care, using graded seams to reduce bulk, finished seams to prolong the life of his shirts. He used topstitching to ensure that the seam stayed in place and also gave his shirts a rakish, slightly decorative look. He used natural, woven fabric but pre-shrunk it by washing it several times before ironing and sewing. Amrit was not as particular about her clothing. She preferred clothes that wore out so that she could buy new ones. Nirmal could wear the same shirt for several years. He sewed a set of ten every four to five years. They washed well and wore well. But he was not interested in sewing clothes for men. He had trained to sew women's clothes – the sari blouses and the tunics, with necklines that ranged from simple Vs and Us, up high and modest, to deep square necklines that scraped a nipple at each right angle and were held together by a narrow strip in the back. He had also learnt to sew English women's clothes. Their long skirts and high-necked blouses with jodhpurs for riding and warm jackets for cool winters. He also made their gowns – silks, chiffon, velvet and soft wool, he had tailored them all. He had copied patterns from books and magazines the women had brought back from England. He had replicated their designs, made them pieces of art, not a single one made again. He didn't know that he could have been the pioneer of couture in India. He only wanted to be a darzi for the refugee housewives of Delhi, making beautiful clothes for them that they would talk about and tell their friends.

After his initial ridicule of the ladies' tailoring idea, Gurdev embraced it and made it so much his own that most people thought he was the artist. First, he learnt about fabric and cuts and finishes and embellishments. Then, he learnt all about sizing and styling and fitting and that special thing that makes a woman turn around and take a second look at herself in the trial room mirror. This last awakening took a long time; it's not easy for men to understand, but Nirmal did.

He taught Gurdev everything. He often wondered if he should. If Gurdev knew all about tailoring and design and fit and fabric, then why would he need anyone else? But Nirmal also realized that what Gurdev did best was talk. The more time he spent with the big man the more he noticed this. Everyone else did the work, Gurdev gave lectures. He also had contacts. Somehow, he had made contacts everywhere. Some were his old friends – but such educated friends, where did he find them? Nirmal wondered. And why had they agreed to be his friends? They seemed to have so little in common, like that Satnam Singh – he was something big in the government now. Nirmal thought a lot about Gurdev, why he had agreed to work with them, who he was, what happened to his wife and children, would he ever get them back – would he even try? But after some time, when Gurdev's ideas began to work, Nirmal began to trust him in a way he had never found anyone to trust before. He began to look to him as a younger brother, someone he could tell the whole truth about his life to.

First, Gurdev began the process of determining what could be allotted to them by the government in exchange for the businesses they had lost.

Nirmal had owned nothing in Lahore.

He had a sewing machine set up in a corner of his small home, a single room and a kitchen, shared with his parents and younger brother and, later, his wife Amrit. He did all his work there. He went to the English women's homes to take measurements and look at designs. Then he worked in his cramped quarters, making sure no one sat on the tiny pleats and the elaborate embroidery. He took the embroidery work to two karigars he had developed in the inner city. The two were brothers, Sultan and Samir, whose grandmother he had heard about from some shopkeepers in Anarkali Bazaar. Both were Muslim and young, sixteen and eighteen. Their mother had died and their grandmother had taken charge of bringing them up. They had learnt their craft from this old lady, a woman who didn't talk much; she only opened old metal trunks to show her grandsons her work. She didn't see so well any more, but she had embroidered gowns and robes for many rajahs and maharajahs. The pieces she had kept were bits of the original fabric, kept separated from each other with almost transparent onion paper that trembled to the touch but didn't crumble. She had kept a sample of every design, and she had sat the boys down and taught them how to recreate each one and then to create their own. Nobody laughed at them. Nobody said it was women's work. They knew that the boys had found a way to make a living that was impossible to copy. But they spent too much time learning their grandmother's skill and no time going to school or playing with friends or learning a little English. Sultan and Samir's grandmother died at the age of ninety-two. She wasn't sick, she hadn't lost her mind and she was still strong enough to climb the steep staircase to her room on the second floor. One evening, after a dinner of lamb korma, saag meat and haleem, she called the two boys up to her room, signalling them to follow her as she climbed, not too slow and not too fast. She didn't stop at the first-floor landing to catch her breath. She went on, one steep step at a time till she reached the heavy wood door to her room. She pushed it open, then held it for the boys, and walked slowly to the bed and lay down.

'Okay, boys. My time is here now,' she said. The teenaged boys had looked at her curiously. 'You have to do this on your own. Make a living, take care of yourselves.' She closed her eyes, breathed in slowly, let out a breath and continued to breath, slowly, softly. The boys ran out of the room, without making a lot of noise. They were sure that their grandma had gone off to sleep. They got their father up from his chair, where he sat cutting his toenails with a pair of scissors, cutting a small slit in each nail with the scissors and then yanking it back with his fingers, cursing under his breath as he drew blood for the third time. He dropped the scissors to the floor when he saw his sons' faces and then heard what they said, talking loudly now, drowning each other's words. He took the steps two at a time, not because he thought he could do anything to save the old lady, but because her last words would give him a blessing. He pushed open the heavy door with one hand and rushed to his mother's side. She was still there, still breathing, but she didn't open her eyes. Her son held her gently to him, hugged her, kissed her on the forehead and that was when she shuddered a little, tried to open her eyes. He could tell she was struggling because of the way her lids fluttered, and then her head sank down into her pillow.

Nirmal knew all this because the boys had told him. Sultan and Samir mourned their grandmother more than anyone else did. They missed her the most. Nobody else sat in her room, day after day, late into the night, learning how to embroider from a simple chain stitch to elaborate cross-stitch to the Parsi gara embroidery to the bead-encrusted dubka and on and on. She brought them fabric – who knows how because she had not left the house since her husband died when she was seventy-eight and he eighty-five – but when they finished a piece, which sometimes took months, she had another waiting. There were beautiful large pieces of satin and raw silk, velvet and even Gandhi's hand-woven khadi. They embroidered around an expertly cut neckline and along the border. Sometimes, they embroidered the entire length and breadth of the fabric, the special pieces for weddings. As the boys completed each piece to grandma's satisfaction, she wrapped it carefully in muslin and stored it in a larger metal trunk. This one didn't go under the bed, it had a corner to itself. After she died, the boys opened the trunk and looked through their work. Many pieces had disappeared – their grandma had been selling their work. They searched carefully through her belongings and found a name and address:

Nirmal Singh, Tailoring and Stitching. He was Sikh and lived in a different part of Lahore. The boys located him, told him the whole story and began working with him. He paid them fair rates, transparently, without hiding the names of clients. They could have gone direct and cut him out, but he was the artist. Without his cuts and designs, their embroidery was lifeless. They needed him as he needed them.

Nirmal could not explain his need to ensure the well-being of those two boys. They had worked tirelessly for him, delivering work that was breathtakingly intricate, and the most beautiful. He wanted them and their work in India, not wasted in Pakistan where they no longer had him to work with them. No one else would understand their thinking, their work ethic and their authenticity. Everyone wanted shortcuts: machine embroidery, cheap thread, untidy knots and dirty hands that left brown imprints on the thread, on the fabric. No one could care for them and for their work like he would.

And then there was his wife and her concern for these boys. She couldn't have her own children. It was probably his fault, but he would never admit that. These boys, children still, she adopted as her own. She cooked for them and taught them how to read and write Urdu. She wore a Burqa and took them to the mosque so that they could understand their religion. In all this, their father had vanished, moved in with another woman it was said, but only after his mother was dead. Samir and Sultan stayed at their home, alone. Nirmal and Amrit had no place to keep them. That was Amrit's biggest regret. She had to leave without them because Nirmal couldn't go and find them. He would have been lynched if he had gone that side with his turban. Only Gurdev could help Nirmal get the boys out. Only he could.

11

AFTER HIS CONVERSATION WITH NIRMAL AND SANGAT, Gurdev was distracted. Thoughts of Simrat and his sons flitted past from time to time, but the idea of creating a new business was thrilling. This venture would be his, Nirmal and Sangat may be the ones with the idea, but he would be the one to make it something big. Just like the small house that Gurdev had built with his own hands that would someday be the biggest house on the street.

Gurdev gave Simrat's clothes and personal things to Amrit to donate to the needy. Her jewellery he packed away and put into his hiding space, stored along with the documents for his plot of land and the dwindling stack of rupees that he had collected from all his relatives and another package that was triple wrapped that even Simrat had not known about.

Nirmal, Sangat and Gurdev began frequenting the offices for Rehabilitation of Refugees daily. They stood in line with hundreds of others like them, day after day, waiting for their turn. Each day the line started earlier, till people began to sleep there to keep their spot. Gurdev knew there was a better way. He saw people going straight in and coming out through a side entrance, wearing smug smiles. How were they getting in, he wondered but only for a minute. He knew, of course, but what could he do? Either they were paying a bribe or they had a contact in the office or most likely both.

The Rehabilitation Office had hired from the camps. They had hired from among them but there were too many of them to know whom. The supervisors were all Delhi locals. He could have asked his friend Satnam for help, but he was in the external affairs ministry, not in the home ministry.

One day, Gurdev followed one of the smug people who came out of the side door. The man had covered his face with one end of his turban. He was walking fast, holding on to a cloth-covered package of documents with his other hand. After a while, the man knew he was being followed and seemed to know Gurdev because he spread the fabric wider to cover a larger portion of his face. Gurdev made no pretence of hiding himself. He pushed through the crowd, at once menacing and courteous, calling 'side', 'side' as he pushed through. The man joined a throng of people as he entered the market area and thought he had finally lost his pursuer. He sat down on a charpoy at a teashop when he felt the ropes on the charpoy sag beside him. He turned to see Gurdev settling next to him, hand reaching out to pull away his face covering. Before the man could push Gurdev away, or hold his cover in place, it was gone. The man behind the mask was Sujjat Singh, Gurdev's former brother-in-law, the same one who had troubled him about returning his money and taunted him about his runaway wife. Even now, he held himself from catching him by his throat and asking him where his wife was. He knew that the embarrassment of a husband whose wife leaves him lasts for some time, but if that wife doesn't seek refuge with her only brother, her only kin, the shame for the brother is even greater. A woman without a husband is a nobody and it is her family's responsibility to take her back to her husband, whoever he may be and whatever he may have done to her.

Gurdev shouted, 'You? What were you doing there? You didn't even move from the other side. You've been living in Delhi all along. What restitution do you want? Or, are you, as usual, trying to steal someone else's money?'

'Nothing, Prahji. Nothing, I had gone to help a friend.'

'You can't go to help a friend, Sujjat – you have to be present yourself. Now, tell me before I thrash you. But never mind that, sorry, sorry. How did you get access to the side entrance? You have to tell me …'

'Okay, okay. I have a friend who is a supervisor.'

'And you couldn't tell me this? You were helping other friends, but your own brother-in-law … So whose papers are those? Whose property are you trying to steal now?'

'Prahji, I was going to tell you only but I just heard from my parents' neighbours. They are Mussalman. They sent a letter but it took months to reach. My parents are dead. They died in a fire. Someone set fire to their house. The family who wrote the letter tried to get them out but they were trapped. They had refused to come this side. I had made arrangements … but what is one to do? They had lived there all their lives. No one could make them move. I was trying to get compensation for their property. Simrat will get half, even though she is a woman.'

'Sujjat, my prayers go out to them. May God give their souls peace. I was thinking though, shouldn't you have come and told us about this, instead of me finding you skulking around at the office? Sujjat Singh, you were trying to take it all for yourself, weren't you?'

Gurdev looked at his brother-in-law with all the sympathy he could muster. This thin ingratiating man, who had not even grown a beard – who knew how he'd even fathered those children of his? Even his own sister had not gone to him for help, that's how useless he was. Despite his anger, Gurdev couldn't help but feel glad for Simrat. Some money would be coming to her, he would make sure of it. If Sujjat got property, he would make him give it to his sister, if they could find her.

'You are a rat, Sujjat. Who knows if you were even able to father your own children,' he said, simply out of spite, to see the look on the other man's face. Sujjat turned red, the colour of the clay tea mug in his hand, and sputtered something unintelligible. Just then his wife, Parveen, walked by, a vegetable bag on one shoulder and a larger shopping basket filled with meat and eggs in the other hand.

'What are you doing here, ji? What happened at the...' she stopped as she realized Gurdev was sitting there, listening intently.

'Oh, Sat Sri Akal, ji. How are you? Any news of...' she asked as Sujjat nudged her hard.

'Everyone is fine, Sister. Everything is fine. How are your children? Sujjat and I were discussing—'

Sujjat burst in, 'Prahji, I was telling you about my friend who works at the Rehabilitation Office.'

Parveen's eyes opened wide, her lips set in a straight line as she looked at her husband expecting to pierce through him with her stare. But Sujjat wouldn't look up at her.

He continued, 'He's a good friend. He only got the job because his uncle is in an important post at the home ministry. Should this be part of the external affairs ministry or home ministry? These are all external people, meaning, no, not. Meaning you are us, only...'

Sujjat kept babbling as his wife rolled her eyes. 'I'm going home. I have work to do, unlike you, who seems to have plenty of time for chai and chit-chat.'

12

ONCE GURDEV GOT THE NAME AND ADDRESS OF SUJJAT'S friend, Ashwin Garg, he proceeded slowly. They had to provide proof of ownership of any property in Pakistan. Gurdev had carried all his documents wrapped first in oilcloth then in newspaper and then in ordinary cloth again. Nirmal and Sangat had nothing. Nirmal had owned no property, even the house they lived in and where he worked from was rented, and the field his father farmed was as a sharecropper. Sangat had his family home and some land but no papers. One of his brothers had all the documents and would probably steal everything.

But in addition to the documents, they also needed something else – a reason for Ashwin Garg to work with them. He could refuse outright or he could turn them in for attempting to influence an officer of the state, or most likely, he would ask for a bribe they couldn't afford.

Gurdev and Nirmal decided to go to his home one evening, after dinner, when the man would be relaxing with his family, stomach full and probably his daily scotch softening the world around him. They would appeal to him on a personal level. Sujjat had given them the general location of the man's home because even he didn't have the exact address. Not many people had addresses to give; mostly it was the name of the person and the locality, and that was enough. Gurdev used the Garg name to find the house, asking only two people along the way. The first one gave them directions to within one hundred feet; the second walked them to the front of the house.

Ashwin lived in Chandni Chowk, in an old house with his wife and children, his parents, two brothers and their families. The house was constructed in the old haveli style, courtyard in the middle, a tulsi plant in a planter ensuring ideal wifehood and motherhood for all the women in the house, and several charpoys for both afternoon naps and evening chit-chat. It was well kept and clean outside, no broken tiles or even that line of dirt that forms where wall meets floor. The front door was polished wood, the shelf to put shoes on before entering the house also solid wood.

Gurdev and Nirmal knocked on the door and were let in by an old servant. They told him they were there to see Mr Garg about an important matter. The servant asked them to wait right there in the entryway while he went inside. The two peered into the haveli; solid brass lights twinkled, casting lace-like shadows on the cement floor. The house shone, fresh paint, polished wood, shiny floors, bright lights, yet Diwali was still far away.

'Yes, what can I do for you, please? And how did you find my house?'

'Good evening, sir. My friend, this man, Mr Gurdev Singh, his wife's brother is Sujjat Singh. He gave us your address. He told us that you can be … helpful,' Nirmal began but Gurdev jumped in, looking around the house, 'For a price.'

'That Sujjat Singh is a crook…'

'Garg Sahib … but he … but he said…'

'Yes, yes, he is my friend but also a crook. And I'm helping him. So what do you think that means?'

'But, sir…'

'So, he's a crook and if he's sent you, that means you are both probably crooks – but you are not my friends. I don't have time for crooks. Please go.'

'But, sir, we are not crooks. He may be, but we are not. We stand there at the Rehabilitation Office, waiting, day after day and nothing happens. The line doesn't move.' Nirmal tried his most pathetic tone, speaking in a low depressed voice.

Then Gurdev stepped in, 'That is because you people are taking all the side-door clients and taking care of them.'

'What are you saying, Mister? Please go now. I can't help you. I don't want to help you.'

'No, no, sir. My friend didn't mean it like that. Please, sir, at least hear our story. It is not at all a complicated case…' Nirmal began placating but was interrupted by Gurdev again.

'Not like that cheat Sujjat Singh who is using your help to get property that doesn't even belong to him alone. What if I report that? What if I file a complaint on that? What do you think will happen then Mr… Mr…'

'Ashwin Garg,' piped in Nirmal but quietly, gently, like he was caressing the man's name.

Ashwin was quiet for a few minutes. They all stood there, looking at each other. Then he said, 'That is Sujjat's parents' property. They died a horrific death, alone. Surely he can be compensated by the state for his tragedy. We are doing nothing wrong. You can file whatever complaint you want. Now please go.'

'Mr Ashwin Garg, I don't think you were paying attention when my friend introduced me. I am Gurdev Singh, Sujjat Singh's brother-in-law, meaning his only sister is my wife, meaning the property doesn't go to him alone…'

'Mr Gurdev Singh, Sujjat is the sole male heir to his parents' property. Our country does not recognize married women as heirs to property unless there is a will. Maybe yours does.'

Gurdev raised his hand high but let it down slowly.

'We are done here, Nirmal. This man is even smaller than that reptile, Sujjat. He is probably taking a share of that property in return for his help – my wife's share, my sons' share. He would not have helped us anyway because, save a small bribe, we have nothing to give him. And a small bribe will do nothing to fill his stomach. After all, wood must be polished and floors shone. Maintaining an old haveli like this to such high standards is expensive.'

Ashwin physically pushed the two men out of his doorway and locked the door. Gurdev spat on the side of his house, a big mouthful of frothy, wet oral excrement. Nirmal sat on the steps of the house next door, head in his hands.

'What have you done, Prahji? You have to control your anger. Now how do we get our money, your money, I mean, whatever. We need money to start our business.'

'I'll tell you what, Nirmal, you start our business in the camp. I'll get you khaddar fabric, homespun, patriotic, Gandhiji – that will be our specialization. Everyone is selling factory-made cloth and clothing made out of it. No one is selling khadi like we will, like you will – I'll find the money, somehow. In the meantime, I'll find some other way to get compensation for my flour mill. We won't stand in that line any more.'

'What are you planning to do, Prahji? Nothing illegal, I hope. I don't want to go to jail with unknowns. At least back home, you knew some people everywhere...'

'Even in jail?' Gurdev broke in. 'What kind of tailoring business did you have Nirmal? And let me remind you, Paaji – home is here now. There is no 'back home' any more. We can never go back.'

'Prahji, rest easy. All I was saying was that when you grow up in one place, there are always those who do well, those who become teachers and doctors and ... tailors but also some who get into a little trouble ... also, khadi – it has some problems ... and embroidery, that is the most important...' Nirmal went on, but Gurdev was no longer listening. He was thinking about where he would find khadi.

'Don't worry, Prahji, I was teasing you. No one is going to jail...' Gurdev mumbled as his mind wandered thinking of khadi suppliers.

13

GURDEV WALKED BACK TO HIS EMPTY SHACK, NOT forlorn, not lonely, not down. He believed that he lost his temper with the right people because getting angry was his way of severing a relationship that had no future. His angry words had such bite that once spoken they broke skin and lodged under, ensuring they released their venom for years. Nirmal, Sangat and others, they never got angry because they wanted to preserve all relationships. Some could be useful sometime; even the people who ended up in jail could be useful. Gurdev went into his shack and went straight to the two bricks under the window. He fished a key out of his salwar pocket and unlocked his locker. He put his hand in and pushed aside the one remaining velvet pouch and pulled out the small handkerchief-bound bundle. He opened it knot after knot and pulled out the sheaf of notes. He held it up and flipped through it like a pack of cards; it was not even as thick as only the high cards in a pack. It was enough for what he wanted to do, but then he would have nothing left. He put his hand back into the safe and stroked the velvet bag. He still didn't want to use that even though from the middle of his head, the stubborn part, he sometimes heard a loud thought: use the money, build your house, start your business, and Simrat will return. He realized that he didn't want her to return. He wanted to begin again and do it differently this time. But if he wasn't going to use the dollars yet, he had to find another way to earn enough to eat.

The next day, Gurdev went to Connaught Place to find khadi, Gandhi's homespun fabric. He had read in the newspapers that khadi was easily available, even after Gandhi's death. He located the offices of the All India Khadi Board and asked them about producers. But when he found them, he learnt that many had slowed down production in the aftermath of India's tragedy. This was January 1950, two years after Gandhi was assassinated, yet the nation still mourned.

After asking many people, Gurdev found his way to the cloth market in Gandhi Nagar, Shahdara, on the banks of the River Yamuna. The area was once predominantly Muslim but looked deserted, many of the two small double doors that led to courtyard homes locked with heavy chains and blackened brass locks. He found several Hindu cloth merchants but they were selling factory-made cloth that the British had dumped in India to staunch the effects of Gandhi's Khadi campaign. But khadi stayed and many Indians were proud to wear khadi, if only it were a little more stylish and cheaper. Khadi was expensive to make, Gurdev discovered as he spoke to the merchants, because it was hand-woven.

After wandering about in the cold for several hours, Gurdev finally found a wholesale storefront with a sign saying it specialized in khadi. He went in tentatively, conscious of his turban and long beard, but the owner was Hindu.

'The Muslims all went to refugee camps and from there to Pakistan,' the man said. 'They locked their doors and fled, most have been gone for over four years. I used to sell khadi but no one is making it now.' The man was young, fresh-faced but wise looking.

Gurdev's face fell. He had thought he had a plan, a good business. But he had failed so easily. He had assumed that khadi, of all things, would be easy to find. He looked at the ground, dusty in the dry winter, the colour of milky tea, and turned to go back across town to tell his friends that they would have to think of something else.

'Prahji, come here,' he heard the man in the shop call out. He turned around and walked back in while the man stood inside and pulled down the shutter. For a minute, the shop was black-dark, and Gurdev put his arms up in a defensive posture, not sure what was about to happen. The man switched on a light, a loud click on a large round switch, a single bulb hanging from the ceiling and pointed to a stool. Gurdev sat down. The man sat before him on a similar stool, a glass-topped counter on one side of them, the downed shutter on the other. He reached over and whispered, 'Not all the Muslims left the neighbourhood and went to Pakistan. Many are hiding with relatives in other parts of India ... some are right here, in Shahdara. My neighbour is one such Muslim who I know is living with a Hindu family.'

Gurdev looked at the man searchingly, but he couldn't wait. 'What does all this have to do with my need for khadi, my good man?'

'Prahji, be patient. Not everyone here knows what is happening and of those who know, many are not happy. There are many Muslim families living with their Hindu neighbours. The women of the house are spinning khadi yarn out of raw cotton and the men are weaving it into fabric, all behind closed doors. I sell the cloth in the market, but nobody knows the source. Now do you understand?'

Gurdev had heard the man. He was young but not naïve or lacking courage. Muslim families were spinning khadi in hiding. This was where he was going to find his suppliers. Desperate people make quality product; they have nothing to lose or gain by not doing so. Nirmal could transform the fabric into stylish yet patriotic garments that they all hoped women would buy and tell each other about. One thought struck him as he imagined their success on the back of this simple homespun. The whole concept was easily copied. Enterprising refugees without fresh ideas of their own could replicate Nirmal's designs easily. Then they would have nothing again.

'Can we be your exclusive buyers of khadi? Meaning the families who spin khaddar for you, can you not sell it to anyone else?' Gurdev asked directly. He had nothing to lose. Competitors could buy khadi fabric anywhere, but this would be better fabric than anyone else's. He knew that.

'If you are ready to buy all that we produce. I represent seven families. Their product is superior because I supply them with the best cotton, unbleached but clean and dense, farmed in the hills of Hyderabad, suitable for hand-weaving.'

'We will buy everything as long as the quality is the same.'

'Then we have a deal.'

Gurdev wondered what his partners would say as he made a partial payment from the skinny stack in his pocket, the rest due in two weeks when the first set of kurtas would be ready – he hoped. He packed up his first bolt of khadi, wrapped up in plain cloth and tied with rough rope, and loaded it on his shoulder. He carried it as long as he could on one shoulder, then switched to the other shoulder and then put it on a rickshaw for the final stretch home. His shoulders burnt, his fingers were red and swollen from grasping the rope that held the bale of fabric together, and his legs trembled from walking so far with that load. His heart was leaden; he had paid for the fabric with his own money and he didn't like the thought of money running out.

Finally, he reached the camp and took the bolt off the rickshaw, paid the man, loaded the weight back on his shoulder and sauntered the last leg over to Nirmal's tent. Nirmal and Sangat sat outside drinking tea. They jumped up, put their tea glasses on the floor and grabbed the bolt of cloth from Gurdev. Nirmal took the precious material inside and laid it on the camp bed. Then he ripped it open and ran his hands across the fabric. It felt rough and nubby, as it should. He tested the weight between his fingers. Again, it felt substantial.

'This is good, good. Now we have to work on it, shrink it, then iron it, then piece dye it, then cut it and then sew.'

'About how long will it take to make the first kurta, not more than a week, right?' Gurdev asked.

'Prahji, I need a month, at least, to get the quality I want. I'll wash it at least three times to let it shrink completely, then I'll cut pieces. Then the dye will be prepared with natural ingredients. Then I'll dye the fabric once. And then dye it all a second time for the colour to be deep and complete.'

Gurdev sat down heavily on the bed, right on the bolt of cloth, head in his hands. Nirmal yanked him back up. 'You can't sit on the cloth.'

'One month, one month! I have to pay the rest of the money in two weeks. I thought one week to prepare everything, a few days to sew and then we sell. This is ... this is going to be bad, bad.'

Then Sangat spoke. 'Paaji, this is my job. I make the deals. I know how to buy fabric. Why don't you take me next time? We'll work out something else with the merchant.'

But Gurdev's face was still pinched, his eyes narrow and unblinking, and his skin the colour of the unbleached beige fabric lying before him.

Nirmal began work on the fabric immediately. He cut the bale into four equal parts. Not too many or they would have waste. Then he took them, one at a time, to the dhobi ghat, the communal washing area. He soaked and he scrubbed and he dried. Then he left the fabric to dry out completely for two days in the pale winter sun while he began on another piece. His hands were red, fingers swollen with chilblains. His monkey cap and muffler covered much of his face, but his trousers were hitched up to above his knees. His sweater had been cast aside and his shirtfront was soaked.

But he went on. Once done, he cut the one hundred metres of fabric into measured pieces. Forty-eight pieces, two slightly larger for the bigger kurtas, came out of that bolt. These pieces he then divided into four groups for four colours – natural, black, red and bottle green. He took these to the dyer, also a camp refugee. The dyer had already got the material ready. All-natural dyes, the black made with walnut hulls, the red dye was made using beetroot and the bottle green from pomegranate skins. He dyed the fabric piece by piece so there were colour variations in each one, the shades and swirls providing a unique look to each piece.

Nirmal took the dyed but wrinkled pieces of fabric to the dhobi, who, with his iron filled with red-hot coals, pressed the shrivelled fabric into flattened submission.

Then came the best part for Nirmal – the cutting. The forty-eight pieces, twelve in each colour were divided into four sizes – small, average, big and bigger. He only cut one piece each of the small and the bigger and five each of the average and big.

———

Just two days short of two weeks, when the fabric was somewhere between dying and cutting, Gurdev and Sangat went back to Shahdara. The cloth merchant shook his head vehemently when they asked him for another two weeks to pay.

'How would you have found me if I didn't want to pay?' Gurdev asked in his usual blunt manner.

'Delhi works on trust ... no, not really. It works on a wide network of friends and associates and like everyone else, I have mine. Plus, I had you followed...'

Gurdev burst out laughing. 'What is your good name, dear man? I like you and that is why I have a proposition for you that might please you.'

'My name is Jagat Nath. My family has lived right here for five generations.'

'Jagat Nath, what if we give you a portion of profit instead of payment for the cloth, make you a partner in the khadi business?'

'No. What if no one buys your product? I have to pay my weavers so that they can eat.'

'Then give us two more weeks. Our tailor is a big khadoos. Fabric must be pre-shrunk, all-natural dyes, precision cutting and sewing with double stitching using high-quality thread – not cheap yarn that will rip across the seams after one extra serving of gulab jamun. Our tailor gives women a little room to grow with double seams and extra length so that anyone can wear the standard size. His measurements are based on measuring hundreds of women over the years, each one written in a pile of notebooks that are stored in a steel trunk that he carried all the way from the other side. His information ... that is what makes the diff—'

'Okay, okay enough. You are boring me to death but tell me one more thing. Is he using walnut hull for the black dye and beetroot for the red?'

'Yes. Yes. That is what he is using. So, which one will it be? Two extra weeks or a share in the profit? This is only a one-time offer. '

'First you pay me what you owe me and take the two weeks. Then sell your product and we'll talk.'

'Jagat Nath, you are testing us. Okay. *Theek hai*,' said Gurdev

Then Sangat, who would have to maintain this relationship, began, 'We are thankful to you. You don't know the kind of people you meet these days … like that man from the Rehabili—'

Gurdev broke in. 'Why are you boring Jagat even more with all our problems? We will manage…'

'My uncle works there – at the Rehabilitation Office. Here is his name and address. He is a Supervisor.' Jagat pulled out a scrap of paper from under the counter and scribbled something on it. 'Go and meet him. Tell him I sent you.'

Gurdev and Sangat looked silently at each other. Gurdev blinked once. Sangat's eyes couldn't stop fluttering. He was fighting back tears. Gurdev could see that he was about to fall at Jagat's feet and possibly kiss them, his lips were puckered so. He gathered up his friend, folded his hands in prayer and thanks to Jagat Nath and walked out of the cloth shop.

———

When he was done sewing and finishing four kurtas, Nirmal stopped work to take a break. He found a scrap of plywood and wrote on it neatly – '*Nirmal Singh Lohti*', and below it 'Ladies' Tailor' – in Gurmukhi and Urdu. Many refugees spoke Punjabi but their script was Urdu. He found a piece of rope, and hung the sign on a small cloth hook that he had sewn on the outside of the tent. He already had several clients from the camp and from outside. These ladies bought their own fabric and brought it to him to stitch. Harleen Madam and Satwinder Madam and Mrs Sharma, Gurdev's neighbour in the camp. And Harleen had told him that she would be sending her best friend. She didn't mention her name.

As he was aligning the sign, he heard Gurdev and Sangat's excited voices from the end of the alley. Their meeting must have gone well. Nirmal was happy for that but felt a little twinge in the base of his stomach, below his belly button. He was nervous about something. He looked again at the sign he had so neatly written and hung and realized that, in his excitement of finishing four kurtas, he had made the sign with only his name. As his two partners approached his tent, he tried to yank off the sign but couldn't. He had hung it in a way that no one could walk away with it. Then, as the two got closer, he stood before the sign, willing them to ignore it.

'Oye, Nirmal, what news we have for you. You won't believe it. We are now in business, Paaji, in business. We have the extra two weeks to pay the money and on our way back we went and met another person who works at the Rehabilitation Office. He told us that Garg is corrupt, the most corrupt. He wants a percentage of everything he gets for you. This man, our cloth vendor's uncle, his name is Inder Nath, he wants money – no one will do anything without money – but he will make sure I get fair compensation for my house and my flour mill.'

14

Noor Ikram Hasan was an imposing woman, tall and garrulous. She knew everyone in her neighbourhood of Nizamuddin, Delhi. She lived not far from the dargah, the main mosque, and considered herself a social worker, the kind who had experienced a tragedy and survived, not the sort who went to the Tata Institute of Social Sciences and lived a life of service. She had gathered together a small group of women whose husbands had suffered a similar fate to her own. They met every week, at a chai shop or in someone's home, drank tea, ate biscuits and discussed the latest films and fashions.

Noor Hasan was a widow; her husband had fought in the Royal Indian Army for the British in Europe. He had been among the first to reach the river Po, bypassing Bologna, a part of the Royal Indian Army's 8th Infantry Division that had engaged in weeks of battle with the retreating Germans. A stray bullet by a lone German sniper in a tree had killed him. The German must have fallen asleep while the rest of his people retreated. Corporal Ikram Hasan's entire battalion turned and fired at that tree as if it was Hitler himself, turning it into a pile of bloody matchsticks punctuated by fragments of human flesh and bone. But it had been of no use to Corporal Hasan. He had bled out from a wound in his neck that had scraped his carotid artery, enough to create a small, scarlet fountain that rose out from below his face, went strong for what seemed like several minutes and then slowed down to a small dribble, taking with it the quivering in Hasan's arms and legs, leaving him unmoving on the soft muddy ground, still thawing under the warm spring sun.

Ikram's comrade Imran had told Noor how he had watched his friend go from tall and strong, marching to victory, to dead in less than three minutes. She had wanted every detail, every stumble, every drop of blood spilt, and every cry of pain. She had loved her husband. They had been married almost four years when he first went to war and more than six when he died. He had come back home over those years of war, but all he had wanted then was to sleep in silence and to eat hot food. She had given him both and sat beside him, reading to him or quietly listening to the news on the radio and only going out to buy more fruit or more mutton. She had expected that he would return physically, and then over time return to himself, the man he had been – an energetic golfer, a lover of Sufi music, the man who could engage the guard at the gate in conversation about cricket for two hours, the man who drew people to himself.

Both Noor and Ikram were only children from wealthy families that had chosen to serve the rulers as part of the bureaucracy. Both their fathers were part of the Indian Civil Services, both were part of the Imperial class of service, serving the central government in Delhi, and both were allotted homes in Lutyens Delhi, not the palatial white structures set on acres of land – those were exclusively for the British – but smaller homes that were set in communities of senior Indian civil servants. These homes shared walls and hedges that separated small gardens but residents could call across to chat, or complain about a wayward dog or sometimes a child.

Noor and Ikram's parents knew each other. They had arranged their marriage and things had gone on well until the war. It had not been surprising for Ikram to join the Royal Indian Army. He had joined the Prince of Wales Royal Indian Military College in Dehradun because he hadn't been able to pass the competitive exam for the ICS and follow his father. He was one of a handful of Indian officers, along with his friend Imran Said, also a lieutenant in the 8th Infantry Division. They were part of a class of people who didn't see anything wrong with serving the rulers. It wasn't as if the British had just come in. They had been in India for decades before even their parents had been born. These were good jobs. They paid well and not anybody could get them. You had to be smart and aggressive and score in the competitive exams. You had to speak English and be comfortable with ruling over your own people, with rules made by outsiders.

Noor didn't exactly agree with her family's decision to serve the British, but her protest was only a niggling thought inside her. She had heard mumbles in school but these too were unformed opinions from young people who had overheard things. After school, she moved away from home, to Aligarh Muslim University's Women's College, where she told no one about her family's occupation. She had begun to be ashamed of her father, but not enough to stage a dialogue of any significance. When her parents proposed marriage to Ikram, also a servant to the rulers, she didn't protest.

However, when Ikram died, Noor moved out of her in-laws' home, now a comfortable bungalow in Civil Lines, allotted to active ICS officers. Civil Lines was a prominent neighbourhood for people who mattered, and Muslims who lived there had been safe, at least at first. She moved to Nizamuddin, a predominantly Muslim community that had arisen around the main mosque. She rented a room at the back of a family home – they called it an annexe. The family, an older couple, lived in the front house. Their married daughter and grandchildren visited occasionally from Lahore. It was more than a room, although that is what they called it and that is what her in-laws called it when she told them what she was doing – '*You are going to live in a room in someone else's house? What is the need for that when we have such a big empty house here? More empty because you and Ikram...*' This exact dialogue was repeated seventeen times, followed by tiny sighs and tinier tears as her in-laws needled her for not getting pregnant while their son was still alive. Sometimes she felt that they had expected their son to die in their lifetime but his dying without an heir was the bigger tragedy. She couldn't live with them and she couldn't go back and live with her parents – that would be all this and matchmaking.

Noor's 'room' was a bedroom, a sitting room, a bathroom and a small kitchen. It had a separate entrance, its own verandah in the back and even a small patch of grass. It was sturdy construction, brick and mortar, with bars on the windows to keep thieves out, kota stone flooring, green and cool, high ceilings and a simple bathroom with an Indian-style toilet. The kitchen was a kerosene stove and a sink with a little counter space and two shelves for spices.

This was December 1945. The big war was over. Indian troops who had fought for the British in the East and the West were returning home. Many were not. Subhash Chandra Bose and his efforts to ally with the Japanese to fight for India's independence against the British were dead in a plane crash. On 6 December, after talks between Jinnah, Nehru and Mountbatten, Jinnah asked for the formation of Pakistan – a partition of India. Indians around the country were still fighting for independence in forms that were labelled acts of terror and their perpetrators terrorists. But people, as long as they followed the rules, were safe in their homes, barring petty crimes for which there were bars on windows and heavy padlocks on doors. Some had the view that the heavier the padlock, the more to steal. So, people put smaller locks to throw off thieves. Noor had nothing of value to anyone. She had left with her everyday clothes and her mojris. Her heavy suits and jewellery from both sides, she had left with her parents. She had brought her marital linens, embroidered bed sheets, table cloths and monogrammed towels, all of which she was supposed to have done herself and, in fact, much of which she had. She liked embroidery. It added to plain cloth beauty and depth that poetry added to simple words. She was usually working on something, cloth entrapped between two concentric wooden rings to keep it stretched, her pattern book on one side of her and her bag of coloured threads on the other. Noor had learnt to embroider from her grandmother, but they had made frivolous things – tea cosies and tray cloths, small wall hangings, dinner napkins with a tiny flower in one corner; later more elaborate work but always for their own pleasure, never for any commercial purpose. Noor didn't show off her embroidery. She worked on pieces, displayed them and let her eyes take in the craft and her execution. Sometimes, she ripped open an often-used towel and redid the work if she found an extra stitch or crooked beading.

Noor settled into her new home, met her neighbours, and made some friends. These were not the sort of people she had met before. They were simple, religious, patriotic people who worked hard at small jobs. Every single person in her neighbourhood wanted the British out. Many came out into the streets and cheered when an Englishman was killed by a freedom fighter – that's what they were called here, not terrorists. She lived on the pension the government gave her as a widow of a fallen soldier. She visited her parents and in-laws from time to time, and both gave her small bundles of money that she tucked away into her purse. Accepting it pleased them, but only after she pushed it away once or twice. She used the pension to live and the gift money to buy clothes. She liked everything about clothing, the fabric, the feel against her skin, how the piece went on her, how it made her feel. For anyone who said that it wasn't the clothes, it was your carriage, she could prove ten different ways that they were wrong. And then there was the embroidery. Sitara and Reshma were two sisters she had found in her neighbourhood: saying their names – *sequin* and *silk* – brought visions of delicate stitches and graceful designs with little shiny bits that drew your eye this way and that. Most of the clothes she wore had been embroidered by the two sisters.

Noor rebuilt her life, connected with old friends and made new friends. She survived post-Partition anti-Muslim riots because she lived in a predominantly Muslim area. Her parents and her in-laws had to seek refuge with neighbours, even in their posh, cosmopolitan areas. She kept to her home and the nearby areas when she heard stories of Muslims being massacred in their homes, set aflame while they slept. Of wealthy Muslims who had to go to Purana Qila camp because they were pushed out of their homes by roaming groups of Sikhs in jeeps, recently returned from abandoning their homes in Pakistan and eager for revenge. If she went out, sometimes she wore a different style of salwar kameez, the shirt more fitted, the salwar with circles of fabric, Patiala-style, and covered her head the way Sikh women do. Sometimes, she wore her dupatta down and put a red bindi on her forehead and even sprinkled a little sindur in her parting. She was comfortable modifying her clothing like this because these were little things; these were all the differences between her and any Sikh or Hindu woman. Her friend Harleen had told her that it was easy for a Muslim woman to pass off as a Sikh but not so easy the other way around. Muslim women had a way about them, a way of draping their dupattas and holding their heads, a way of carrying themselves that Sikh women in their matter-of-fact simplicity could not copy.

15

Noor was studying Sufism, not to become a Sufi because that would be impossible. She could never give up anything worldly and beautiful. She was studying the practice of Sufism as an intellectual pursuit. She was particularly enamoured by Amir Khousrau, whose tomb was right there, next to the tomb of Hazrat Nizamuddin Auliya, also a Sufi saint, one of the most well known in India, of the Chishti Order after whom that area was named. Amir Khousrau was Nizamuddin's most beloved disciple. They died six months apart in the early 14th century. She had a desire to visit Ajodhan, the place that Nizamuddin went to every year for Ramzan since he was twenty and became a disciple of Baba Farid, a Sufi saint. Ajodhan was now in Pakistan, so this desire, that had taken years to develop, in a matter of moments had become impossible.

Noor was a reformist Muslim who had studied at Aligarh Muslim University. She was an intellectual, an interesting woman, or so she had fashioned herself to be. She wore her black hair long, parted in the middle and swept over to one side. She had begun to grey a little at the temples and above her ears, springy coarse new hair that stood straight up as much as she tried to comb it down. She let it be. She had skin the colour and texture of dates, smooth and brown, tiny lines appearing but smoothed down with her beauty concoctions.

Noor was vain, unlike what she was expected to be as a widow and an aspiring Sufi. She collected orange and apple peels in the winter, dried them and powdered them. She used this as a scrub for her face and body. Fresh cream mixed with turmeric, she used as a mask for her face, and the pulp of aloe vera as a tonic for her hair. She smelt of jasmine, sandalwood, rose, honeysuckle, lavender or something equally redolent of femininity and mystique. She dressed in beautifully embroidered flowing kurtas and pyjamas or salwars in the West Punjab style. She would have to start calling it Pakistani style now, or refugee style as worn by the more stylish refugees who had made their way to Delhi.

———

This was the style that Nirmal had mastered. Word of his skill with cutting a kurta had spread across Delhi. His fabric was plain and unadorned, so his appeal was not universal. Most early settlers as well as the more well-off refugees preferred embroidery and other enhancements on their kurtas. But he had a following of women who preferred fit to fashion and who came all the way to the refugee camp to buy his khadi kurtas.

———

Noor's friend Harleen had told her about this tailor, who had moved from the other side but had no shop. So, Noor, ever in search of nice things, went. She found the camp with her rickshaw walla's help but once there, she had to ask passers-by for Nirmal the tailor. After three lefts, four rights, two more lefts and a T-Junction, she found his tent. It had a small handmade sign on it that said *Nirmal Singh Lohti, Ladies' Tailor*. The tent flap was down and a small lock secured the flaps together. Noor laughed out loud at the ludicrousness of the scene but this was what people did – cursory as it was, if a tent was locked, no one tried to enter. And the place was so busy; someone immediately called out a new face.

'Yes, Madam. What do you want? Tailoring of clothes? You must come back tomorrow. Ladies' Tailor has gone to his shop in Khan Market,' said a voice from behind her.

'What shop? I thought he didn't have a shop.'

'That, madam, you will ask him please, tomorrow.'

Noor was sure she would come back, she had to. But she wondered if she could even find her way out of the maze today, let alone find her way back again tomorrow. As she mulled over the directions, she heard the same man call out to her.

'Oh, madam, Gurdev is coming. See there he is with Sangat. You can talk to them.'

'Who is Gurdev? I was looking for Nirmal the tailor.'

'Gurdev is his partner, madam. You can talk to him.'

Noor looked to the end of the alley and saw a tall Sardar walking with a shorter man. They were walking towards Nirmal's tent. Noor stepped out of their way, intent as they were, although she was not usually one to step out of anyone's way.

The shorter man fished out a key from his baggy western-style pants and unlocked the lock, parting the tent flap. He went in and brought out a big metal box, wide at the base and narrower on top. The tall man brought out two metal boxes, also large but rectangular. Each of these boxes had a lock about three times the size of the one on the tent. These he swung into his arms as if they were empty vegetable bags.

'What is this? What are you doing with all that? Where is the tailor?' Noor was distressed. She was watching something important happen, but she didn't know what.

'Madam, we have set up our shop in the new market. Some little work is still pending but we are more or less ready. The road in front is bad though. Please come and see us in two or three weeks. Everything will be arranged by then,' the shorter of the two spoke; the tall man looked at Noor in silence.

'I can't keep coming back to this side. You know how much I had to pay the rickshaw walla and then to find this new shop of yours! Finding anything in this refugee jhamela...' She clamped her hand to her mouth. 'So sorry, I shouldn't have said that. After all, you have been displaced, you've lost everything...' Her voice trailed off as she realized that the tall Sardar was staring at her unblinkingly.

'Madam, don't worry. We'll put a big board on the shop and small-small boards at ea—ea—each turning to guide people...' the short man stuttered.

'Bibiji, you can come with us now. We'll show you where we will be,' the tall man finally spoke. He addressed her as one would address an older woman, a Sikh woman. Noor adjusted her dupatta over her head, said 'Hanji' like any Punjabi woman and followed the two men out of the camp.

Noor knew what she was doing when she had decided to come alone to this Hindu and Sikh refugee camp. She had wanted Harleen to come along, but her friend was busy with guests at home. Noor was impetuous and impatient so she had carefully drawn a bindi on her forehead and taken care to say Namaste and Sat Sri Akal, depending on whether she was talking to a Hindu or Sikh and walked straight, all the way up to her full height.

Noor was nervous now though, following these two men. After they came out of the camp, they walked three abreast whenever possible, single file amid crowds.

'What are your names, please? I don't want to refer to you as 'brothers' because you are not my brothers and clearing my throat to get your attention will make my perfectly sound throat sore.'

'I am Gurdev,' said the tall man. 'I am Sangat. Nirmal is our third partner. He is the real ladies' tailor.'

'And what are the two of you doing in this ladies' tailoring business? Watching Nirmal take measurements?' She laughed out loud, a deep-throated unselfconscious laugh as she watched the two men blush – even Gurdev went pink under his thick black beard but he recovered quickly.

'Bibiji, there are many other things to do when setting up a business like this. Where do you think the shop came from? That was my effort. Where do you think all the mulmul and lace and silk and brocade is coming from? Sangat is in charge of that and finding the right craftsmen. Right now, Sangat is trying to find two of the best embroiderers in the world.'

'Who? Sitara and Reshma? They are the best embroiderers in Delhi. I know them.'

'Bibiji, we are not just darzis. We will bring you work like you have never seen before.' Gurdev looked at Noor, straight at her, like he hadn't done so far. 'As for our embroiderers, this trunk has some samples. Two boys who are the best in the world do them. Your Sitara and Reshma only have ornamental names. They cannot match the work. The only problem is that these boys are in Pakistan and we have to find a way to get them out.'

Sangat stared at his friend, wondering why he was telling this strange woman so much.

Without thinking, Noor blurted out, 'I can go and find them for you. They'll let me go to Pakistan and come back.'

'Bibiji, I mean, why … would you want to go there. Those Mussalmans, they are out for our blood. A woman like you, I can see you are educated, but it is not like that now. They have been kidnapping and raping our women – you must have heard. Our men have also brought Mussalman women … Bibiji, this is not a joke.'

'Gurdevji, I can go … because … I can go because I am a Mussalman.' She turned around to look for a rickshaw to take her home.

'She's a Mussalman? But she doesn't look like one. So openly she is walking into our camp. What about that bindi? Do Mussalman women wear them? No. She was trying to deceive us. And where is her Burqa? Is she a real Mussalman even? She looks like our women only.' The two men whispered back and forth, Sangat doing most of the talking, Gurdev nodding absentmindedly.

'Bibiji, wait a minute, please. We don't care whether you are a Mussalman or a bhoot. If you will wear our clothes and bring us more customers, why should we care? Right, Sangat? Sangat stood there, stunned. He pulled Gurdev aside. 'One minute, Bibiji. Bhai Sahib, if anyone finds out, our business will close down before it even starts,' he mumbled under his breath.

'Speak up, Sangat. You don't need to mumble. Bibiji can help us. You will help us, won't you, Bibiji?'

'Gurdev, I will help you but please stop calling me Bibiji. I feel like my friend Harleen's grandmother, who sits on a charpoy in the courtyard shouting orders.'

'Oh ho, you also have a Sikh friend,' Sangat finally spoke out loud. 'Good, ji. Chalo, everything is perfect. Now, we need to get a rickshaw and take all this to the shop.'

Sangat hailed two rickshaws and loaded the three boxes in one. He indicated to Gurdev to get on with him. Gurdev looked at the heavy load already in the rickshaw. He looked at the short sinuous man who stood aside ready to pedal. He looked over at Noor and then he looked around for another rickshaw.

As if reading his mind, Noor said, 'We can share a rickshaw, no need to get a third one for me.'

Gurdev and Noor sat side by side, pressed against each other in one rickshaw as Sunder balanced the three boxes in another. Both rickshaws moved slowly at first, then gathered speed as the road cleared outside the refugee camp.

'Noorji, you took a big risk coming here.'

'I know. I should have come with Harleen.'

'No, Noorji. You should not have come here at all.'

'I meant what I said about going to Pakistan to look for your two boys. I can go to Lahore easily. I know people...'

'Noorji, it is too dangerous. I cannot let you take such a risk. Anyway, why should you? You don't even know us. I also don't know how good these boys are. Nirmal has set his mind on them but it will not be easy...'

'I know, Gurdevji. Let's leave that for the time being. Where did you come from? Did you ... what happened to you? Where are you now? At the camp?

'Noorji, I will answer all your questions but now we are reaching the shop. Please be careful. The road is not made yet.'

Gurdev jumped out of the rickshaw and held out a hand for Noor to help her. She waved it away and stepped right off. Gurdev walked over to Sangat's rickshaw and picked up the two large boxes.

Noor looked around. The area looked like a child's sand pile with bits of coloured doodads buried here and there, a sandcastle the main feature, still under construction. There were large piles of rubble, rocks and mud, piles of trees and brush and shallow holes in the ground for foundations yet to be built. There was an air of frenetic activity but in slow motion, colourful trucks moving here and there, men shouting instructions, women carrying iron bowls filled with rubble on their heads. But on one side of this melee, construction was complete. One row of shops, fifteen-feet-by-fifteen-feet was all done. There was a bookstore coming up across four shops, a double-wide sweet shop and then two shops for Gurdev and his partners. They had pulled the shutter down on one while carpenters worked on the other one, making shelves and display cupboards and cushioned diwans for the sales staff to show the delicate fabric and low plush stools with backrests for their customers. They had named the shop Nilibar.

'Why Nilibar?' Noor asked.

Gurdev turned pensive and distant. 'The Punjabi word 'bar' means a threshold, an outside space, an area somewhere between civilization and the wild. The Punjab that all three of us hail from was built around the banks of five rivers. Each area between two rivers is referred to as a different bar. Nilibar is the area on the East and West of the Sutlej River. It is the love for our emotional and spiritual home, our land, our soil that has made us bring a part of it to what is now only our practical home.' Gurdev continued talking as if he was somewhere else, 'There was also a famous cloth shop named Nilibar in Lahore run by a well-known Sikh family. My mother went there before a wedding or other function and bought cloth from them. I went with her, watching as these boys draped fabric around themselves, covered their heads with the beautiful dupattas, modelling for their clients. I used to giggle sitting by my mother till, one day, one less timid young man had me up modelling a dupatta draped around my head.' Gurdev's voice became low and soft. 'That whole Nilibar family was slaughtered, including the children, with machetes and swords, as they slept. The old man who sat at the cash register in the shop, always asleep, the young man, one of the sons who knew my mother best – all butchered in their beds. They should have moved when all of us came, but they thought they could survive because they were rich.'

Noor said nothing.

'And that is why no one is going to Pakistan.' Gurdev's mouth twitched, his whiskers quivered, the coarse hair moving around as if in a storm.

'And here's your tailor, Nirmal. Nirmal, Bibiji here has been looking for you. She was referred to you by Bibi Harleen Kaur.'

'Sat Sri Akal Bibiji. Come this side, please.' Nirmal guided Noor into the shuttered side of the shop. The wall between the two had a door that looked like it was part of the glass wall. This second half of the shop was all finished. It was the workshop; set up with six, foot-pedal operated sewing machines in one half of the room and thick mattresses on the floor on the other half. This is where the craftsmen would do the handwork, buttons, hemming, embroidery, and all that. There were also two trial rooms.

Sangat and Gurdev brought the boxes they had collected from Nirmal's tent and set them on the floor. Nirmal gently dusted all three and unlocked them with a set of keys he kept pinned inside his pants pocket. He opened them with prayer-like reverence, hands on heart, then on head and then on the closed lid.

Noor saw in these three men, whom she had only known for a few hours, a hunger for something much more than money. She saw spirituality in their actions, a purposeful method to each movement. And she couldn't help but imagine herself in the beautiful clothes that this short, oddly dressed man was going to make for her.

At thirty-four, Noor's middle was thickening and her upper arms had become shapeless. Her belly was getting soft and her upper legs were dimpled. It was a good thing she hadn't had children – or things would have been much worse – but there hadn't been any time. Her husband had been shipped off to war. Nice clothes helped and they helped her feel young ... maybe comfortable. There was a lot she could say about being comfortable. It was all about how you felt when you saw yourself in a mirror inadvertently, in a shop window, perhaps, as you walked down the street. It was also how much you felt you needed to suck your stomach in to create a smooth side profile. It was how square or slouchy the stitching of your kurta made your shoulders look. And then there was the fabric. Billowy gave you inches where you had none and clingy showed curves you preferred remained hidden.

'Bibiji, Bibiji, where did you get lost? Come, I'll show you what I've been doing.' She broke out of her reverie and heard Nirmal's voice calling out to her but she also heard whispering behind her, in the other half of the shop. 'Why didn't you tell Nirmal that she's a Mussalman, Gurdev? You are letting him think she's one of us. Why? You think there will be a problem, no?'

Noor sat on the mattress as Nirmal laid out kurtas in Khadi fabric, simply tailored, in four sizes and four colours.

'All-natural, homespun fabric, all-natural India-made dyes and I pre-shrunk the fabric and tested the colour in hot and cold water.' Nirmal went on as Noor examined the stitching, the finishing, turning the garment inside out.

'You can buy my "ready-mades",' Nirmal giggled at the term, 'or you can buy fabric from our shop and we will stitch according to your measurements and design. But then, don't ask for designing because for us, design is our investment – that is what we do for our own clothes, based on our experience. Gurdev's idea was to go only "ready-mades",' Nirmal giggled again, 'but I think women are used to stitching – they don't believe a good fit is possible with anything else. They don't know me, though. They don't know what I can do…'

'Why didn't you go with Gurdev's idea then? You agreed with him and you believe you know how to do it.'

'Bibiji, I am confident but not stupid. He's the one who has invested everything. It is his property in Pakistan that has brought us all this. We have to get him his money back, no? Slowly slowly, we'll do everything.'

Noor went into the changing room to try on the 'ready-made' khadi kurtas. The room was spotless, a small stool in one corner, hooks on the door, mirrors all around. She had never seen anything like it. But she found it strange to take off her clothes, alone, in this strange place. What if someone was looking … through a peephole or something?

What if this was all a scam to get women to undress? She shook her head to blow out the silly thought and took off her top. She tried on two styles, a fitted and a loose one. She liked them both. One made her look sleek and svelte, with no lumps and bumps, the other gave her a more casual, earthy look. She came out and paid for both and walked into the other half of the store, where Gurdev and Sangat were watching the carpenters put finishing touches on the woodwork. Now, they had to buy their stock and they were in business.

'Bibiji, what do you think? Do you like the tailor? Your friend sent you to a good place, no? You haven't seen our main thing yet. Those trunks have...'

'No, no,' Nirmal interrupted Gurdev. 'Don't say anything about that. Those are only samples. We still have to get Sultan and Samir out before we can start talking about that part.'

Noor knew they were talking about their embroidery samples and the master craftsmen, but she kept quiet. She also didn't correct Gurdev. Subconsciously, she felt for the bindi on her forehead, the texture rough against her finger and quietly said, 'Sat Sri Akal ji. I will tell my friends.'

After Noor got back home and sat down with a cup of tea, she felt a little rumbling sensation in the base of her stomach cavity that rose in waves all the way up to her throat. It wasn't nausea. It was joy. She felt joyous. It was that thrill of buying something new, but no, that was a different feeling and it went away quickly. That feeling couldn't penetrate the joy that kept coming back in waves. She closed her eyes and Gurdev's face appeared before her – strong, bearded, small, sharp, almost ink-black eyes that blinked so infrequently, she thought there was something wrong with them. She would have to ask him about his eyes the next time she met him. His moustache hung over his lips, never trimmed, smoothed on either side. He had this way, like many men with moustaches, of running his middle finger and thumb down the top of his lips, urging the coarse hair into a smooth curve above his lip line. Each time he did that, she saw his lips, like a bow, the upper shapely but narrow, the lower full and red.

Noor shook her head. What was she doing? She knew nothing more about this man except for that he was enterprising, polite, level-headed and secular. He was probably married to a shy Sikh woman and had a bevvy of children. She wondered where they lived, what his wife looked like, what made him not even flinch when she had said she was Muslim.

For days after, Noor couldn't focus on her Sufi studies or her meetings. She ate perfunctorily and wore the same two khadi kurtas every day, in turn. Her young maid laid out something else for her, an older embroidered kurta and brocade salwar but she screamed at the young woman and asked her to iron the khadi.

'But, Noor Bibi, you've already worn it three times this week. People will think you have no other clothes.' But Noor shook her head and sat in her bathrobe till the maid ironed the kurta.

When Harleen came over on Saturday to ask Noor to come out for golgappas, Noor finally snapped out of it.

'Aha! Someone went shopping, I see. Nice, na? Not fancy but comfortable.'

'That's exactly what I said. No embroidery, no fuss but comfortable.'

Harleen and Noor had been friends since they were in school together. Harleen had an older brother, but she and Noor were sisters bound by something else. Harleen had been with Noor at her wedding, when news of her husband came and when Noor decided she would live alone, not with her in-laws or with her parents.

Harleen's own life was conventional – an arranged marriage, three boys, in-laws and all the pandemonium that comes from living in a closed box.

'I heard that they are doing well with their ready-mades – the tailors, I mean. So odd, no? Those would not fit me, but looks like they fit you well.'

Harleen looked down at her own body, under five feet, stocky but not fat. She never missed her early morning walk with her otherwise disinterested husband. It was their time to gossip.

'They'll fit you, Harleen. That man, Nirmal, he is a genius. He has determined a formula for women's sizes. He's measured so many women of our type that his clothes will fit anyone. Let's go and buy something for you.'

'I can't go. I got away for a little while to see you. My husband's Bhuaji and her family are here from Gurdaspur and will stay for some time, till things settle down. That's what she said – 'We'll see when we are able to go back.' All five of us are squeezed into one room and one bathroom. But the stories they have, you won't believe...'

'Harleen, at least you have a home and your own bathroom. I went to the refugee camp. You can't imagine. The toilets and bathrooms are common, men on one side and women on the other...'

'Noor, I know about the conditions. Those are my people...'

'They are also my people. I'm also Indian.'

'But it was your people...'

'Stop with this, Harleen. I know what happened in Gurdaspur. I know what happened to the Muslims there. Many have come to Delhi. They have also lost everything, and they get nothing in compensation because they haven't come from Pakistan. I know what happened on the train from Gurdaspur to Lahore, Harleen. I know. So don't talk to me about my people and your people.' Noor shook her head to say *never mind* and hugged her best friend. 'Speaking of your people, I met a Sardar. A tall, handsome Sardar. He is the tailor's business partner.'

Harleen squealed with glee but immediately sobered up. 'Noor, no. No. You can't. You don't know what will happen.'

'Relax, Harleen. He's probably married with many children. I felt something, that's all. First time ... after five years ... I felt a flutter, so I thought I would tell you.'

'Okay, okay. Good. Fluttering is good but find someone else to flutter after, I beg you. A Muslim, even a Christian or a Parsi – but no Hindus or Sikhs. Understood?'

'Yes, Harleen. Understood.'

16

Despite her promise to her friend, Noor couldn't stop fluttering after Gurdev. What she didn't know was that Gurdev was fluttering after her as well. He was distracted, not eating his food, listening to his partners for a minute then drifting away. For a while he didn't know what was happening to him till Sangat touched him on the shoulder and asked, 'Is everything all right, Prahji? I've never seen you like this. You haven't eaten anything – and it's your favourite makki ki roti and saag. Amrit sent it especially for you. Why these women like you so much, I don't understand.'

Sangat chatted away with Gurdev, slowly taking bites of the food. Nirmal stayed silent.

Gurdev closed his eyes, his moustache fluttered about with his exhalations. He held on to the sides of the chair he was sitting on till his palms hurt. He opened his mouth for one big breath in and spoke slowly, 'Two long years have passed, since Simrat left me. I don't know where she is or how she is doing. To tell you the truth, I haven't tried to find her. If I had, I would have. Funny thing is, even her brother doesn't know where she is. I hope she is well and taking care of her children. I want her to get her share of her parents' property – that Sujjat Singh will take it all if he can. I think I owe her that much. Then, I must move on.'

Nirmal and Sangat both nodded their agreement. Gurdev never spoke about his personal life – even that first time they met him, he knew they had overheard his conversation with Sujjat and with Mrs Sharma but he had not offered anything. Without saying anything else, he left them both at the shop and took a rickshaw back to his house.

The night chill had set in and Gurdev's shack was cold. Little fingers of cold wind made their way in through tiny cracks, even though Anandi, the neighbour's daughter, had stuffed them with kneaded dough. The dough dried up after a while and either got wedged in nice and tight, or shrunk down and got pushed back into the shack leaving a clear but tiny pathway for the billows of icy wind.

The shack had one large bed now. Gurdev had removed the second bed that he had set up for the boys. It was high off the floor, the area below used to store his meagre wardrobes and a few books. There was one thick, fluffy quilt lying folded on one end of the bed. This night, he got into bed and tucked the quilt under his chin, his knees up, feet as close to him as he could manage. He slid one foot down the cold sheet, warming it along the way. As his foot made its way down the bed, the sheet turned toasty right at the end and there it was, the warm soft cloth that covered a hot water bottle, tucked under the sheet and under the folded quilt so it would stay hot. Anandi had been at work again. He had to do something about her. Her attention was embarrassing, but other thoughts distracted him.

On this cold night, colder than most, he wondered if Noor was warm. He wondered what she would think of his humble shack. He wondered where he would keep her if she ever agreed to be with him. And, just like that, his head moved from Anandi working to keep him warm to Noor. He said his prayers, something that Simrat had taught the boys, the first verse of Japji Sahib, the morning prayer of the Sikhs. He didn't usually pray, but Simrat's voice reciting the verse with the boys flitted in and out of his conscience.

After prayer, Gurdev tried to invoke images of the Gurus or even of a recent visit to a Gurdwara but he couldn't. Noor's face, sideways, sitting next to him on the rickshaw was right there. He found her interesting and entertaining. He liked that she was bold yet unassuming. He liked that she was stylish yet understated. He liked the way she smelt when they sat close to each other on that rickshaw. Simrat had never smelt like that. He couldn't say whether he had relished the ride or hated it, but by the time they reached Khan Market, he was aroused and uncomfortably so. Fortunately, he still wore loose-fitting Pathan suits, a long shirt with a man's salwar, remnants of his life in rural Pakistan, worn down and faded, but useful that day.

Gurdev had not been with any woman since Simrat had left. He had been busy and preoccupied and not interested. Once or twice, he had looked at Anandi – her strong body as she hung clothes to dry or carried a heavy bucket of water to swab the floors. His neighbours had approached the subject of her marriage with him several months after Simrat had left, but Gurdev had politely declined. They had insisted she help him out, do a little housework and cooking for him, and he had reluctantly agreed but only as long as she did the work while he was out. The young woman had lost her husband during Partition. She had suffered, but Noor had suffered too. She had also lost her husband. Gurdev's thoughts pivoted right back to the woman he was completely enamoured with, but he was troubled by his own past.

No one, not even Simrat, had known what he had done. What would Noor do if she found out? Some nights he woke up with a start, couldn't breathe properly. He felt stifled. But most days, he ensured exhaustion so that dreamless sleep had to come. He also didn't drink as his friends did. He gave up alcohol after that night in Lahore. If he put it to his lips, he wouldn't be able to stop – for it was the perfect antidote to pain. And once he was drunk, he would open his mouth and tell everybody what he had done, who he was – but he wasn't that. He wasn't that man. He wasn't. He wasn't. As he repeated those words in his head, he finally fell asleep.

———

The next day, Gurdev went to Nirmal's barrack at the camp to speak to his wife, Amrit, and asked Sangat's wife, Paramjit, to come as well.

'Amrit, Paramjit, I need your help.'

'Prahji, what do you need? I hear you are ready to marry again,' said Amrit, the outspoken one.

'Yes, tell us, Prahji, what do you need from us?' said Paramjit.

'I'll tell you who's perfect for you, Gurdev – Anandi, your neighbour's daughter. The old lady came to me and to Paramjit, but we both told her you were not ready.'

'I need your help to find a husband for her. Last night, she put a hot water bottle on my bed. It's too much. The bottle was still hot so she must have come right before I returned, which was late. It's not good for her to keep doing these things.'

'But, Prahji, who knows what all she's been through? Her parents have been trying to find someone for her for long. What can we do?' said Paramjit.

Amrit was blunter. Gurdev usually liked her directness, but not this time. 'You should marry her, Prahji. She is right for you and knows your ways. Besides, what will you do without a woman around to take care of things?'

'Bibi Amrit, I can hire a boy to take care of my home. I don't need to ruin a young woman's life for that. I don't feel anything like that for her. She's like my daughter. So, is that fair?'

'But, Prahji, there are no options also, no? What else can she do? I have heard of some things … that she was taken … by some Mussalman men. Her husband died trying to rescue her … that is what I've heard. Now, who will marry her? That is why her parents are struggling. But you are a good man … and she's already been taking care of you…'

'So, it sounds like you will not help me?'

'See, Prahji, we cannot approach anyone knowing the history of this girl. Everyone will assume … you know … that she's been with you and who knows what else? There is already that talk.'

'Bibi Amrit, what are you saying? Everyone will think the worst if you let them. If you tell them the truth, they will know the truth. If you shrug your shoulders and say 'who knows' or 'it is only natural' or something equally idiotic, they'll think the worst.'

Amrit and Paramjit tried to calm Gurdev down, but he was done listening. These were backward women with backward minds that would take generations to change. His Simrat was not like them. For the first time, he let himself miss her. And then, when her face slowly morphed into Noor's in his mind, he had to jump up rudely and walk away from the two women. Later, he asked his friends to apologize to their wives on his behalf. He had not been himself.

Gurdev walked alone for a long time, slowly at first, then faster, and he kept walking. Before he knew it, he had reached Jagat Nath's shop.

'Namaste, Jagat Nath. Hope the spinning and weaving is going well. Nirmal's kurtas are selling faster than we can make them. Luckily, thanks to your uncle, I've received a good settlement and our new shop in Khan Market is almost ready.'

'Gurdevji, you were here yesterday and told me all this. Have you forgotten? Are you feeling okay?'

'I am a little disturbed, Jagatji. Now that you've agreed to become our partner, I can tell you.' Gurdev told Jagat about his wife, her sudden departure, Anandi, his house, everything. And now it was up to him to find a husband for Anandi. He didn't say anything about Noor, of course – although he was desperate to talk to someone about his feelings. Should he be having such feelings after one meeting? Should he forget about her? He wanted someone to tell him what to do, but he couldn't ask Jagat.

'Gurdevji, this is a small matter. You give me specifics, caste, sub-caste, date and time of birth, mother's name, father's name, their Janam patris, etc., and we will find someone suitable. You said she's been married before – then husband's name...'

Gurdev's face fell. Poor Anandi would maybe fit these qualifications, but what would happen when more questions came? This man was like everyone else. He couldn't believe him. He couldn't believe that he had misjudged him.

'Gurdevji, you look like a dog who ran away from home and can't find his way back. I was only joking with you. Please don't take me so seriously. We don't believe in all this. Why would I be helping so many Muslims if I did? Why then would my own wife be Muslim? Of course, in order to live here peaceably, we changed her name from Umrao to Urmila. But that had to be done or someone would have killed us both. But I know what I have done and I am proud of it. I'll put the word out and let you know. Don't worry. Sometimes, us Delhi people are not so bad.'

'Jagatji, thank you. You have saved me yet again.'

Offers for Anandi began coming right away. There were men who Gurdev rejected – too old, too serious, too timid. Finally, after three months, Jagat sent his boy to the shop with a message that said he had found the perfect match. It was a doctor. A young doctor. His name was Dr Vinod Bhargava, Simrat's young doctor who had recommended she see a specialist who then recommended an operation after which she had run away.

The young doctor was a good man. When Gurdev finally met him and introduced him to Anandi, he felt goodness spread through him, goodness that he hoped would begin to undo the events of her past.

Dr Bhargava and Anandi got married in a court ceremony. Gurdev got Nirmal to give up one of his embroidered treasures to make a sari for Anandi. It was a khadi sari, in keeping with the times, but the border had embroidery that brought tears to Gurdev's eyes. For the first time since he had met Nirmal, he truly appreciated workmanship that was almost as if angels had sewed. Before he had met Nirmal, women's clothing was one of those things such as sewage systems or a newspaper printing press. They worked, somehow, but nobody cared to learn too much more about them.

When Nirmal opened his second trunk to take out the embroidered border that he had decided on, he gently caressed all the other pieces – never to be used except for special people for special occasions – at least until he could get Sultan and Samir to India, assuming they even wanted to come to what was now a strange and hostile country that didn't want them.

But he had to try. Their world would change even more than it already had if they could become masters of embroidery. Jagat Nath, their fourth partner, was pleased with the success of the khadi line and wanted nothing more: he could not grasp the importance of embroidery to their business. Gurdev saw the beauty in what Nirmal kept in his boxes, and he understood that women wanted this kind of embellishment for their clothing, but he didn't understand why they couldn't find someone who was already in Delhi to do it. He would even go to parts of Uttar Pradesh or Punjab, where they had heard the embroidery was impeccable, and find the craftsmen himself. They would come to Delhi readily if they found a place to stay and good pay. But Nirmal would not budge.

'I'll make khadi kurtas day and night. I'll come up with new styles, ditto from the films, but no chiffon like the films, only khadi and maybe mulmul, another fabric that Jagat Nath can get his hands on at a good price and with reliable delivery. But I will not create an embroidery line without my boys. We have to find them, convince them to come here and take care of them.'

'Nirmal, we all want to make the business grow. There is nothing else to do but that. We are not artists, after all, we are businessmen, are we not? If we don't expand our product line, we'll go stale and old, and people will stop buying our product, even if it is the best. But first tell me why we have to go into embroidery? Each piece can take days—'

Nirmal interrupted Gurdev, 'Days, Gurdev? No, no. Each piece can take weeks, even months.'

'That is what I am saying, Nirmal. You finish one khadi kurta in hours and we can sell as many as we can make, for now. We have to come up with something like that, that you can make quickly and sell quickly.'

'Gurdev, you are like my brother but, brother, you don't know anything. After some time, all women want clothes for functions, for weddings, for special events at the Gurudawara. They want to show off to their friends they have something different – not all same silk with same embroidery. Then, after some more time, they want more for their daughters' weddings: embroidered clothes that the in-laws will be jealous of. In the olden days, girls, their mothers, grandmothers, bhuas, maasis and chachis all sat and embroidered their trousseau – all giving the bride their blessings in this way. Now, who has the time for all that? They want us to do it – but where are we? Same old Sitara and Reshma, same old designs, nothing new, nothing different. For something different, we need Samir and Sultan. They are like those women of the olden days. They put love into their work. They will give work from the maasi and from the grandmother, and your ladies will pay for it. Ask your Noor madam, she will tell you. If we don't do it, they will keep buying daily wear from us and go somewhere else to spend big money.'

'Nirmal, I understand, I think. No need to ask Noor madam anything. But you know it might be impossible to get those boys here. There has already been one war fought, and with difficulty that ended in 1948. I know that was only in Kashmir and things have settled down again, but it is not so easy to get visas for either country. Have you thought of something? If you have an idea, tell us.'

'Gurdev, I have not thought of anything but I was thinking of asking Noor Madam. She seemed to know a lot about Pakistan.'

'Nirmal, Noor Madam is a customer. Why would you involve her? No, definitely do not ask her anything. She's a talker. Everyone will know what you are trying to do and then you'll be in jail. She was saying she knew about Pakistan. And how long ago was that? Two years, at least. Everything is changing. She knows nothing. Let her keep buying your clothes and bringing her friends. That, she's good at. I will come up with a plan and I don't need anyone's help, especially not hers.'

Nirmal stared at him, his face blank, his eyes blinking slowly. Gurdev stared back, a questioning look on his face. He looked away first. Neither said anything. Nirmal liked Noor, Gurdev knew that. She had brought him a lot of business and she told him what worked and what he needed to fix. And she talked to him as an equal, not like a rich customer like many Delhi women did. Not the refugees, they spoke with respect. It was the locals. They bought his clothes and enjoyed them but thought him nothing but a refugee shopkeeper. Rude Delhi women didn't bother Gurdev. He put them in their place, in his soft turban and his scruffy beard and his old Pathan suits that he kept washing and wearing. Someday, he would need to get something new but for now, he was fine. He was fine as far as his appearance was concerned but inside, he was not. Noor was irritating him. She came to the shop often, drank endless cups of tea, tried on new kurta styles even before Nirmal had sewn the pieces together and chattered non-stop with Nirmal, with Sangat, with all the young craftsmen who worked on the cutting and sewing. One day, he had walked into the workshop to find her standing before a mirror, draped in two pieces of fabric over her own clothes, with Nirmal standing by her side, pinching and pinning the fabric around her as she told him where she liked it to fit and where to flare. Gurdev got angry seeing her like that. He wasn't sure why, but he felt this knocking in his head that quickly spread to his arms and his chest, which suddenly felt constrained under his loose kurta as if he was wrapped in tight elastic that squeezed him tighter with each breath. He turned around and walked out and went into the bookstore next door. He found a cool spot in the back shelves where he took out a Perry Mason novel by Erle Stanley Gardner, *The Case of the Sulky Girl,* and he had to smile. It should have read *The Case of the Sulky Sardar.*

Gurdev went back into the workshop in a better mood. He greeted Noor casually and sat down with Sangat to discuss business matters.

18

NIRMAL HAD NOT TOLD HIS PARTNERS THAT HE HAD BEEN in touch with Sultan and Samir almost since they had first reached Delhi and got settled in the refugee camp. He had not even told Amrit that he was writing to them. His letters had reached them and they had replied, which meant that they were still in Lahore, still in the family house. He knew their grandmother was dead but he wondered about their father. He had not been that old but, in these times, age mattered little where death was concerned. In his letters, he wrote nothing about inviting the brothers to India in case someone was reading their mail. People were still writing letters across the border, to friends, neighbours, relatives left behind. Some were even sending parcels of food, books, even music records wrapped carefully in old petticoats.

The border, aside from Kashmir, was not yet secured; four years on, people still went back and forth but it was not easy. If they were caught, they could be tried for treason and shot by a firing squad before anybody heard anything about the incident. Officially, the Pakistani government was letting in

Muslims from India with a proper application and proof of
family and property in Pakistan. The Indian government was
doing the same for Hindus and Sikhs. Muslims who wanted
to leave Pakistan for India, Muslims who had only been in
Pakistan for a trip or on holiday, for instance, couldn't come
back through official channels. India continually denied their
visas. There was talk about special visas on both sides, for
weddings or other special occasions, also to visit religious
sites. But these visas were only given on specific authority of
a senior official in the Indian government, and the visiting
party had to check in with the local police and then confirm
their departure.

The possibility of bringing Sultan and Samir to India
looked bleak but Nirmal was sure Gurdev would come up
with something, especially since he had been angry. Gurdev
was hard to control when he got angry but he came up with
good ideas in that anger.

Gurdev did have a plan. It was a complicated plan with
little chance of success. It would take months to execute and
he would need active and hence potentially incriminating
support from everyone – Nirmal and Sangat, Jagat, Anandi,
her Dr Vinod Bhargava and even Noor. He asked Nirmal to
call everyone for a meeting at his house. Nirmal could tell that
he was nervous, not about his plan but about his shack. And
he had asked to invite Noor. Nirmal had not even brought
up her name. She had come to the shop, many times with
friends and talked to him, what she liked, what they wanted
him to make next time. Gurdev had been there once. He had
left looking angry. With Gurdev, it was hard to tell what got
him angry. Nirmal and Sangat had learnt to leave him alone

when he was in that mood. No point. Sometimes he shouted at them. Sometimes he even said mean things about them not contributing anything. Sangat would get sad but Nirmal didn't mind. He knew that the only way to get his boys to India was if Gurdev made the plan. He set the meeting in a week, making sure everyone was able to come.

'Thank you all for coming,' Gurdev announced in his booming voice. Please sit wherever you can find place and please excuse my humble dwelling. Someday, you will all come to the house I will build on this land...'

'Get on with it, Gurdev,' shouted Jagat, drowning out Gurdev's platitudes.

'Okay, okay. You are all here to help us achieve our next major milestone – to add embroidery and an assortment of fabric to our collection. Remember that this is not ordinary embroidery...' He was interrupted again, this time by Anandi.

'We know, Prahji. Angels have done this embroidery. I have proof. Go on now.'

'All right, the task is to bring two of the finest embroiderers from Lahore to Delhi, without raising suspicions – meaning we don't want them to be fugitives being hunted by the police of two countries. We also want to ensure for them a comfortable life in India, doing the work they are so good at but also taking on some apprentices who they teach their craft to. Noor, your Sitara and Reshma could be candidates and, if possible, much more than candidates for the two young men.'

Everyone laughed out loud.

'Sitara and Reshma are both in their forties and have seven or eight children between them.,' said Noor.

'Oho, as good as one foot in the grave,' retorted Gurdev and everyone laughed again.

'We'll get to the apprentices later. As it is, this plan will only work one step at a time. Each time we take a step, we have to see the result and then plan the next step. This cannot be a big plan from beginning to end because so many things keep moving and changing. But I want everyone to be involved in every step – we need many good heads working together to make this work.

'One: Nirmal will write another letter to Sultan and Samir – he's already done that, in fact. Two: in this letter he will invite them to the wedding of his daughter Anandi with the good doctor. There was a loud 'whaaat?' from Anandi on this point but Gurdev put a finger on his lips, indicating to her to let him finish. Three: Noor will make preparations for a proper wedding. Four: Jagat will offer his expert comments on everything. Nirmal, why don't you read the letter you have written?'

My dear sons, (for what are you but my sons, as close as you are to my heart?)

I write to you to share my great joy with you. My daughter, Anandi, your childhood playmate, is getting married. We have found a match well suited to her fiery temperament, don't worry. It is a young doctor, handsome and cool as the water in the river Sutlej. For this grand occasion, I would like to invite you to be my personal guests.

Myself, along with two partners, have been able to stand up a business, our own cloth and tailoring shop for women. Needless to say, the shop will be busy with

*Anandi's dowry and marriage clothes for some time –
for, as you know, she is demanding.*

*Anandi wants you, her brothers, my sons, for her
marriage ceremony. She says she will not marry if you
cannot come. You are her only remaining brothers since
her own two died, tragic, a tree fell on them while they
slept. Both with one tree, imagine the sorrow.*

I await your early response. Write soon.

*Your beloved father
Nirmal Singh Lohti*

Everyone in the room burst out laughing and talking at the
same time. 'I'm your daughter, Nirmal, and what about my
never-born two brothers who were felled by one tree...'

'Anandi is demanding...'

'And she definitely has a fiery temperament...'

'And what about her cool as the waters of Sutlej husband –
how lucky you are Anandi.'

Gurdev let everyone giggle and laugh and then he cleared
his throat, speaking loudly over the continuing snickers
and chatter, 'We must have wedding invitations that go
with this letter – not one – three or four. Noor, since you
are organizing the wedding, you'll have to get the wedding
invitations printed – quickly. We'll do the ceremony here, on
the empty part of my plot. We'll get tents put properly and
have the halwais in this corner here, behind the shack. We'll
use the shack as the bride's dressing area. No need to rent
a marriage hall and all that. The wedding has to be at least
three months away – Noor, tell her she can't ... you know ...
before that.'

Noor and Anandi tried to interrupt, but Gurdev shushed them and went on. 'It needs to be a proper wedding, in case someone comes to check. Now, you can ask questions.'

Anandi and Noor shook their heads in mock disgust.

Sangat said, 'It's a good idea – but two Mussalman boys coming to a Sikh girl's wedding – why?'

'Gurdevji, let me answer that question, please,' said Jagat. Gurdev nodded his agreement. 'Sangat, this was what our country was only a few years ago. The Muslims were with us until Jinnah lit a fire in the forest that burnt so hard and so fast that even though he later wanted to, he couldn't put it out. We turned against each other for no reason but political manipulation. We were fooled by our leaders – brothers who played together and grew up on the same soil turned against each other.' As Jagat said this, he turned away from the group, looked up and blinked rapidly and then turned back to face them again.

Nirmal continued where Jagat left off. 'I was not lying about them being like my sons. They were diligent and hardworking and eager. I didn't teach them anything about embroidery – that they learnt from their grandmother – I taught them how to deal with the world. They knew nothing, couldn't even say a simple 'hullo', sitting as they were with their grandmother, night and day. They didn't go to school – embroidery was their life, and it became like that because of their devotion to their grandmother who took care of them after their mother died of … something …'

Nirmal was happy with the meeting. At least they had started something. Everyone was not only focused on making money. Now, they all had their own small homes, except Gurdev. He still lived in his shack. And they all had small savings and their business would continue, with or without embroidery, but his boys, they were going to get lost. That man, their father, he had no understanding of their talent. He would put them to work as carpenters or painters or worse – sweepers, unskilled labour, if he was even living.

19

Noor sat in Gurdev's shack, listening to the hullabaloo around her. Suddenly, from customer, she had become one of them and she was pleased. It brought her close to Gurdev. But as she looked around his home, she wondered. He had referred to it as a shack and she had thought he was being modest. But this place was actually a shack, one large room that included everything. There were no private spaces except the bathroom, which was outside. Fortunately, Gurdev had now connected it to the sewage pipe on the street and had proper plumbing. She had heard that initially the toilet for the family was a hole in the ground over which they poured mud after going. This man was a little too rustic, a little too rough but she sensed that there was someone else hidden beneath that rough, worn-out Pathan suit. It was a sense, though. She had no proof and now, as she looked around his home, she saw nothing that could tell her any more about the man.

After Anandi left to live with her new husband, Gurdev had hired another woman to cook, clean and take care of his home. He was particular, she noticed. Surely it wasn't Anandi who had known how to make the bed so neatly. Gurdev must have taught her. The bed was large, much bigger than a normal double bed. It was a simple bed without any frills but it looked solid. Under the bed lay three metal trunks, each inscribed with the owner's name. These, she assumed, were the family's wardrobes that his wife had left behind. Separate from the three trunks that looked shiny and new, there was another trunk, an old trunk, which looked like it was made of a denser metal and had some weight to it. It had a big lock on it, the others didn't. It had been painted black over the original silver but the black paint had worn off and Gurdev Singh, S/O Pritam Singh showed through. Atop each trunk were a few books, schoolbooks for the boys but contemporary fiction on top of Gurdev's trunk, English books, bought from English bookshops. A couple of Thomas Hardys, several P.G. Wodehouse and E.M. Forster's *A Passage to India*, plus a few more whose titles she couldn't make out. She could see under the bed because she sat on a low stool, the dining chairs and other perches were all taken. Gurdev most certainly did not intend for his books to be seen by his most frequent visitors – his business partners. Although, Noor thought, a little condescendingly, that they wouldn't know what the books were. But Noor was intrigued, more than intrigued, she was flummoxed and curious, desperately curious.

She got back to the conversation when she heard her name and nodded for something; it was important, it seemed, so she nudged Jagat and asked him what she had missed.

'Oh, you are organizing Anandi and Dr Bhargava's wedding and getting the cards printed. Pay attention. Gurdev is not tolerant of daydreaming' Jagat whispered with a smile.

'Only that much, huh! Organize a wedding for two people who are already married…' she whispered back.

Gurdev's plan was good, at least this first part. But he was right. She desperately wanted to ask him what would happen to those boys once they got to Delhi and decided to violate their temporary visa and stay on? But she didn't say anything more, listened to Gurdev speak authoritatively on who was doing what. He looked at her once or twice but only as if he was scanning the room, like a good speaker does. Once again, she wondered how he knew how to do that, to hold an audience, to scan the room and look at everyone. Maybe it was a natural thing with him. He never learnt but had an innate gift of leadership. Either way, Noor had almost completely convinced herself that this man was definitely no flour-mill owner.

Once the meeting was over, she dallied a little hoping Gurdev would seek her out, but he didn't. His partners came to him to talk about some supply issue since Jagat was also there. Noor observed their exchange for as long as she could but then realized she was the only other person still in the shack. She wrapped herself up and made her way out with the rest. She would need to find a rickshaw to take her back home. It was dark, and was thinking when she heard Gurdev's voice behind her.

'I'll come with you. We don't want anything to happen to you out here, do we?'

The two went out to the main street and found a rickshaw stand that was well populated. They got into one and Noor asked the man to go to Nizamuddin. Gurdev told the man that this was a round trip, a good deal for the man because he would probably be coming back empty.

When Gurdev got into the rickshaw with her, Noor felt the whole side of his body against hers. She tried to move, open up an inch or two between them but it was not possible. The rickshaw was too narrow and she needed to make sure her dupatta didn't get caught in the wheel. She also needed to wrap her shawl tightly around her because even though the cycle rickshaw moved slowly, it raised enough of a cool breeze to get her teeth clattering. Her arm brushed against Gurdev's chest as she rewrapped her shawl and she recoiled. Her side came to rest on his side, comfortably, like children's blocks fitting into each other, providing warmth at least along one side. Yet she shivered. She sensed Gurdev's stillness. He was not bothered by the proximity it seemed. He seemed comfortable.

'I saw your books – under your bed, the ones lying on top of your trunk.'

'Oh, those were my wife's. She liked to read so I bought her whatever I could afford from used book stores in Lahore.'

And there it was, a simple enough explanation.

'Have you read them as well?' Noor asked

'What, Noorji! I don't have time for all this reading and writing. Let the children learn to do that and maybe make something of their lives.'

'But, Gurdevji, you can read and write English, no? I've heard you speak, but only a little. Do you speak fluently?'

'You have a lot of questions about my English. Why?' Gurdev responded in perfect English, better than Noor's – the one who had grown up in an almost-British household.

Noor flinched. She didn't know what to say – that she had thought that his English was basic, his accent vernacular. She had thought he was this rough, uneducated man with a heart of gold, or something like that.

'Cat got your tongue, young lady?' said Gurdev

'Why the subterfuge, Gurdev? Why act like something you are not? Why are you trying to fool all these people? They've been good to you.'

'Noor, it's like this. I was born in Lahore. My parents were like yours, attached to the British, they received large land grants right by the Beas, fertile land. And it was tilled by sharecroppers – renters who automatically paid a portion of their harvest to my parents. That portion was an absolute amount, not a percentage of the total. Meaning, if they had a poor harvest, they still had to pay the fixed amount. I lived in luxury. We had a large house in Model Town, where all the Indian elite in the city lived back then. I went to an English school, with a lot of English children and a few Indian children. After school, I went to University College London and studied Business, to come back and handle the family business. But what family business was there? It was a collections business, collecting money from people who couldn't afford to pay. But my father wanted to start something, a newspaper or a publishing house or a factory making something, anything. He had money, lots of it, and didn't know what to do with it. I was the only surviving child. I had a younger sister but she died soon after she was born. I heard whispers about other miscarriages that my mother had. I was the lucky one – the one who survived. And look at me; I probably took everything she had to give – all of her poured into one child, with no more to give to any others. And that is who I am. Happy?'

'No, no. Not happy. What happened then? You came back from studying in England and then what? Did you start anything?'

'No. Of course not. My father didn't have the courage. He was happy to take handouts from the English, but to actually spend some of that money to do something for his community and country? No.'

The rickshaw pulled up outside Noor's house. Gurdev got off and held out a hand for Noor. As always, she ignored it and got off on her own.

'You need to come inside and tell me the rest of this story.'

'No, Noor. I'll go back now. You can't have a Sardar go into your house with you so late at night. I'll speak to you soon.'

Noor demurred and let him get back on the rickshaw and ride away. She stood outside for a few minutes stirring around everything she had heard. Was it all true, she wondered? But why would he lie to her? He had no reason to. But then, why was he lying to everyone else? Technically, he wasn't lying. He hadn't told them everything. Nobody spoke English around him because they couldn't so it was easy to stay with Punjabi, and broken English. Like many others, he could read and write English – Nirmal and Sangat could not, one of the many ways he was useful to them.

So, he had a reason for all this and he would tell her, Noor thought as she entered her home. But this didn't mean that he was interested in her, not at all. He was a Sikh – as he had pointed out himself. Maybe his tolerance didn't go as far as a romantic liaison with a Muslim. Maybe he was scared of what people would say. She shook her head. Gurdev was not scared of anything. As she sat at her dressing table, removing her earrings and her rings, she thought about the task that had been assigned to her. She would do it, distracted as she was. She would put him completely out of her mind in that way, until he made a move.

Noor undid the braid and brushed her thick black hair, the silver muted under the dim light of the dressing table. She had learnt this trick from her mother – the dim light softened the lines on her face and pressed most of the strands of silver into blackness. She took off her shawl and dupatta and laid them on an armchair by the dressing table. She kept her sweater on – the room was not warm – and upturned a bottle of cleansing milk on to a ball of cotton. She rubbed the cotton on her face in gentle circles, and then moved down to her neck. Her face was clean but her neck was black, almost as if dust particles wanted to hide away in the dark corners, behind her ears and on the back of her neck. It was the same as every day. Each day that she spent running out to East Patel Nagar or Khan Market in a rickshaw caused her skin to darken with dust, grime and work.

She changed her clothes and put on a soft sweater over her pyjamas – her night sweater. She checked the doors, switched off the lights except her bedside lamp and got into bed. She pulled out a notebook from the drawer in her bedside table and began to make a list – everything she needed to do to plan a wedding.

20

GURDEV GOT BACK IN THE RICKSHAW AND DIDN'T LOOK back. He had to get away from Noor. He had already told her too much. Next, she would want to know why he left his parents and when he had met them last and whether they were safe and why his wife left him and what was in his trunks – not the new one, she probably could guess what that contained: five sets of worn-down Pathan suits, some underwear and undershirts for the winter months, two sweaters and four pairs of black socks. No, she would want to know what had been the contents of the other trunk, the contents that were now locked up in his wall safe. And if he told her that, he would have to tell her the whole story. He couldn't do that because there were consequences, actions, next steps that she would make him take – that's what women do, they make men do things. Things that were inevitable and things that men would probably get around to eventually – women make men do them right away.

Gurdev had left home without taking anything from his parents. He had been twenty-three, still young and inexperienced. He had no interest in marriage but his parents were determined. Bella's father needed their money for his hotel. And he wanted Gurdev to take over his business. Gurdev's father needed to put his money into something and give his son something worthy of his London education. Gurdev didn't agree with either father so he had finally taken a stand and left home. He went into the hinterland and worked as a labourer. He lived with farm labour, built shacks to shelter them in the winter and learnt everything there was to learn about farming wheat and rice and sugarcane and cotton. He spent five years doing this, staying in one village for at least a year. He earned money with his labour and later by advising farmers on things he learnt in the previous village. He met his wife, Simrat, in one of these villages, in the far reaches of Punjab. He was working on her father's farm. Their marriage was her father's idea. Gurdev liked her quiet confidence, her simplicity and the way she worked at the farm. She took care of the livestock – six buffaloes, one goat and a dozen chickens. They got married in a village ceremony, without the drama of the big city. Gurdev didn't invite his parents. His representatives at the wedding were the villagers he worked with every day. A few people even came from neighbouring villages, people he had worked with in the past.

Simrat and Gurdev settled in the outskirts of Sukho, some distance away from Simrat's parents. That was where Gurdev set up his flour mill and his oil press. That was the home they had to leave after Partition. Simrat's parents refused to leave their home. Her older brother, Sujjat had left the village and gone to the big city of Delhi many years ago. He had come for their wedding but didn't stay long. He said that village life didn't suit him. His wife, Parveen, didn't come with him. She was a Delhi girl. Village life definitely didn't suit her.

In the end, Simrat and Gurdev left the newly formed Pakistan with their children, leaving her parents behind. Gurdev learnt later, from Sujjat, that the old couple had been burnt alive in their house.

That was his story, or most of it. There were parts that he wasn't ready to share, even with himself, but if Noor wanted to know more, this is what he had to tell her, and he did. He told her about his wife and her illness. He told her that he willfully ignored her condition because he had no choice. They had to leave Pakistan. Had they stayed, their fate would have been no different from that of her parents'. But Noor wanted to know even more.

'I know all about your wife, Gurdev. Everyone knew her. She was a wonderful person. People still talk about her fondly at the camp. I can understand how you feel about her but I'm sure she had her reasons. I also understand why you left home, but why did you never go back? Why aren't you at least trying to find out what happened to your parents? In any case, whatever happened, that property…'

That's where Gurdev had to stop her. 'Property – all anyone cares about is property. I don't care about their property. I left it all, don't you see?'

'But if you are practical about it and claim it, you'll get money to build your house…'

'I don't want to build my house with that money. That money bore the blood of poor Indians who served rich Indians. I want to build my house with money that I earn.'

'Okay, but at least find out if they made it out…'

'I know what happened to them. There is no need for me to find out anything.'

'What happened to them, Gurdev? What are you hiding? What are you afraid of? I won't judge you, for whatever may have happened. Why should I?'

'There is nothing to judge and you are no one to judge me. It's just that things happened in anger, wild-burning anger that came from somewhere deep inside. Those bastards who called themselves our leaders, they were able to draw it out. I think we had all buried it deep, or extinguished it together. But they brought it back with a force that no one had expected.'

21

NIRMAL SENT THE LETTER TO SULTAN AND SAMIR A WEEK after he had first written it. Noor had designed and printed the wedding invitations, making sure she had the names of the bride and groom and their parents right, the venue – Gurdev's plot, the different ceremonies – the Sikh wedding ceremony – morning, followed by lunch and a farewell to the bride. She had designed the card in a simple ivory and gold colour scheme. She planned to use the same colours in the tent but with splashes of red, an auspicious colour for weddings.

One month later, Nirmal received a response:

Dear Nirmal Papaji,

You are as much our father for without you, we only knew what our grandmother was teaching us. You taught us so much more. We are much eager to attend the wedding of our younger sister and your daughter Anandi. We have duly applied for our special visa even before we wrote this letter. We will tell you when the

visa is received. Sometimes that can take over a year,
we've heard.

Forever grateful
Sultan and Samir

Nirmal read and reread the letter to make sure he understood
the implication. First, they wanted to come to India – meaning
they had not found a tailor who could use their skills or give
them a good price for theirs. Second, getting a visa could take
much longer than two months. Hence wedding plans needed
to be halted, for now. He wrote a response to the young men.

Dear Sultan and Samir,
  I am happy to receive your letter. It brings me great
joy that I am still remembered by you. If you say the
visa can take a long time, we will stop the wedding for
the time being. We will begin planning once we get a
letter from you saying you have visa and are definitely
coming. Please tell the people at the visa place this –
that the wedding is on hold till you two can come.

Forever your beloved Father
Nirmal Singh Lohti

Nirmal was going to mail it, but decided to show it to Gurdev
once. Gurdev read the letter and looked up and around. He
tugged at his long beard and tucked imaginary hair into his
turban.

'Something is not right. I can't tell you what, but something
tells me that these boys are now being watched. They will

never get their visas. But don't say anything to anyone. Send this letter and we'll see what happens.'

Nirmal had to tell Noor to put everything on hold, the halwai, the tent man, the band and the flowers. But they could go ahead with the bride's dress and jewellery. The jewellery was all gold-washed silver, but of good quality, looked as good as real. Nirmal was making the dress, a salwar kameez; this time he agreed to change from his khadi and asked Sunder to buy brocade from the market, and raw silk and chiffon for the dupatta – which he embroidered painstakingly. His work was good, he thought, as he looked at the plain piece of cloth with little bits of gold and tinsel appearing as his hand moved slowly up and down. He had to sit on a straight-backed chair and push his reading glasses first up his nose then down to look for the right place to magnify the tiny stitches. His short legs rested on a stool, all the lights in the workshop were switched on – and then he could embroider. He also made a wedding dress for the groom: an outfit that made the short man look like a Maharajah. This one was plain brocade, no embroidery. Nirmal's poor eyes and his aching fingers couldn't have done any more. Once he had finished making both dresses, the group went back to waiting. Nirmal displayed the fancy clothing in glass cabinets in his shop to show off his work and to tell people he could make more than khadi but had to take them out because of demand. The trouble with embroidery is that once you show something good, people, meaning women, can't resist. And to ensure that you make something good, you can do nothing else – otherwise you lose the flow, the connection with the garment. He understood this and he knew his boys did, but none of the local embroiderers did. They did piece work, bits and pieces of the embroidery. One person did the beadwork, another did the satin work, a third did the zari work and a fourth did the final finishing. That was not Nirmal's way, and that's what made the difference.

When everything was ready, they all waited but days and weeks passed without a word from Pakistan, then months. Then Nirmal got worried. He hoped he wasn't getting the boys into trouble. As long as he had known Gurdev, he had been right about most things. Maybe he was right this time too. He sat with his chin in one hand, the other tucking in bits of his turban that were already tucked in, thinking aloud.

'What if they found out that the letters were all lies and realized that the boys want to stay in India? What if they have arrested the boys? What if they are before a firing squad right now? What if they are coming for us too? They must have spies here. They can send a code and tell them to kill us. And I foolishly put our shop address on the envelope – but I wanted the boys to know where the letter was coming from. Gurdev, Gurdev, are you listening? We have to do something. Please do something.'

Gurdev focused his eyes on the newspaper he was reading. This plan had failed but he would think of something else. He needed some time.

Meanwhile, Sangat had begun buying all kinds of fabric directly from weavers and craftsmen. He travelled across the country looking for the best. There was a steady stream of customers. Most were there to buy the ready-made kurtas, which had been expanded to include other fabrics, though khadi remained the mainstay of the ready-made business. Khadi was not what people preferred. The fabric was rough and had a casual look, no matter the cut. But Gurdev and Sangat pushed people to buy khadi, milking the patriotic angle and the Made-In-India angle. More important, khadi fed Jagat Nath's Muslim families, now more than doubled from seven to sixteen. Nilibar's khadi had an edge over fabric available everywhere else because production was restricted to these families and Jagat Nath still bought the best raw cotton for weaving.

22

JAGAT NATH WAS A YOUNG MAN, SOMEWHERE IN HIS LATE twenties. He was the youngest of the group. He was a Punjabi Hindu whose family had lived in Shahdara for generations. In the old days, Hindus had been a minority in the neighbourhood. Muslims had dominated it. But nobody in the neighbourhood had felt that anything was wrong. The Hindus were not strict vegetarian, as was the case in some neighbourhoods, and the Muslims while practising, lived comfortably with their Hindu neighbours. They had a separate area for slaughtering goats during Bakr-Id so the blood was hidden from sight. Everyone was invited to the feast thereafter and most families joined in.

Jagat Nath had grown up with children of both religions. There were no restrictions on play or eating in a neighbour's home. He married a young woman named Umrao, whose family also lived in the neighbourhood. Everyone attended the wedding although there were a few rumblings among the older Hindus. The family ignored them and went on with their celebrations. Neither converted to the other's religion although it was customary for non-Muslims to convert to Islam. In their case, the kazi didn't object and neither did the Hindu priest. They were married according to the customs of both religions.

Everything changed in 1946, however. The Muslim League grew in prominence. Muslims across India were called to action. Overnight, the Muslims of Shahdara became more militant, more insistent about their religion, and the Hindus did the same. The friendships and neighbourly love dwindled, and minor arguments on everything from garbage to drying clothes turned into communal clashes. Talks about partitioning the country on the basis of religion had begun and were gathering fervour. Large groups of Hindus descended upon primarily Muslim neighbourhoods such as Shahdara, shouting 'Hindustan Zindabad.' It was at this time that Umrao's parents advised Jagat Nath to change their daughter's name from Umrao to Urmila. They told her that they were going to leave for West Punjab before things got any worse. Urmila's mother's sister lived there and was advising them to come. They left right at the beginning of 1947, but by October of 1947, all of Shahdara had emptied out. Some of the inhabitants had gone to relatives in other parts of India but most had joined refugee caravans to the newly formed Pakistan. People had locked their doors, expecting to return soon – but those who left never came back. Several families stayed, helped by their Hindu neighbours, but they stayed hidden, making khadi fabric for years after Independence.

Jagat Nath and his family didn't have anyone staying with them but they helped many families make a living while in hiding. It was Jagat's job to ensure that they got the best raw material and the best price for their product.

When Jagat first met Gurdev, he wondered if the Sardar had lost his way. But soon he found out that the man knew exactly where he was going and what he was doing – at all times. He wondered about Gurdev, about his past, about his experiences as a refugee, about his wife who wasn't there, but he didn't ask. Young as he was, he was taken more seriously than men twice his age. Gurdev particularly looked to him for answers or second opinions. But, in order to give sage advice, Jagat had learnt that he had to speak as little as possible – so when he did speak, it sounded weighty and sensible.

Jagat had not brought his wife to meet the group so far. He would soon, he wanted to. He wanted her to be part of this new cohort. They wanted him to be part of the new embroidery business but he had nothing to add there. With the khadi, he was an integral part and his partnership had given him more money than he would have earned as a supplier of fabric. But now, things were getting complicated. They wanted to get these boys out of Lahore. The thing was that his Urmila could help them. Her parents, aunt and uncle and several cousins were in Lahore. Given that her parents were liberal Muslims who went to Lahore from Shahdara, they wouldn't object to two Pakistanis wanting to move to India for commerce – unless, their beliefs had changed with their address. But he hesitated in offering her help. He had to speak to her first. He was afraid of all these India–Pakistan conversations with his wife. She always looked torn – knowing she had to take India's side, but a big part of her was in Pakistan. He understood that but with everything that had happened during Partition, he couldn't sympathize too much with her predicament. In fact, he felt a hot fever run through his body whenever he thought about his in-laws – it was probably anger, although

Jagat Nath was not capable of expressing it. They shouldn't have left and now that they had, he couldn't care less. He tried not to let Urmila see what he was feeling but he was sure she did. Maybe, if she participated in this plan, got her parents to help, he would feel more connected to them.

When he asked her, she agreed to come and join the next meeting and even offered to bring her special mutton biryani to share with everyone, but she was clear that she would have to see about helping.

23

GURDEV WAS WORRIED ABOUT THE NEXT MEETING. HE had no plan, only some very basic information about the border that he had got from his friend Satnam. He did the thing many people do when they want to avoid what they are supposed to do. He didn't go to the shop for several days and spent time with an architect about plans for his house. Money was coming in, not enough to begin construction – he would need embroidery for that – but enough to pay an architect. But without embroidery, there would be no construction so paying an architect and discussing plans for a house that would never be built was just a distraction. He could build a smaller house, a simpler house but that wouldn't do. He wanted to build his parents' house, not just any house. If he couldn't do that, he would stay in his shack.

The meeting was in Gurdev's shack again, this time with food. Noor was bringing chicken korma, Jagat was bringing mutton biryani, Sangat was getting saag and makki ki roti and Anandi was bringing daal. Nirmal was the only one who had not offered to bring anything.

'I have been busy, working … you people … one is meeting architects, the other one is travelling everywhere buying fabric, beautiful fabric, mind you, but when you give people so many options, you have to stand there and let them choose. I am losing my mind with some of these women. They will shortlist something, buy something else. Then the measurements…'

The whole group broke out in guffaws at the word.

'Don't laugh, everyone. It is no longer funny. You don't know the women who come to the shop. One wanted me to put a bedsheet over her before I could measure. 'Madam, you want fitted clothing or a bedsheet, I asked her. If you won't let me measure you, I can sell you this bedsheet to wear.'

Everyone laughed again. Nirmal also joined in. 'Another one asked me if I had a lady tailor. The sign outside says you have one, she said. I went out to see what we had put on the sign. It said: 'Nilibar – Khadi and other Fine Fabrics and Ladies' Tailor'. Madamji, I told her, the sign says that I am a ladies' tailor, not that I have a lady tailor. She left the shop – good luck finding a good lady tailor. They don't exist. Ladies are clever. They don't want to do tailoring for other ladies. It is fools like me who end up in this profession – taking curses if clothes are too tight and getting frowns if they are too loose – which they never are. It's not my fault that these ladies come and give measurements and then go and eat laddoos and samosas for two weeks and come back and say their clothes don't fit.'

Noor had fallen to the floor, slipping off her low stool, her legs up in the air, she was laughing so hard when Jagat and his wife Urmila walked in. Urmila had a big degchi in her hand that she set on the counter in the kitchen. She looked around politely with hands folded and dupatta-covered head lowered. Noor picked herself off the floor and sat down again. Her dupatta had fallen off her neck and into her lap. She picked it back up and threw it over her chest. She walked over to the young woman and welcomed her. Then everyone stood up and said something to welcome Jagat's wife.

Anandi was the first to speak. 'Didi, welcome. I am Anandi. This is my current husband and future bridegroom – if you don't know the whole story, get comfortable and we'll tell you.'

Jagat jumped in, 'Don't worry Anandi. Urmila is up to date with everything. Urmi, Gurdev, the mastermind; Nirmal, as you heard, the Ladies' Tailor; Sangat, the third partner; and me the fourth. Then we have the lovely Noor, who is our best customer and advertiser and the equally lovely Anandi and her husband who will run away anytime during the evening … why don't you eat your food, doctor sahib? You never know when you may be called away.'

Gurdev took charge. 'Nirmal, anything?' he asked hopefully.

Nirmal rummaged in his pocket and pulled out an envelope. 'Actually, one letter came today only. Amrit handed it to me as I walked in to change and wash up. I get covered by the smell of ladies' perfume…'

'Open the envelope,' the whole room yelled in unison.

'Okay, okay. Here we go.'

Dear Nirmal Papaji,

We are well but we have no news. Six months have passed but there is no news from the Indian Consulate. We heard about a man asking about us in the neighbourhood – but then nothing. Our father was

embarrassed by our work so no one knows what we do.
    We'll keep waiting but if there is another way, please
try to find it.

Your grateful sons
Sultan and Samir

Nirmal spoke first, 'Oh no! This is most unfortunate. They will never get visas. Why should they? If their special skill is discovered, why won't the Pakistanis keep them there? There are stylish women in Pakistan also. But can't we tell the Indian government that we want them because they have a special skill...'

Gurdev guffawed. 'Embroidery – that special skill is embroidery! The Indian government will allow scientists and PhDs, Civil Engineers maybe, or Doctors – how can you convince anyone that embroidery is a skill that is in short supply in India and so we have to import it from Pakistan...'

'If women were running the world, we would not have had a problem,' said Nirmal.

'If women were running the world, there would have been no Partition,' asserted Noor, 'or any wars. We don't believe in killing and bloodshed. We know where all that flesh and blood comes from, how it's nurtured and nourished and cared for.'

'How do you know, Noor? You haven't had any children,' said Sangat, but regretted it the minute he had. All three women present, including quiet Urmila jumped on him, despite the fact that none of them had themselves borne children yet.

'What do you think maternal instinct is about? We are mothers in our hearts when we are born; we don't need to give birth to know that bloodshed to feed egos and political objectives is not the answer...' said Noor.

'Okay, okay. Embroidery as a special skill is not the answer in this world. Any other ideas?' Gurdev brought the room back to coherence again.

'I think we'll have to go there and bring them back,' said Noor. We'll need someone to help us. I'll have to ask my father for help. I'm not sure if I want to do that. He wants me back at home but ... that's another story. But I can ask if it will help.'

'How do you plan to do that? And how can your father help? I know the borders are still open but if you get caught – treason, death by firing squad, all that stuff that Nirmal usually comes up with,' said Gurdev.

'What do you mean? Nirmal isn't crazy. If he comes up with that stuff, it is probably true, as it is in this case,' said Nirmal.

'So, any other thoughts on this suggestion? Any other suggestions?' asked Gurdev.

'Why does someone have to go and bring them? Why can't they come out themselves? I mean, it's dangerous for an Indian to go to Pakistan, particularly a non-Muslim,' asked Urmila.

'They can't come out on their own. They are like babies, sheltered and coddled, they have never been to school, and they've hardly ever left the house. The old woman used to send me their work with a servant. After she died, the servant continued to bring me their work until I asked him to bring them along. I wanted them to see what happens to their work, I wanted them to meet their clients. Every time I took them out, they stood quietly together, not saying much at all. So, you see, they will definitely not be able to come out on their own. If anyone asks them one question, they'll start trembling, maybe even urinate in their pants.'

A few people giggled until they realized that Nirmal was not joking.

Urmila spoke softly once everyone was quiet. 'I'm not sure I can help you. I'm not even sure I want to. My parents live in Lahore. I haven't seen them in about two years. I'll probably never see them. Jagat must have told you that I'm Muslim but changed my name. My parents felt this was the best way. Our letters take months to reach, sometimes a page is missing, sometimes there are wet blotches that spread the ink and then dry, and sometimes it looks like a dog bit off one corner of the envelope. I don't know if they do it on purpose or if the system is still so stretched, having broken in two but not joined up into two separate units yet,' said Urmila, in a soft voice, and as she recounted the condition of the letters, her voice went quieter and quieter, almost silent as she analysed the reasons for her letters being mishandled.

'It's okay, Urmila, or would you like us to call you by your Muslim name, Umrao, right? We don't mind. We have Noor here, who ensures that we don't say or do anything that'll get us in trouble, right, Noor?' said Gurdev.

'Urmila, if you are uncomfortable helping us because you think there might be some retaliation against your parents then don't help us but understand that these boys are eager to get out. With this latest letter, I'm getting a little concerned about them. I don't think it's the letters to India that are getting them in trouble. I think they are already in trouble. They probably have no work. Remaining parent is gone, more than likely, and they are not able to do the work they are trained to do. If you do decide to help us, do it for them, not so that this lot can launch their embroidery line – I'm sick of hearing about it. In the meantime, I'm not permitted to wear embroidered clothes, I'm not permitted to buy embroidered clothes…' said Noor, slightly agitated.

'Who dare stop you from doing anything, Noor?' said Gurdev.

'Ask your friend, the embroidery policeman. If I wear something I've had for years, he comments, if I talk about my Sitara and Reshma doing something new for me, he makes this nasty face. I'm stuck wearing these nice and comfortable khadi kurtas – but for Allah's sake, they are khadi. I need to wear something special – silk or tissue or brocade or something, no?'

'I'll do it,' said Urmila softly. 'I'll help you. At least I'll do my best. The rest, who knows. And please call me Urmila. That is my name now,' she said smiling shyly at her husband.

The whole group cleared their throats all at once; one or two progressing into coughing fits, marking their acknowledgement of a shared romantic moment between husband and wife.

Urmila blushed but Jagat laughed. 'You can't pay too much attention to this lot. Go about your business. Do what you can and learn not to take yourself too seriously. That is what I've learnt from them.'

'I have thought of a plan that might work. Do you all want to hear it?' said Urmila.

The group said all together, 'Yes, we want you hear your plan, Urmila. Sorry, Urmila.'

She ignored them and went on. 'We need a couple to do this. It has to be someone who can pass off as Muslim – meaning you have to speak Urdu and know a lot about places in West Punj—I mean Pakistan. This couple will go as my parents' guests – I will write to them to let them know but we don't have to wait for their response. They'll gladly receive anyone who can give them news about their daughter. By the way, whoever goes can tell them that we are expecting our first child...'

The room broke into a paroxysm of congratulations and other wishes. Noor hugged Urmila first, then Anandi held her and then the men – Gurdev patted her gently on the head, Sangat folded his hands before him and said 'Mubarkan', Nirmal drew her into a big bear hug that startled her, giving her face the look of a balloon being squeezed from one end. She squirmed out of his hug and said, 'You were going to squeeze the baby out of me right now.'

'Oh, this young lady, so quiet, so serious, she has a sense of humour. Good, Jagat. Good choice. Courageous and a little funny – that's all you need in a wife, right Dr Bhargava?'

Dr Bhargava had made his way over to the food and was pouring Urmila's biryani down his throat followed by bits of Noor's korma. 'I have to say, Urmila and Noor, your cooking, your food, the flavours, the spices, I have eaten nothing like this before. Anandi, you must taste everything. It is something else.'

Anandi looked a little annoyed but Gurdev caught her eye and gave her a look. She nodded. A group of Muslims had kidnapped her and had killed Anandi's first husband. He was trying to get her away from them. After his death, Anandi came to India in a foot caravan with her parents but they couldn't keep up with the walking and fell behind. They urged her to go on, that they would come slowly. She didn't want to but they insisted, so she found a group of women and joined them. She still didn't know what had become of her parents. The people she lived with, Gurdev's neighbours, were not her parents. They gave her a home when she realized she was all alone and arrived in Delhi without will, more as part of a human waterfall spitting into the refugee camps. She had an intense dislike for Muslims, but with Gurdev's help and counselling, she was trying to see people beyond their religion. The food that her husband was praising was typical frontier food, lots of meat cooked over slow flame for a long time, with masalas that were unique to the region – food that was provided to her during her captivity, food that she could no longer push down her gullet. She ate the daal she had brought and Paramjit's saag and makki ki roti.

Everyone served themselves in Gurdev's tiny kitchen and sat down to eat. There was silence in the room for the time it took for everyone to eat their first helping.

'Who's going to go? I thought I would ask the question as you are all getting up to get more food. As you begin eating again, please think. Don't eat with a blank mind,' said Nirmal in his trademark confrontational style.

'Noor and I are going to go,' Gurdev announced quietly. 'I'll make some changes to my appearance, which my grandfather's soul, if it's still wandering around, will not like much. Noor you will help me do that. I already speak Urdu and so do you.'

Gurdev went on without waiting for acknowledgement from Noor. 'There is a village, right at the border. We have to make it to this village. It's called Kasur. From there, we can literally walk across the border.'

'How did you find this information? Had you already decided that this was the only way?' Noor asked Gurdev.

'I knew that the visa way would not work. The Indian Consulate is not giving visas to Pakistanis, even for special circumstances. They simply don't respond. I discovered this because of our case and also because I also know someone in the foreign ministry,' Gurdev said with a wink.

'Who do you know? If you know someone there, then why do we need to go at all? Why can't we arrange a visa for them?'

'Noor, it is not that simple. My friend can't do that without getting into serious trouble himself. He can help us with information, but nothing secret. This we will have to do – as husband and wife, okay? It's pretend of course, but we'll have to appear authentic. Those two boys are our nephews, your poor sister's children. Their mother died. They are going to come and live with us. Urmila, we'll need a place to stay and maybe even to hide if things go wrong – but we won't implicate your parents. We'll leave if things get out of control. Noor, are you listening? Or are you daydreaming again?' Gurdev said with a hint of a smile.

'Of course, I'm listening. This is probably the most important thing I have done, will ever do, in my life. I am listening. Please go on. By the way, I think I have to practise being a much more orthodox Muslim than I am accustomed to. Urmila, can you help?' said Noor.

Gurdev turned his attention back to Nirmal. 'Nirmal, you please keep an eye on the mail. Read all letters the day you receive them. Maybe the Indian Consulate will come through for the boys. Sangat, you don't have to do anything at this time. Urmila, you are writing a letter to your parents introducing us, a married couple. Anandi, looks like your grand wedding is off for the time being. But you know what we can do? We can decide a date, print cards for a reception instead, and go ahead with it, regardless of the embroidery boys. Noor?' said Gurdev finishing up his instructions.

'Yes, why not? I think we deserve a nice function – and that's what the wedding will be. Plus, we should entertain a little. That's how connections get built,' said Noor.

'Jagat, you have to coach me, hold my hand and tell me we will make it – also tell me everything you think might be wrong with the plan. That's your job. And if anything goes wrong, you have to keep these two in line. We are all business partners also, remember that,' said Gurdev, not sure what he was getting everyone into. Urmila's plan had become his plan.

24

NOOR KNEW RIGHT AT THE TIME THAT SANGAT AND Nirmal had spoken about their embroidery boys that to get them out was not going to be easy for the three Sikh men. That's why she had offered to go to Pakistan and bring them out with her. At that time, she had thought it would be an adventure. She had known that she could go in without a problem but bringing the two young men out, she hadn't thought that part through – it hadn't occurred to her that they would require documents to enter India. Gurdev's plan of getting to the village of Kasur and walking across the border seemed possible. Whatever little information he had was usually reliable. After Partition, both countries were issuing new passports but old Indian passports still worked for Indians and both Noor and Gurdev had them. They could go to Pakistan if they got visas – if they got into trouble, they could leave the way they came, legally. The trouble was that Gurdev would never get a visa with his current passport and very obviously Sikh name on it. He could change his appearance but what about his passport? She couldn't believe he hadn't thought of that. They could also walk into Pakistan through Kasur and walk out with the boys. That thought had entered her head but she had kept it to herself. This was not going to be an adventure, it was going to be risky and dangerous. She felt herself shiver at the thought of what would happen if things went wrong but then the thought of being with Gurdev made her smile.

Noor and Gurdev decided to meet regularly to update each other and get comfortable talking to each other. At the first meeting at a chai shop in Khan Market, on Gurdev's insistence, Noor sat waiting for him. She was there for almost ten minutes before she got up to walk over to the shop to ask Nirmal where Gurdev was. As she picked up her purse, she heard a voice behind her.

'Keep sitting, Noorji. Let's have some chai.'

She turned around to look for Gurdev, for that was his voice but she couldn't see the tall, bearded Sardar with his lopsided turban anywhere.

'Look here, Noorji, right here, under your nose.'

She looked down and to the left and there he was – still tall, even while seated but the turban was gone and the beard was clean shaved. His face looked smooth and sharp, his nose and cheeks, free of the dark backdrop, were pronounced, like drawn in ink instead of faded pencil. The worn-out Pathan suit was gone and instead he wore a western-style shirt and trousers, shirt tucked in, belt in place, well fitted unlike the ones Sangat walked around in, constantly hitching them up his non-existent behind and rolling belly. Gurdev had no belly and he had shoulders, broad shoulders that she had noticed in his Pathan suit. The fitted shirt covering the flat stomach made her go weak at the knees so she sat down.

'Gurdev Singh, there was no reason to shock me like this. What have you done to yourself? I thought you were only going to trim your beard and shave your moustache. You've gone for a full transformation. I was expecting to see a scruffy Sardar transition into a scruffy Mussalman, not this.' As she looked at him again, she instinctively gaped.

'Bibiji, you should close your mouth now. There are a lot of flies in this chai shop, one will fly in and then you'll have a nest growing in your stomach.'

'What nonsense you talk. Where are we planning to meet? Why this whole drama of the chai shop. I know you wanted to see my reaction. So let's go to the inside room in the shop?'

'Yes. We'll meet there. Safest. I don't want anyone to hear our conversation and try to make something of it.'

They walked slowly to the shop, Noor continuing to steal glances at this man walking next to her. He had been imposing and attractive before but he had never bothered with his appearance. He didn't trim his beard and she sensed that he took off his turban at night, like a hat, and slipped it back on in the morning, till Sunday, which she knew was hair-washing day. She had happened by for something for Anandi around the time of her wedding and seen this giant yeti-like creature with flowing hair, sitting on a chair outside in the sun. He had parted his hair, given her a thumbs-up and gone back to dozing, hair covering his face.

As they entered the shop, Nirmal looked up from a deep conversation with a customer and cursorily said, 'One minute, please' and went back to his conversation. He was clearly not moved at the sight of a stunningly handsome man as she had been. Then, he saw her and waved, a friendly movement of fingers, not cursory at all. He looked up again and adjusted his turban. He mumbled something to his customer and walked over to them in three giant strides. 'Come with me, please,' he ordered.

Noor and Gurdev followed Nirmal into the inner room behind the mirror.

'Oye, Sardar, what have you done? You have ruined yourself. This sacrifice is too much, too much. I can't bear it. I can't bear to look at you. Where is your hair, where is your beard? Have you taken off your Karha as well? This is what distinguished us from the enemy in battle, my brother. This is what made us Sikhs. You have destroyed your religion. You have ... you have ... disrespected your father and his father and all your Sikh ancestors if there were any more...'

'Calm down, Prahji. My appearance is not what makes me a Sikh. It never has. And we are no longer in battle. I've done this before, in front of my father, and my grandfather, although he was too old to notice any difference.'

'This is not funny, Gurdev. I will not allow it. You grow everything back, or...'

'Or what, Nirmal? I'm going to Pakistan. I even have a new passport. Noor, before you ask, I told you I have contacts in the government.'

Gurdev took out a blue booklet from his pocket. Both Noor and Nirmal peered at it. It was crisp, the pages tightly bound, never been opened, except the first page that had his name and photograph. It was the clean-shaven, shorthaired Gurdev but his name was Shakirullah Hasan.

'And what is this name, Gurdev? Babaji will never forgive you for this transgression. You can go to Bangla Sahib Gurudawara for the rest of your life, but you will not be forgiven. First of all, they won't let you in with that name.' Nirmal was quaking with anger, his face was puffy and he squirted spit, large splats of it, every time he made the 'F' sound.

'Prahji, they don't check identification at the Gurudawara. But listen, jokes aside. Calm down. It doesn't change anything about me. It's only my appearance. My heart still says "Wahe Guru Wahe Guru". Okay?'

Noor watched the whole interaction quietly, trying to blend into the wall. She was impressed with Gurdev. She wondered who his resource was. Getting a second passport like that, he had to know someone important.

'Now that we've got all that out of the way, let's do our planning. Nirmal, you go back to the customer. That poor lady must be wondering where you've gone off. So, Noor, my first step is done. What is your first action?'

Noor looked around. 'I was supposed to do something? I didn't … know.' This was the first time she had been grilled by Gurdev. He grilled everyone around him, Nirmal, Sangat, Anandi, Jagat, even the young doctor, but he had never put her on the spot like this.

'Oho, don't panic. Nothing, you don't have to do anything. Actually, yes, you do. You have to get to know Jagat's wife, Urmila. No, this is not about religion. You need to find out where her parents live, what kind of people they are and all that. Also, find out about her mother's sister and her husband and children. What do they do? We don't want any overzealous relatives to find out anything and turn us in. And actually, this is slightly about religion. You'll need to find out how you should dress in Lahore – they may be more conservative than … you.'

Noor felt like she should have had a notebook and taken notes. But Gurdev was right. They needed to know all this, and who better to help her than Urmila?

'I'll go and meet her and find out everything. When do we meet again to update each other?'

'Take a week. See her as much as possible. You can't learn all this and remember it by meeting one day for a few hours. Then, we'll meet again. Right here. One week.'

25

Noor set out for Shahdara a few days later. She
had never been there before and didn't want to ask
Gurdev, so she spent the time mapping her journey. She could
take a tram for a part of the way, up to Paharganj but from
there, she had a long tonga ride followed by a rickshaw ride. It
took her almost two hours to get there, and she arrived feeling
grimy and sweaty. She had to ask for Jagat's house only once,
at the local vegetable shop. A boy from the shop brought her
right to Jagat's door. She rang the doorbell, a brass bell that
hung outside, a tiny bell that she wondered would be heard
inside or not. It was and she heard footsteps in flip-flops
hurry to the door a few seconds later. It was Urmila, hands
covered in wet flour. She had used her left hand to unlock the
door and held it open with her rear end as she motioned Noor
to come inside.

'I was expecting you,' she said with a faint smile. 'Give me a
few minutes to finish up, I'll join you here.' She led Noor into
a drawing-room, quaintly furnished room filled with antique
furniture of a Mughal look. It looked like it had been handed

down and no family member had tired of it enough to replace it with newer pieces. There were sepia-coloured photographs of several generations of Naths, portraits of both men and women and family photos down the generations. The carpet on the floor was old Kashmiri wool on cotton, worn down to the thread but the pattern still alive. There were small knick-knacks from rare travels – a large shell from some beach, an ivory elephant, a pair of miniature tablas, not at all gaudy. Noor got joy out of looking at beautiful things, beautiful people, and beautiful scenes. She appreciated comfort and a sense of things being where they should be, without excess. As Noor ruminated, Urmila came back to the room for a quick, 'Tea or Coffee? Or something cold? You look like you could use a glass of khus sherbet?'

Noor, startled a bit, replied, 'Khus sherbet would be lovely. Thank you.'

Urmila went off again and came back almost immediately. She sat down on one of the sofas, indicating to Noor to sit as well. Noor sat down on the comfortable seat and smiled at her new friend.

'How are you, Noor? I enjoyed meeting you all the other night. It was a different experience for me. Usually, at get-togethers, people talk about children and servants and upcoming weddings, even recent deaths. Usually these get-togethers are with family, mostly Jagat's family because mine has all left, every single person has moved to Pakistan. Sometimes I wonder if I should have gone too.'

'Why do you think that, Urmila? Are you not happy in India?'

Noor felt that the conversation was getting a bit too personal but then this girl was probably lonely.

'I am happy but you know that in India you don't just marry the man, you marry the whole family but what about my family. Doesn't the man have to marry his wife's family? He doesn't ask about them, he doesn't write to them, calling them is difficult anyway but he won't even try to book a call. Because they have gone over to the other side, they have become the enemy. He could enquire about their health once in a while, no?'

'That doesn't sound like Jagat at all, Urmila. He seems so sensitive. Maybe he is looking out for you, doesn't want any trouble for you. Talk to him and find out. You may be surprised.'

'I'll try. Men can be different outside than they are with their wives. But you are here for a purpose. Let's talk about what you need to know.'

'Tell me a little about yourself, Urmila. Where did you study and what? Tell me about your parents and all the relatives you've been close to and whom we, as your friends, might be expected to meet in Lahore – to give your best wishes to, that is.'

Urmila told Noor all that she could. Her father had a cloth shop same as he had in Shahdara. He had borrowed money from his brother-in-law, his wife's sister's husband who was a rich landowner who had invested his money in a cinema hall. Her mother helped out in the shop and her mother's sister was a rich socialite.

They continued to talk, Noor seeking out more details about Lahore that Urmila was not able to provide because the last time she had been there, she had been young. 'What do women wear, Urmila? Is it like here, head covered except in orthodox families where full Burqa is required?'

'What are you asking me, Noor Aapa? Are you asking me if Sharia Law has been instituted in Pakistan and women have to be covered from head to toe and hands are being cut off for stealing? From what I understand from my father, who is following all this closely, the Pakistani constitution has a whole section on Islamic provisions – this, from a leader who promised religious freedom for all religions in Pakistan. But I can tell you this: women are dressing like they did before. That part has not changed. Ghararas and farshis are in fashion, if you want to know. Also short, narrow pants. That loose salwar you are wearing, very unfashionable,' she said with a smile.

'Urmila, now you are making more trouble. As it is that Nirmal won't let me shop anywhere else … and I am noticing that you are on to his khadi kurtas as well…'

'I have no choice, Noor Aapa; we are giving him the khadi cloth that's helping so many people. Jagat won't even let me wear anything old. Day and night I wear this khadi, but I can tell you, this won't work in Lahore. You better ask Nirmal to make you something else. Here…' She took out a photo from a drawer next to her. 'This is my mother with her sister and her friends. Show this to Nirmal and ask him to copy this style. Then, you'll fit right in and won't draw attention because of your droopy clothes … but please bring the photo back to me. I don't have too many,' she said with a sad laugh.

Noor turned her attention to a wood tray covered by a lace doily with two Venetian glass tumblers. She could tell they were old, but not at all chipped. The khus sherbet within was the perfect temperature, sweet enough, not cloying.

'Urmila, your home is lovely. I like every bit of it and this service, for a glass of a cold beverage, impeccable. Where did you learn to do all this?'

'Aapa, this is not me but I've learnt. This was Jagat's mother. My mother also learnt from her. She had a friend or more likely, she worked for an Englishwoman who taught her these things – but the family likes to say she had a friend. Jagat was also influenced by all things English but he realized it was a farce – not who we were. He went the other extreme, with his support of khadi and the freedom movement. He participated actively you know, the slogans and the hunger strikes and the marches, he did so many. His mother was not happy about it but then she became a convert too – but she kept her ways.'

'I have to be honest, Urmila. That is exactly how it is in my house too. We are so British. My father was in ICS. He studied in England and has a clipped accent; he puts it on, of course. You can't acquire a British accent after two years in the country in your early twenties. Your accent is set already. You can pick up a few words and intonations, but that's it. But who am I to judge? I'm snobby about accents. Yours, for instant, you speak differently from Jagat who is a pukka chota sahib. Yours is more … more…'

'Vernacular?'

'No, no. Indian, I would say, not vernacular at all. Chalo, I must be going now. I'll see you soon.'

Noor left Urmila's house to begin the long journey back home. She was not going to see Gurdev for a week and was already missing him. Why was he not saying anything, she wondered? Independent as she was, this was not something she was going to do. He would have to make the first move. Now it wouldn't happen till they got back from Pakistan. He was too stressed. She was excited. She would get some new clothes stitched, take the flight from Delhi to Lahore – she had already got her visa, no problem at all. She had said she was going to visit friends in Lahore. They had the address for the boys. How hard was it going to be to find them and then cross the border to Kasur village, stay in Amritsar for a few days and then come back to Delhi? She wasn't stressed at all. She was excited about being around Gurdev all the time for days and days.

Noor spent the whole two-hour journey back home daydreaming about Gurdev and lamenting the fact that she wasn't going to see him till Sunday, which was a still a few days away. She tried to analyse the complications in the plan but all she could think about was the prospect of being with Gurdev and to be wandering the gullies of Lahore with him, maybe even dodging some bad people. She had to stop herself and go back to wondering how everything would work, what poor Gurdev was worrying about.

As she walked home from the Nizamuddin tram station, her mind cleared a little and she began to realize that Gurdev had reason to be worried. She turned the corner on to her street and saw the same worrier pacing up and down around her front gate.

'Gurdev, is everything all right? Why are you here? I thought we weren't going to meet till Sunday.'

'Everything is fine. I got my visa today – that means I have to start getting used to my new name – Shakirullah Hasan.'

'You can refer to yourself as Shakir. I'll have to start calling you that as well. We are a modern couple, right? Reformist, right? Not conservative, please tell me, not conservative.'

'No, not conservative. I couldn't pull that off either. My Urdu is good, but I can't recite verses of the Quran at a moment's notice, although we did study it a little in school, so some vague memories remain. But that is not why I'm here. It's late. It's dark. I wanted to check if you were home and you were not, so I waited. I've been here for an hour. Why are you coming back so late?'

'You know, that Urmila was most helpful. We got talking about fashion and how I need to have some gararas and farshis made because my salwars are so old fashioned and what did she call my khadi kurtas – yes, droopy. She said droopy wouldn't do in Lahore. I'd stand out as a foreigner because everyone there is so stylish!'

'Oh, come on, Noor! You can discuss all the fashion stuff with Nirmal. You are not a naïve young woman. You know how this city is. There are safe places and not-so-safe places and you need to be home before dark … and that's that … otherwise…'

'Otherwise what?'

'Otherwise, I worry. That's it. Now, I can go home and let you get back in and rest. It's been a long day for you.'

'No, no, I'm fine. Come inside. I'll give you dinner. My girl made everything. I'll make fresh rotis…'

'Noor, I can't…'

'Oh come on, Gurdev. You can come inside and have dinner. No one is going to say anything. And you are not even a Sardar any more. Anyway, I don't care what people say…'

'But it may upset your chances of, you know…'

'Of what? Getting married again? I don't want to get married again, unless…'

'Unless what?'

'Nothing. Let's change the subject. Come and have dinner if you want. Don't if you don't want.'

Noor pulled open the screen door, unlocked the wood door and stepped inside. She reached right behind the door and switched on the light. She waited, expecting him to follow. She had dropped all the hints she could think of; he should have picked them up and followed her in. She wouldn't have asked him in if he hadn't been standing outside her door waiting for her. He wouldn't do that if he weren't interested. Maybe he was only interested in her safety so that the mission wouldn't be jeopardized. Noor felt disappointment fall on her like a heavy quilt. She didn't know what she was so disappointed about. He may have come in and eaten and left but that wouldn't have changed anything. She wanted something to change. She wanted him to want her, not as a client or a friend but that's what they were, friends. Even that was remarkable. She knew no other Muslim woman in her circle who was friends with a man let alone with a Sikh man. So, maybe that was it. They would be friends. Eventually, he would find a nice Sikh woman to marry and she would find a Muslim man. They would each stay on their side of the boundary wall, meeting every now and then but never eating together because that couldn't happen. Gurdev's Sikh wife wouldn't allow it, Noor was sure of that. In fact, his new wife would probably forbid her from shopping at Nilibar, stop her from ever seeing Gurdev. Noor burst into tears with loud sobbing noises, crying for having lost something she had never had. She let herself sob and even wail a little. She let herself sink deeper into this nightmare, wondering how far down she could go. She hadn't cried like this when she got news of her husband. She hadn't cried like this for anything. She let herself go on till she couldn't cry any more. Then she straightened up, smiled and went on with her dinner and bedtime.

26

GURDEV TOOK A RICKSHAW HOME, ROCKING SIDE TO SIDE on the stiff red vinyl seat. In his head, he counted the things still to be done. He had been worried about Noor – there was no one else he could take with him. He had also wanted to go in and eat with her, to be with her. He could have but he didn't want to get distracted. More important, he didn't want her to get any ideas now. It was better if they stayed the way they were.

Noor and Gurdev were going to Pakistan as a wealthy Muslim couple visiting old friends. That's all they said on their visa applications. Both got their visas easily, without too many questions but didn't think anything of it. Both needed the right clothes and other props to make sure they looked the part. The whole team was working to get them ready. Nirmal had framed the photograph that Urmila had given to Noor as reference for current fashion in Lahore and hung it up on the wall in the inside room. Then, after gazing at it for a while, he began to draw some designs. Then he brought out reams of fabric from the other side to decide what would look rich but understated when khadi wouldn't do. He decided on cooler Tussar silk, a knobby fabric that looks a little like khadi but is much more polished, smoother Chinese silk and chiffon and fine imported cotton.

'Oh no no no! I can't wear all this. It's sacrilegious. It's unpatriotic. I can't do it.' Then she touched the fabric and held it against her skin. 'Okay, the Tussar and the Chinese silk but definitely not the English cotton.'

'But it's not English. It's American, Noor.'

'Well, then I can wear it since they too were once a British colony.'

Nirmal smiled at no one in particular. Women were so easy to manipulate, especially when it came to clothing. They'd believe anything as long as it made them look good – but good varied by woman. For some women, good was comfortable, for others it was form-fitting and sexy, still others believed it was all about the fabric and how it felt on their skin. He had women clients who got a rash if they wore fabric as rough as khadi. He had to put a satin lining – inside a khadi kurta – to make it wearable.

Noor wasn't fussy, of course, but she was particular about the fit. And now this new wrinkle with the latest fashions – gararas and farshis. The former were divided pants, snug on top and flared starting from mid-thigh, the latter were flared pants all the way. Both had to sweep the floor on the back, but not so much that the women tripped over the fabric. He was excited and apprehensive. He wanted to get everything right so that Noor fit in but he also wanted to make her stand out, in a good way. She deserved that, he felt. His clothes deserved it too. He wanted her to come back and say that so many people wanted to know where she had her clothes done.

And then there was the matter of Gurdev's clothes. Shakir – that's what he was calling himself these days. Just getting the name out of his gullet was a challenge for Nirmal. But he said it, to get Gurdev accustomed to hearing himself called that. His clothes also had to be cut in a Pakistani style and for that Nirmal had no photographs to model on. He had to assume that western clothes were pretty consistent across the two countries, both equally influenced by the British and both feeling removed from that influence at about the same time. So, that's what he decided to go with. Summer clothes were less expensive, no woollen jackets and smart overcoats, only casual gabardine suits, nicely fitted shirts and slim pants, as was the style. Nirmal could do all this. He didn't like to do it but ready-mades for men were terrible, made of cheap synthetic material and nothing would fit Gurdev's build anyway. So, he asked Sangat to source some summer suiting fabric.

It took three weeks to get everything ready. Noor's clothes needed embroidery to suit her station so Nirmal did it himself. He was so close to getting the real thing – he simply wouldn't settle for imposters. The workshop next to the shop was abuzz with activity. Nirmal saw it as he had visualized it. All six sewing machines were occupied, the mattresses on the floor were crammed with people doing finishing work, buttons, hemming and so on.

Nirmal went about checking everything for quality, peering over this shoulder and snatching a piece out of another person's hands to correct the alignment. He was excited, not nervous at all. He was soon to get everything he had ever wanted; he already had most of it but embroidery, oh embroidery, he thought, how it transformed the look of a piece and how it surrounded the person wearing the clothing with an aura that said, I care and I have good taste.

Just to be clear, there were many talented embroiderers available in Delhi, but Nirmal shunned them all. Nothing could be as good as what his boys produced, nothing, not even the work he himself was doing. And then there were the boys. He longed to see the look on Amrit's face when she saw them, and see them she would. Gurdev would ensure that.

27

FINALLY, IT WAS TIME TO LEAVE. NOOR AND GURDEV looked like low-level royalty. They had matching leather luggage that Jagat had brought out from his mother's collection and polished up. Noor wore a brooch to keep her dupatta in place, which modestly covered her head and then wrapped around her neck. If you paid close attention, you would see that the brooch was engraved with the face of Queen Victoria, another one of Jagat's contributions from his mother's collection.

Noor and Gurdev stayed in their respective homes that night, bags packed, alarms set, even though the flight to Amritsar was at noon. She had thought they would fly straight from Delhi to Lahore but all flights to Pakistan had been suspended. They had jointly decided that it was best that they fly to Amritsar instead of taking the train. Flying was faster and less tiring: their beautiful clothing would fit in well with other flyers' and stay crisp, not train-stained and crumpled. In Amritsar, a relative of Sangat's would meet them at the airport and take them to Wagah, a village only one kilometre from the boundary line with Pakistan. This was an official checkpost right on the National Highway that connected both countries. It had earlier been one continuous road, with no gates and checkpoints and the same road that Gurdev had walked on to cross into India and make his way to Amritsar and later to Delhi.

At Wagah, Urmila's parents would pick them up and take them to their home – and then the real work would begin.

Noor waited by her door, suitcase by her side, stepping from one foot to the other. She peered out through the screen door, waiting for Gurdev to arrive. They would need a lot of time because they would have to go by tram first and then take a rickshaw to the airport, balancing their bags on their toes. She waited ten, then fifteen minutes and was beginning to get angry, the kind of anger she knew she could not express to Gurdev. She thought back to the last several days – Gurdev had behaved like a man on a mission, only talking about tickets and timings and Model Town, Lahore. She thought she would bristle and be coy after their last meeting at her home but she had decided against it. He had not responded to her attempts to draw him in and he was not about to. Instead, she thought about what may have happened if he had come in and stayed. She thought about his broad chest, wondered how hairy it was. Going by his beard, she imagined soft and thick. She imagined her head on it, her hair spread over him, his legs intertwined in hers, his hand on her ... when she heard loud honking. It was Gurdev in a brand-new Fiat 1100. A middle-aged Sikh man got out of the car and folded his hands in a polite gesture of greeting. Then, he stepped back and opened the trunk. It easily accommodated both suitcases. The man shut the trunk gently like one would a velvet-lined jewellery box. It didn't connect so he banged it closed and got back into the driver's seat. Gurdev opened the back door for Noor and got into the front seat next to the driver himself.

So, clearly this man wasn't a driver. Noor wondered whose car it was.

'I decided that since we were going to fly to Amritsar, we should also go to the airport in style. What do you think of this latest Indian beauty – well not exactly Indian, more Italian but assembled in India?'

Noor looked at the leather seats, the smart steering wheel, and the way the tongas and rickshaws almost jumped out of their way when the driver blew the horn.

'It's nice, not that I have a lot of experience with cars, or anything.'

As they approached Safdar Jung Airport, Noor felt that now-familiar feeling of terror. She had one new thing to worry about, one that she had put out of her mind so far. She had never flown in an aeroplane. She didn't think Gurdev had either, but he had studied in England. She wondered if he had got there by ship or by BOAC.

When they finally reached and Gurdev had said his thank you and a polite Sat Sri Akal, Noor burst out, 'So who was that? How were you able to get a car at such short notice?'

'How do you know it was short notice? I could have been planning this all along.'

'You couldn't have been because all your plans have been written down in triplicate and shared with everyone. This was not on the plan. We were to drag our suitcases to the tram station and then take a rickshaw to the airport. You would have told me about this yesterday if you had planned it. No, this was arranged this morning. I'll find out how, don't you worry.'

'Okay, you do your detective work, but for now, we need to get checked in and make sure the flight is on time.'

'I'm nervous. What if Urmila's parents aren't there to receive us? What if something has happened and they can't come?' said Noor as they walked around doing this and that as instructed.

'Don't worry, Noor. If that happens, they'll send us back to India. You need a sponsor to go into Pakistan. Without one, they won't let you in. So, we have to try.'

The flight was not too full. Noor and Gurdev sat next to each other, their hands by their sides, both gripping the seat below them. Neither was feeling confident about anything. It was a short flight, about an hour. Both sat glued to their seats, seat belts fastened, as they had been told to do, and didn't release their grip on their seats. At one point, Gurdev tried to behave like a seasoned flyer and got up to go to the bathroom. The plane lurched to the right and Gurdev rocked around as if he was on a camel's back. He quickly got back into his seat and sat down again, grabbing hold of the bottom of his seat again.

'Relax, big man, it's only a little wind,' said Noor. Then the plane rocked to one side again, making the contents of her stomach rise up a little. She grabbed hold of Gurdev's hand and held on so tight that he had to dig her long nails out of the callused flesh on his palms.

Eventually, they reached and the plane landed flawlessly. The two didn't know what Sangat's Uncle looked like so they searched for older Sardars who also seemed to be searching for someone. They found several and circled each one, cautiously mumbling Sangat's name every so often till one circled them equally cautiously. The two men walked around each other, looking down, neither saying anything until Noor finally said, 'Sangat's uncleji, Jagtap Singh?'

'Haanji,' said the man they had thought to be Sangat's uncle. The two men greeted each other with folded hands and as Noor's hand went up to her forehead, she corrected herself and folded her hands. Best to minimize the number of big lies and begin pretending they were a couple.

'Bibiji, come this way. Any need for bathrooms and all that? I can take you to my home – on the way to Wagah.'

'No, Uncle. You can take us directly to the border.'

'Sangat told me not to ask any questions but I have to ask – why are you going to Pakistan? I now understand why you had to cut your hair – they will not let a Sardar into the gate, but why do you have to go at all? Okay, don't answer that or Sangat will eat my head. All I can say is may Guru Nanak shine his light on you through whatever you are trying to do and may you come back victorious.'

Noor and Gurdev thanked him, for his blessings and for not asking for more information. What would they say anyway? That they were going to bring two embroiderers out? He would have laughed at them. He would have called all the elderly Sikhs in the airport and told them, and they would have laughed at them. An important property matter maybe, or a sick grandmother, or even a family wedding, but this reason, anybody would tell them that it was not worth the risk.

Jagtap drove an ancient Dodge Desoto that creaked and moaned as they put the two suitcases in the trunk. Gurdev made a mental note to buy a car when he got back to Delhi. He had the money now but it had never occurred to him. The

Fiat 1100 that he had borrowed for the ride to the airport belonged to his neighbour in Khan Market. He had borrowed it on a whim, to make the journey to the airport a little easier for Noor. They got into Jagtap's car, which was well worn, but clean on the outside and immaculate on the inside.

'Where did you buy this car Jagtapji? It is so well maintained. Are you able to get parts here?'

'Gurdev, I bought this car from a British family; actually bought may be the wrong word. They had abandoned it when they left. It was in bad shape, tires flat, birds had got into the bonnet and there was oil leaking from the engine block. Fortunately, the windows were up and the doors locked. I found a locksmith to make me a key after seeing the car on the side of the road, in the same place, never moving for months. I restored it, and now it still groans a little but mostly it hums. Wait till we get out of the city and on the open road. Then you'll see. These Americans know how to make cars.'

'Will you sell it to me?'

'Why, Gurdev? What do you want with a car? You know nothing about them, you don't even know how to drive,' said Noor. She smiled at the thought of riding in it, though – hair flying with the wind blowing through the open window, all the foot traffic parting for them, the curiosity in people's eyes – who is it? Who is inside that big car?

'Why would I want to sell it? Didn't you hear me tell you how I got it? It's like my child.'

'But you can find another one and restore it, then another one. There must be dozens of abandoned cars all around Amritsar. And then make a business of it. You can make a nice profit, maybe once you run out of abandoned cars in Amritsar, you can come to Delhi and do the same thing?'

'No, not Delhi. Delhi people are too smart. They must have already figured this out,' said Jagtap pensively. 'Maybe I will sell you this car and restore another for myself. Maybe I can restore a few more. Gurdev Singh, you know how to stir people up. You come back from Lahore and we'll talk.'

They set a date and time for their return. This time, it wouldn't be at the Wagah Border. It would be at Kasur village, about thirty kilometres from Lahore and twenty-six kilometres from Amritsar. The village was right at the border but far enough from Wagah that there wouldn't be any security patrols, Gurdev's source had told him. She later learnt that Gurdev's friend Satnam Singh, the one who had run the relocation business, had joined the government. His clients, the departing Englishmen, had helped him connect with the right people.

At Wagah, Gurdev and Noor got out of the car a short distance from the checkpost. Gurdev picked up both suitcases and Noor put her handbag on her shoulder. Both walked confidently towards the soldiers of the Indian Army, standing four abreast in front of the pulley operated gate. The gate was nothing but a long sturdy bamboo, weighed down by rocks on one side that lifted up with the weight and down with a rope. There was little activity at this checkpost now: the legal movement of people was long over, but a trickle continued through the back roads, both ways.

'What is your name?'

'Shakirullah Hasan and Noor Hasan.'

'Are you husband and wife?'

'Yes, we are.'

'What is the purpose of your visit to Pakistan?'

'They've given us a visa…'

'I am asking you…'

'We are going to visit our relatives in Lahore.'

'Do you know that Pakistan doesn't grant visas to Indians, even Muslims, easily?'

'No. We got ours without any trouble.'

The guards looked at both passports. They carefully examined Gurdev's brand-new document, turned the pages carefully till they found the Pakistani visa, examined the stamp, turned the document over and handed it back. They did the same for Noor's passport. Both the Pakistani visa stamps were identical but the passports were vastly different. Noor's was old and authentic and Gurdev's was brand new and also authentic – exactly the new design that the government had announced recently.

The guards lifted the gate and let both of them through into no-man's land. They walked slowly, Noor wondering what she had got herself into. Gurdev looked at her till she looked up and met his eyes. He blinked, several times and she remembered – he never used to blink much. She still had to ask him about that. Thus distracted, she walked confidently to the other side, Gurdev a step behind her. The path in no-man's land was unkempt and rocky, yellow dust swirled about. It felt desolate and lonely even though it was no more than ten metres wide with guards on both ends of it.

On the Pakistani side, the questioning was oddly enough, more friendly than on the Indian side. The difference struck Noor somewhere but she couldn't trace it. Her subconscious filed away the feeling without any specific reaction. She looked at Shakir – she had to think of him as Shakir even in her thoughts – to see if he had any particular reaction. His face was blank with concentration, no emotion visible whatsoever.

'*As salamu alaikum wa rahmatullah wa barakatuhu.*'

'*Wa alaikum salam wa rahmatullah wa barakatuhu.*'

Noor had clenched her fists with the first greeting even though Shakir had practised this longer version several times.

'What are your names, please?'

'Shakirullah and Noor Hasan.'

'And you are visiting relatives in Lahore?'

'Well, they are not exactly relatives, they were close family friends, dearer than relatives. You know how that happens sometimes.'

'What are the names of these good people you are going to meet?'

'Riaz and Shakeela Baig.'

'How long do you plan to be in Lahore?'

'Only one week. It's been many years since we've met but we have to go back to our children,' said Noor.

'How many children do you have?'

'Only two boys, so far. We pray to Allah for a girl,' Noor looked at Shakir shyly.

Then a sudden gust of wind blew up a swirl of dust right up into the group. Shakir sneezed, his classic deep-throated, shake-the-walls, lift-the-floors sneeze. Noor panicked. Gurdev's instinctive words after a sneeze were 'Wahe Guru'. She held her breath, afraid to touch him for that itself might be taken the wrong way. His mouth opened, teeth on lower lip to pronounce the 'W' sound, he changed his mind and sneezed again, then again, followed by a natural-sounding '*Alhamdulillah*'.

'*Yah hamuk Allah,*' replied Noor, 'May Allah have mercy on you,' and smiled.

Shakir held a handkerchief to his nose to keep from sneezing again. His eyes were red and watery. He mumbled something about a dust allergy and continued to drip. The security men stamped their passports and ushered them through, making noises about feeling better.

Once across, Noor searched for Urmila's parents. They weren't hard to find. Theirs was the only car waiting by the side of the Grand Trunk Road. Like Jagtap on the other side of the border, they didn't get out of the car. Theirs was a Buick LaSalle, also ancient but not nearly as well kept as Jagtap's. Riaz reached down as they approached and Gurdev saw the trunk pop up at the back. He walked towards it and placed their two suitcases inside and pushed the lid shut. They went to two sides of the car and opened the passenger doors to get in but only one side opened. Noor walked over to Gurdev's side and slid in as he held the door. The two people who sat in the front of the car remained silent. Once they were inside and the door was closed, they got a warmer welcome.

28

'GURDEVJI, WE'VE HEARD SO MUCH ABOUT YOU FROM Jagat and Urmila. So much good you are doing for our people in Shahdara. Poor souls stayed in India and now they are prisoners in their own homes making your khadi. Welcome to Pakistan!' said Riaz.

'Thank you, ji. Very kind of you to extend your hospitality,' said Gurdev. 'Just so you know, I am Shakirullah Hasan and this is my wife, Noor Hasan. Naturally, I could not get a passport as a Sikh ... so...'

'Shakir Bhai, please don't tell us any more. It only puts us at risk. You are welcome to stay at our home for a few days but please don't tell us where you are going or what you are doing. It is better that way. And make sure you do some good shopping for shawls and our local fashions – that'll make you seem more authentic.'

'Don't worry Baig Saab, my begum here has never been to Lahore. She has spent time with your daughter and made a list – Anarkali Bazaar for suits, Liberty Market for dupattas

... and who knows what else. I hope these are still the right places.'

Gurdev could sense Riaz Baig's unease. His wife, Shakeela, stayed quiet through the entire journey. Later they learnt that she wasn't a fluent English speaker and preferred to stay quiet till she could convey that she preferred Urdu. They drove from Wagah on GT Road towards the city but turned on to Firozepur Road towards Model Town. Gurdev's parents' home had also been in Model Town. And it had been only five years since the incident. He looked out of the window, his last trip flashing before his eyes. But the last time, he had been walking, not riding in a big car. His perspective had been different. As they entered Model Town now, they passed one large house after another. Gurdev heard Mr Baig say something about a large white house as they passed it. He heard something about Urmila's auntie's house but he was too busy looking at the house three doors after – but Mr Baig had sped up and the house passed by in a blur, still enough for Gurdev to know that it was his parents' house. It was no longer a burnt-down ruin, the house had been rebuilt to its original grandeur, almost identical to what it had been in the old days. In fact, it looked exactly the same. Gurdev wondered about that. A new owner, a refugee from India, wouldn't have known about the original design.

They drove past many more mansions and then turned left to still nice but smaller homes. Riaz Baig pulled into the driveway of one of these homes, a pretty free-standing villa, old but well maintained, with a garden in front that looked like it was cared for by someone who knew a little about gardening. As they walked into the cool entryway, out of the simmering heat, Gurdev wondered how they would get around in this city. He had not seen rickshaws on their way here but knew there would be in the city. He had heard that there were still taxis in Lahore, old cars of similar vintage as the LaSalle, but they were dwindling as parts were getting harder to get. He asked.

'What's the best way to get around in the city, Baig Saab?'

'If you have enough money, I can get you a car and driver. If not, you'll have to walk to the main road and hail a taxi to get to the city centre and then move around by rickshaw.'

Noor replied, 'We have Indian money. There was no way to get our hands on Pakistani money. It's not available for exchange anywhere.'

'Your Indian money is no good here, although some black marketers will give you fifty to sixty paisa on the rupee. Any time you create these artificial restrictions, people will find ways around them. Do you want me to ask around?'

'No, no. That won't be necessary. I have American dollars. Those won't be a problem exchanging here, will they?' Gurdev had finally pulled the two bricks out and reached into his wall safe, pulled out the velvet bag and taken half the money and put it into the inside pocket of his jacket. It was time.

'Arre Gurdev Saab, for dollars you will get a premium on the market price. No one knows about the Pakistani rupee – will it be valued based on the market or will the government control the value based on foreign reserves, of which we have none, by the way.'

'But it is my understanding that all reserves were divided between the two countries based on population distribution.'

'That you are right about. But Pakistan, since Jinnah's death, has been moving backwards instead of forward. But never mind all that. I cannot say anything bad about my country: if I do, I'll consider myself a traitor. I had a choice and I made a decision, the one that Shakeela wanted, and I'm happy with the one we made, even though we had to leave our daughter behind. Although...'

'What?' prodded Gurdev.

'I wish Partition had never happened,' said Riaz

'Why?' asked Gurdev.

'I'm not sure why, but I've heard that Jinnah tried to pull it back but the forest was on fire, and there was nothing he could do to put the fire out. Mind you, we escaped the worst of Partition. We moved long before the date of Independence and lost nothing. I even got a good price on my house in India, thanks to Jagat. But I saw what Muslims were doing to Sikhs and Hindus here. I saw it before my own eyes. We gave shelter to one family also, but not for too long or we would be marked. Everybody knew we had only just arrived in Pakistan.'

Gurdev learnt that he would still need to change his dollars for Pakistani Rupees. Riaz Baig was happy to take some off his hands, for future emergencies. Gurdev kept avoiding Noor's questioning glances. He knew she wanted to know how he got the dollars. He raised his eyebrows and pointed them in the direction of the rest of the house, assuming that the bedrooms would be somewhere back there. She finally understood.

'We've been travelling all day now, Shakeela Bibi. Is it okay if we rest for sometime? Then we can come and arrange everything,' asked Noor.

Shakeela, who had been absolutely quiet until then, said softly in Urdu, 'What news of my daughter, Noor? Tell me everything. I haven't seen her in over five years now. Sit down and eat something and tell me. Then you can take your rest. And please call me Aapa. I'm not that old.'

'Shakeela Aapa, your daughter is well. She's an intelligent girl, and I'm getting to know her. She has a sense of humour but she keeps it hidden and oh, this should have been the first thing to say, she's expecting...'

'What! What! Did you hear that, Riaz? Our little girl is going to be a mother...' Shakeela wiped tears out of her eyes with the end of her dupatta and shook her head. 'Look at me. I can't help myself; it's joy of course, so much joy. Maybe someday I'll be able to see my grandchild. Come, come. Come and sit down. I've prepared a light snack.'

Shakeela led Noor and Gurdev into a cool and pleasing home. The Baigs had brought a lot of their furniture with them. What they couldn't fit into the truck they had left for Urmila. Gurdev was impressed with the way things were laid out and how comfortable and well used everything looked. They sat at a dining table where the straight-backed chairs perfectly supported his large back. Mrs Baig had laid out samosas and gulab jamuns, even some hot jalebis. A beautiful tea kettle covered with a rose-vine printed tea cosy sat on one end of the table. Teacups and saucers matched the tea cosy, pink roses with green vines holding them together. Gurdev watched as Noor's eyes widened with appreciation. Naturally, the Baigs' taste and care of things was limited to their home. Their car was not a reflection – or maybe it was Mrs Baig who was the fastidious one. She poured tea into the cups, added milk and asked about sugar.

'Two for me,' said Gurdev.

'Only one for me,' said Noor.

They drank the tea and ate the confections and savouries, all made by a local halwai, the taste so similar to that of food found in India but yet different. There is a thing called 'zaika', an Urdu word that means 'taste'. But it means 'a particular taste'. The taste of these particular samosas reminded Gurdev of his childhood. The samosas he might eat in Khan Market didn't so much.

Gurdev savored all the food, each bite taking him back into his mother's kitchen, taking out hot samosas from a brown paper bag that also had, hidden at the bottom, a small plastic baggie filled with chutney and tied up with string. He remembered taking out the chutney, turning the bag upside down and piercing it with a knife, letting the sweet and tart condiment flow into a bowl. His mother always untied the string and slowly released the chutney into a bowl but Gurdev was too impatient to unwrap the string. He remembered dipping the hot samosa directly into the bowl of chutney, no plate, just his other hand cupped below his eating hand to catch runaway peas and pieces of potato. He remembered the other brown paper bag – the one with the jalebi, also piping hot. These were treats that his father brought home rarely, and he brought home only a little bit of each. He didn't want anyone to overindulge and stop appreciating these finer pleasures. Gurdev was so savouring the food that he almost didn't notice the leaves shaking outside the living room window, a slight movement that blocked the sun for a moment.

Gurdev felt a kick under the table and turned to Noor, 'Yes, sorry, I missed that.'

'Shakeela was saying that our room is ready.'

'This is a two-bedroom house, but it looks much bigger from the outside. Also not as expensive as the three and four bedroom homes on either side of us – but you could never tell, no? It is better to buy a small house in the best neighbourhood than the biggest house in a bad place, don't you think?' said Shakeela.

'Yes, yes of course. That's perfectly true, Shakeela Bibi. One request. I have been having trouble with my back and may need to sleep on the floor,' said Gurdev, casting a small glance towards Noor. Urmila wouldn't have told them too much about them if she thought the letters were being read, only that they were a Muslim couple she knew in Delhi. That's why Riaz Baig had told them not to say anything.

'Gurdev Bhai Saab, I will make the arrangement. Come, follow me.'

Noor and Gurdev followed Shakeela. Gurdev carried both bags through the narrow corridor, wondering if Noor was going to make anything of being in the same room. Something had changed with her after that night at her house. He had been worried about her travelling around the city at night on an errand he had sent her on. He still felt she had no business in all this, but she had been best suited. She had cooled towards him, he felt. It was a relief, actually. That momentary attraction he had felt was now under control but still present. Any pressure from her and he could crack.

The room that Shakeela directed them to was fastidiously furnished, every little detail addressed. There was a double bed with a chintz-covered headboard, a dust ruffle below the mattress to hide old suitcases stored below, bedside tables with reading lamps on both sides and a dressing table with a mirror and a nice bright light. The bed was high and accompanied by a two-step footstool.

'My mother had much of this furniture made by copying photos from English magazines. It's so well made; it survived the journey with barely a nick. Towels are in the bathroom. If there is anything else you need, please do let me know.'

Gurdev and Noor shut the door behind their host and sat down on the bed, which was at once soft and firm.

'How do they do it? Both of them – mother and daughter are exactly the same. Their homes are replicas of each other. But more important, where did these dollars come from? Brand new cars to take us to the airport, fake passport, now American dollars. I'm beginning to get a little afraid of you. Do I know you, the real you or are you some currency smuggling tycoon who lives in a shack to distract the authorities?'

'Oh ho, Noor. I'm nothing like that, a little resourceful. And don't be jealous. You too are a good housekeeper … sometimes. You are good at directing people. Different people have different strengths. Yours are to get things done without doing anything yourself…' Gurdev laughed softly till he was hit in the head with a pillow that was perfect, not too soft, not too hard.

'If that's the case, Gurdev, then I'll go shopping tomorrow and you go looking for your embroidery boys. How about that?'

'No, no. Sorry, sorry! You are resourceful and caring and you can get people to open up to you and your fashion sense is impeccable and …what else can I say?

Gurdev went suddenly quiet. His parent's old home kept flashing by as if they were still driving in Riaz's car. He sat down with his head in his hands. He had to tell Noor about what had happened. He wouldn't be able to go there if she didn't know the background. He began mumbling to himself the pros and cons of talking or not talking, telling or not telling, if telling, then what. Where should he start? Where should he end?'

Noor stiffened, wondering if something had already gone wrong. 'What is it, Gurdev? You are scaring me.'

Gurdev looked up at her from his seated position, his eyes looking up, then down. He wasn't blinking and his breathing was quick and shallow.

'A few weeks before we left Pakistan for India, I went to Lahore. Things were already bad, even though the boundaries had not been declared yet. I went to see what my parents wanted to do. I reached their home at night. I found it alight, burning with a force that couldn't possibly be natural or caused by accident. I wondered if they were out. I saw a figure in the window, trying desperately to get out. I saw that there was a lock on the door outside and most of the other exits out of the house had been blocked by debris. I saw that there were men outside, three men, who were ensuring that the people inside couldn't get out – that they burnt inside. I waited silently in the darkness because I couldn't do anything. There was no point calling the police, they wouldn't come. I waited for the men outside to finish their grizzly task. I followed them. They didn't go home directly. First, they went to a dhaba to eat. I watched them as they twisted their roti to break off a piece, as they scooped up the curry, as they put it into their mouths, as little bits dribbled down their chins, as they wiped off the brown drops with the back of their palms, as they rubbed those hands on their salwars. I watched them so closely because I wanted to see what was in them that made them do what they did. I saw nothing different. After watching them for some time, I left. I didn't go back to my parents' house. They were gone, I was sure.'

What Gurdev didn't tell Noor was that he followed the men to their home. He waited till they were inside. He waited for three hours after that, till 2 a.m. Then he wedged their front door shut and poured petrol that he had bought at a petrol pump on the way there and set their house on fire. He heard their screams – women, children. They had tried to come out of windows but he had wired them shut. He did to them what they had done to his parents. They were Muslims. Their screams still rang in his ears, every night.

'Gurdev, everybody did something, didn't they? Talk to my friend Harleen and she'll tell you what happened in Gurdaspur, how Sikhs derailed a train going to Lahore and how all the Hindus and Sikhs had quietly got off the train at the last station, how hundreds of Sikhs suddenly materialized from the surrounding fields and massacred each and every passenger on that train. Ask her what went on in Muslim homes in Gurdaspur that night. Then ask her what the Muslims on the other side of the new border did to the Sikhs who were trying to get out of there. It was the time, Gurdev. I'm so sorry about your parents.'

'I saw my parents' house as we were driving in today. The weird part is that their house has been rebuilt but it's exactly the way I remember it. Why would someone rebuild a house they've occupied and make it look exactly like it did before? How would they know what it looked like before if they were refugees from India – unless they were not? Unless it was occupied by someone from here, someone who had seen the house before – but that would be illegal. You can't go and occupy a vacant or burnt-out house because the occupants have fled, or in this case … died … in the fire. Right?'

'Gurdev, that's how it was in India, at least. Remember Shahdara. The locks that people left on their doors are still there. The government hasn't reached that part of the city, but that doesn't mean anybody can occupy those homes. I don't know if that's the case here. Maybe the Baigs know more. They must have been here at the time of the fire.'

'Yes, they came before we left for India. They would've been here. I don't want to ask them, though. I'm not sure I want to know second-hand information. I would like to go to the house and find out for myself.'

'It's not that far, we can go for a walk later, maybe say Adaab to a few neighbours along the way.'

'Can we go now?'

'It's still hot. Let's wait till 6 p.m. People sleep in the afternoons.'

But with 6 p.m. came visitors. Shakeela Baig's sister, Nusrat, and her husband, Ali Zafar, the cinema hall tycoon. Nusrat was much like her sister in looks. They were both petite with delicate features. Nusrat's complexion was light, the colour of a full moon with strong blue undertones. Shakeela's was more like an egg, with yellow undertones. But Shakeela, once she opened up to people, exuded warmth. Nusrat, on the other hand, was as cold as a malai kulfi. She had come to her sister's house to meet these special guests from Delhi. Guests from Delhi in Lahore had been a common enough occurrence in the past, but now it was as though they were the divine presence – God-like creatures who had somehow broken through the barriers and come across. People from India who wandered over into Pakistan were usually shepherds with no understanding of national boundaries, or soldiers who had a specific purpose for going into a particular area.

They sat in the perfectly designed living room where each person seated could see everyone else and hear everyone else. Each person had access to a small table to keep their sherbet on and on which Shakeela placed two small individual servings of nuts, freshly roasted and perfectly spiced. Once everyone was comfortable, the talk began with politics and then moved on to films. Indian cinema still made its way to Pakistan and everyone was talking about Nargis Dutt and Raj Kapoor in *Awaara* and then talk turned to Dilip Kumar and Nargis in *Babul*. Ali Zafar referred to Dilip Kumar as Yusuf Bhai.

'Why did that man feel the need to change his name to a Hindu one? He would have been popular with any name. And why do Hindu men need to marry our women?'

'Bhaijaan, let's talk about the wonderful acting in these films. This new boy, Dev Anand, in *Baazi* with Geeta Bali as a dancer, who would have thought that India was capable of producing crime dramas? Romance and running around trees is all that we've been good for,' said Gurdev.

Noor opened her eyes wide but then narrowed them again. Gurdev had not seen a single movie in all the time that she had known him. When they went as a group, he refused to go. He said real life was more interesting. He said he didn't have three hours to waste sitting in a dark room that smelt bad and he didn't like tucking pants into his socks so rats wouldn't run up his leg and bite his ankles. Noor had shaken her head and told him there were no rats in movie theatres but he had never gone. And never had he discussed popular cinema with Sangat and Nirmal either.

'Bhaijaan, wait till Pakistani cinema gets its feet. Then you'll see what real films are all about. Noor Jehan's new film *Chan Way* is a blockbuster. But only when we stop Hindi films from coming to Pakistan will our industry grow,' said Ali Zafar.

'Ali Bhai, why do you want to control art and artists. Let them flourish everywhere. Send your films to us and keep watching ours. That's how we all stay in touch with each other, no? Our governments have not made it easy for even family members to see each other,' said Gurdev.

Noor, Shakeela, Nusrat and Riaz watched the conversation, silently sipping their sherbet and absentmindedly popping nuts into their mouths. Once a sound came out of Riaz's mouth, but Ali quickly pounced on him. 'You are still an Indian at heart. How can you be a Pakistani when your only daughter and soon-to-be grandchild still live in India? You don't know anything about this side.'

'Arre, Bhai Sahib, let him speak. It was all one country not that many years ago, wasn't it? There was no difference between West Punjab and East Punjab. We ate the same food, spoke the same language, watched the same films, lived the same lives, made the same stories – the stories that Saadat Hasan Manto wrote in Bombay and the stories that he came and wrote here, they are about the same people, our people. How different are your films going to be?' said Gurdev. Noor could see the other man's face redden. He was not accustomed to being stood up to. And Gurdev knew that. That's why he was needling him. She smiled.

'Both of you are right in your way. Now, can we discuss shopping,' she said, laughing.

Nusrat also laughed. 'I'll tell you all the best places, Noor. My sister, she's meticulous, gets it from our mother, but she's staid in her style. Look at her now, she's still wearing last year's style of salwar – beautiful embroidery, I have to say, but you have to update as styles change, no?'

'I can't throw out perfectly good clothes because styles have changed. Speaking about changing styles, tell me the latest about your neighbours,' Shakeela asked her sister and then turned to Noor to explain. 'Nusrat's neighbours, we showed you their house as we drove in, the house about two or three doors down...'

Noor saw Gurdev stiffen in his chair. Nusrat took over the story.

'Some new people came and occupied that house. They looked familiar but I couldn't remember where I had seen them before. I still can't. We all thought they were refugees from the other side. So we had Riaz go speak to them, to understand where they had come from, some common experiences, you know, since they had also come recently. But those people acted strange. They said they had come from Gurdaspur, but Riaz has been to Gurdaspur many times and he didn't know the locality they said they were from.'

Gurdev sat absolutely still. Nusrat continued. 'See, that's a big beautiful house, a large plot in an expensive locality. It had to be given to someone who had left behind a property of equal size and value, right? But this case seemed strange so Riaz and Ali went and filed a complaint with the Rehabilitation Office. Now there is an enquiry. The thing is that these people had money, old Indian money that they were able to change to Pakistani money early on, and foreign currency – dollars and pounds, lots. So, they kept throwing it around at everyone. Bribes, but also to show that they had money to rebuild the burnt house so it's rightfully theirs. We think they are lying but can't prove anything. They are so uncultured and gaudy. The house looks nice from the outside because they made the same thing that Sardar family had before – slightly ostentatious but nice enough. You should see the inside, terrible...'

Everyone was listening with rapt attention but the story ended there, for now. Gurdev broke into the silence, 'Do you know what happened to the Sardar family?'

Ali answered, 'Sad story, that. Someone set fire to their house with both husband and wife inside. They had one son but he lived somewhere else. Good boy, they always said. They never got out is all we know. Nobody did much checking because the times were such. Fires were burning everywhere. The police didn't know what to do. They did find bones after the fire but barely. It was a bad time, a bad time.'

Noor sat there thinking that Gurdev had got everything he needed without stepping out in the heat. She wondered what would have happened if he had actually gone there and rung the bell.

Shakeela had stepped out of the room for a few minutes while Nusrat was telling the story. She came back in to say that dinner was served at the dining table. They could sit down and eat, six seats at the table.

The group sat down to a dinner of mutton biryani, keema cutlets, bhindi and daal. Shakeela served everybody the rice dish from the head of the table and passed the plates around. They all helped themselves to everything else. Once again, Gurdev noticed a movement outside the window in the dining room, a flicker of light, a flashlight, outside. The curtain, he noticed was kept slightly apart on one side, not at all in keeping with the fastidiousness of the rest of the house.

'Shakeela Bibi, Indian or Pakistani, your cooking is the best, like nothing I've tasted anywhere,' said Ali, cupping his fingers and shovelling rice and mutton into his mouth.

Gurdev ate with his hands too. Noor watched him, fascinated as he made perfect morsels with his fingers and flicked the food into his mouth. They ate chapatti with meat and vegetables, which was okay to eat with your fingers, but eating rice in this manner took a special skill. After cleaning his plate once, getting a second helping and cleaning his plate again, Gurdev sat back in his chair. His face looked purposeful, like he was here not just to eat but for some other reason.

'Nusrat Bibi, you were telling us about your neighbours. What's wrong with their house?'

'You know, gaudy and gauche, like someone who has a lot of money and doesn't know what to do with it. Everything is covered in gold leaf. And the place is filled with things – statues and odds and ends, but large, and if you forgive me, not to my taste at all.'

'How many people in the household, Bibi?' probed Gurdev.

'I haven't seen them all at the same time, but looks like there's a couple and two children. I see an old lady sitting on the verandah from time to time. I've also noticed activity in the back, where the servants' quarters are, smoke from the chimney every day, from cooking probably. I also notice that the clothes hanging to dry change every day. I haven't actually seen anyone back there and the family seems to be doing their own work. A gardener comes around to clear the lawn and take care of the few plants that survived the fire. They haven't planted anything new.'

Gurdev seemed satisfied, so Noor jumped in. 'Nusrat Aapa, you were to tell me about the best places to shop. Somebody told me that I should look for two embroiderers, young boys, in Anarkali Bazaar. Their work is the best.'

Gurdev stared at Noor in awe. She was getting these people to do their work for them.

'Do you mean Sultan and Samir? Yes, I've heard a little bit about them, but they got into some kind of trouble and disappeared.'

'What do you mean, disappeared? And what kind of trouble? Nothing serious, I hope.'

'Noor Bibi, we have many other shops that will give you beautiful suits with embroidery. Why only these two? Best to leave them alone, especially because you are here for only a few days, you know what I'm saying, I'm sure,' said Ali Zafar, glancing narrowly at his wife. 'We have heard rumours that these two boys are Indian spies, sending information to their handlers in India via regular mail, in code. Imagine, such young boys.'

'Oh, that can't be. I've heard that these boys don't even leave their house. They've not even gone to school. All they know is embroidery. They don't know anything about spies and codes – how could they? Who taught them? Why can't people do a little more digging before throwing around accusations like this? The poor boys. No wonder they have no work … that's what … um, I've heard.

'Our Noor Bibi gets a little emotional sometimes. What she means is that if they are the best then why not search for their work, why settle for anything else?' said Gurdev.

'No, no, nothing like that. I'm not stubborn or … I feel bad for them,' said Noor.

'Sorry, say that again, please, madam. You are or you are not stubborn?' Gurdev teased Noor.

'Here, I've written down some names for you. You will have to go to the market and ask for the places,' said Nusrat.

Gurdev wondered if Ali Zafar actually knew about the boys or if he was irritated that Noor had come with her own intelligence. In any case, they would have to locate the boys on their own.

Shakeela served dessert to which Gurdev shook his head vehemently and then wiped two bowls clean. She had made phirni, a rice pudding variant made with rice flour, cardamom, saffron and milk. Noor wondered who had stood there and stirred the milk till it thickened, not Shakeela because she had been right there with them for most of the evening.

After dinner and a few burps, Gurdev wanted to step outside for a walk, to aid digestion, he said, but Noor wanted to sleep. It had been a long day and she was tired. Gurdev agreed not to go out alone and came to the room with Noor. They locked the door, washed up, changed their clothes in the bathroom, one at a time and Noor lay down on the bed. Gurdev went around to the other side to find a comfortable bed laid out for him on the floor. He smiled. This lady was something else, but there was more to her than her fastidious housekeeping, he could sense it.

29

THE NEXT MORNING, THEY WOKE UP TO THE SMELL OF eggs cooking, toast browning, something being blended and a low cacophony of voices. The Baig house was up. The Indian visitors jumped up and rushed around to bathe and get ready. Gurdev cursed his additional chore – shaving. He had never ever shaved, had never seen his father shave or any of his friends or other relatives. It was not easy to start shaving this late in life. Plus, each time he did, he felt guilt at the base of his neck, which he had to lift and hang back behind him to release. Once the guilt left, he went on, listing down what he hoped they could accomplish that day. One item on the list was to visit A-8, his parents' former home.

'Ouch,' he whimpered. He had cut himself, another thing he could not get used to, this daily bloodletting.

They took turns in the bathroom, Noor taking extra care she didn't touch Gurdev in his pyjamas as she swept past him for her turn. It was that awkward sideways walk through the bathroom door, ensuring that not even a bit of fabric touched. He knew what she was doing and he was beginning to understand why. But they had to go on and she was doing that well. He would have to rearrange his mind once they got back.

'Good morning, dear guests. I have arranged your car. It's waiting outside for you.' Riaz Baig was happy. He had his stash of American dollars. Life was good. Noor and Gurdev ate heartily. They couldn't help it. This was one, he wanted to say Indian but had to change it to Pakistani home, where no one forced you to eat anything. You sat there and ate because the food was pleasing and smelt and tasted like something one simply had to put into one's mouth. After they were done eating, Gurdev went back to the room, made the bed, checked his pockets, hid their passports and other documents at the bottom of his bag, made a mental note of what was at the top of the bag, picked up Noor's purse and came back out again. Noor took her purse from him sheepishly, and they walked out into 40 degree Celsius heat at 9:45 a.m.

Riaz had got them another Buick LaSalle, this one in better condition than the one he had but still old. The driver was a Punjabi from Gujarkhan, not far from Gurdev's Sukho. He wanted to ask him questions but he put on his Shakirullah persona and greeted the driver whose name was Akbar with the traditional Urdu greeting. Akbar was friendly, with a crooked toothy smile, and possibly not aware that his clients were from India. It didn't make sense to tell anyone, Gurdev concurred in his head. Especially since they looked like everyone else, spoke more or less the same language and thanks to Urmila's guidance, Noor's clothing didn't give them away. Fortunately for Gurdev, there were plenty of men wearing western clothes.

Akbar himself wore white pants and a white shirt, a chauffer's uniform, but it was stained in places and more pale yellow than white. But he had a way about him that was warm and friendly; some people have that more than others, some people not at all. Gurdev and Noor had already discussed and decided that they were visiting Lahore from out of the country. America, but only if the driver asked specifically. They kept Ali's warning in mind, people may be watching. The driver was probably okay but not necessarily so. It didn't take long to buy someone off or threaten in a way that ensured compliance.

Akbar started the car. It rumbled at first, but then as they backed up and got on the road, it hummed like Jagtap's Desoto.

'Akbar Bhai, is this your car? It is so well kept and the hum of the engine, it is so smooth, a baby would sleep through it,' said Gurdev.

'Yes, Bhaijaan, it is mine. My old boss, Mr Alan Wickman, he lived here in Lahore many years. I was driver. He left car for me. Now, I take care of it – even better than before, because it is mine,' he said, laughing. 'It makes, difference, no?'

'Yes, Akbar. If you own something, you naturally value it more. What was Mr Wickman doing here, Akbar?'

'He was a history professor at university, big university here, you know. And Mr Wickman's wife, she was also always busy, always going from here to there. She made clothes, not like a darzi but fancy. English ladies go back to England and order her clothes – such was quality, done all by our people, here only, in Anarkali Bazaar.'

Gurdev and Noor looked at each other and smiled.

'Akbar Bhai, take madam to one of those embroidery people, no? She wants to make some suits. How many suits these ladies need, I won't understand. She wanted to take them with her.' As he said these words, Gurdev realized that he had given Akbar an opening to ask where Noor wants to take the suits. But he didn't. He looked at Noor and shook his head as if in wonder, now aware that Akbar was observing them in the rearview mirror whenever he got a chance.

'Why don't we go to Liberty Market first? I want to buy some dupattas,' said Noor, sort of understanding Gurdev's look.

'Yes, Bibi.'

They got to Liberty Market, which was a brightly coloured beehive of tiny cells filled with glass bangles, embroidered shoes, dupatta borders, artificial jewellery that looked better than the real thing, and tiny tea shops embedded in their own fractional cells at regular intervals.

'Bibi, I will wait here only, otherwise not easy to find car. You do your shopping and come here,' said Akbar.

'Shakir Bhai, you go with Noor Bibi or sit here? This is women's work, no?'

Gurdev didn't remember telling Akbar his name or Noor's. Maybe Riaz had told him. But the slip of paper Akbar was holding when they went to the car said 'BAIG'.

'I'll go with her, Akbar. I'll hurry her along. Otherwise, you and I will be sitting here till tomorrow.' They both laughed.

Gurdev hurried after Noor, who had already begun browsing in a shop that sold glass bangles.

'Listen, let's have some tea,' Gurdev said as he tapped Noor on the shoulder.

'What, now? We just got here. And you just ate breakfast … with tea.'

'Let's keep browsing and then let's sit in a tea shop for a few minutes. We need to plan.'

'Oh okay.'

She examined the bangles, tried on a few. She struggled to get them up her wide hand, wide in the middle but her fingers were long and slim, not stubby, as one would expect with such a wide hand. She asked for a bigger size, speaking Punjabi and Urdu with the young saleswoman. 'Bibi, the bangles will be too big for your wrist then. Take smaller size and use ghee or soap to slip them on.'

'No, no. Then I'll never wear them,' Noor went on as if nothing was wrong. Gurdev had both his hands under his armpits, his hands covering his chest, his fingers flapping up and down. He let out a small sound every few seconds, like a deep exhale. Noor was ignoring him, he knew, and for good reason. That driver, or whoever he was, was watching them, he was sure. He let his hands out from their cocoon and bent over Noor, making like he was deeply engrossed in whatever she was looking at.

'I think you should buy bangles that you can put on and take off easily. So what if they hang on your wrist. You will complain every time you put them on and after one or two times, you'll stop wearing them.'

'You are right, G—Shakir.' She had almost done it. He nudged her, not too gently and she winced. The shop girl turned around to see if everything was okay. 'Yes, yes. Shakir, you are absolutely right, as always. The smaller size will hurt to put on and take off. Here take these back. I'll take one dozen of this one and one dozen of this other one, both in the larger size. Shakir, please pay,' and she walked out of the shop, stepping into a narrow alley that took them away from Akbar's prying eyes.

Gurdev paid for the bangles with the Pakistani rupees that Riaz Baig had given him the previous night in exchange for dollars. The shop owner, sitting at the cash register, held up each note against the light to ensure that it was genuine. Both countries had introduced a metal thread to be a part of the paper bill. This metal thread was visible when the note was held up to light. A fake bill had a line drawn in where the metal thread should be. Most small shopkeepers had become adept at identifying fake notes.

He checked his pockets, making sure he was keeping the Pakistani money and change separate from the dollars. He had the dollars in an inside pocket within his pocket that Nirmal had sewed for him. A pickpocket would only get to the first pocket. He walked into the alley that Noor had gone into and found her standing outside a leather shop, examining handmade, hand-embroidered shoes.

Gurdev pointed towards a teashop with two small tables inside and two outside. He went inside, a tin-roofed shelter, but cool because of the shade and ordered two glasses of tea. They sat down on two wooden chairs and a small table turned black with layers of paint mixed with grime. A young man brought their tea, holding both glasses in one dirty hand, pinching the two glasses together with his thumb and forefinger, each digit slightly immersed in the beige liquid. He placed the two glasses on the table, splashing a little and wiping the spill away with his already dirty shirt tail.

Gurdev could see Noor squirm as she pushed away her glass. He nodded gently and picked up his glass. He drained it, placed the empty glass before her and then drank from the other one slowly.

'Akbar knew our names, Shakir and Noor. The piece of paper that had the Baigs' address only said BAIG, not our names. Someone must have told him our names and where we are from. That means he's somehow connected with the government. I wonder what they want. They don't know anything except that you are obsessed with embroidery. Which there is nothing wrong with. Many women have a similar obsession…' He felt a kick on his shin and he winced. 'Ouch, did I say something wrong? I know what you did for Khadi kurtas. Imagine what you'll do for good embroidery,' this Gurdev said loudly. Noor caught on. She didn't kick him again.

'Bibi, I know a place for excellent embroidery, not here. In Anarkali Bazaar. I'll have to take you – fifty rupees only, for bakshish, okay?' It was the young man who had brought the tea. 'We go on rickshaw.'

'But we have a car and driver.'

'I know, Bibi. Everyone in the bazaar knows that some rich people have come for shopping. No car in Anarkali Bazaar. We will go by rickshaw from the backside.'

Noor suppressed her laugh and got a kick in the shin from Gurdev; he had always told her to watch her superiority with the English language. 'There's more to a person than the way he talks, you know,' he had said in his perfect English.

'Okay, you guide us. What is your name?'

'It is Imran, Bibi.'

Gurdev noticed that the young man was directing all his comments to Noor. He knew who would be driving this expedition.

30

GURDEV AND NOOR MADE THEIR WAY BEHIND YOUNG Imran, who would be about the same age as Nirmal's Sultan and Samir. They walked through alleyways crammed with shops, their merchandise hanging off the doorway and spilling on to the narrow path. Boxes covered with less expensive clothing and other adornments lay outside. More expensive items were pinned up on satin and locked behind glass doors. No one had mannequins but everyone had at least one glass cabinet in which sat the most exclusive outfit in the shop, pinned on white satin as if draped on two-dimensional model.

They went through more alleys, moving further and further away from the LaSalle and Akbar. Noor could see that Gurdev was concerned. She wasn't. After all, they had valid visas. Gurdev's passport was India's problem. They couldn't catch him on that here in Pakistan. What if they did when they tried to go back to India? Oh, but they weren't going to go through the checkpoint. They couldn't if the boys were with them. And if the boys weren't with them, they would have failed in their mission. Maybe that is why Gurdev was concerned. She was certain that this man she loved could not tolerate failure.

Her thoughts stopped abruptly when they entered the Dupatta alley, a whole street devoted to the long scarf that both Indian and Pakistani women wore for both modesty and fashion. She had to stop here and feel the phulkari, the zigzag design that is a Punjabi trademark. Girls embroider their own dupattas for their wedding – not an inch of the base fabric is left uncovered. Noor wanted one.

She called out to Gurdev, 'Shakir, I want to see this.'

He turned around, an irritated look on his face – his mission interrupted. But he softened and asked Imran to stop for a few minutes. Noor saw Imran whisper something in Gurdev's ear and walked over to them.

'What is this? You men are conspiring against a lone woman who simply wants to buy a pretty phulkari for her own wedd—'

'For your sister's wedding, you mean, Noor,' Gurdev interjected, but Imran was not paying attention. He was busy chatting with another young man his age, probably telling him how easily he had made fifty rupees.

'Oh, Gu—Shakir, this is hard. We should have practised more. I noticed that you were about to say 'Harleen', a solid Sikh name. We have to be more careful.'

Gurdev nodded and told Noor that the phulkari is better in Anarkali Bazaar. 'Imran knows a guy...'

'Let's go then.'

They finally came out of the market and into the heat. Imran hailed a cycle rickshaw and told the man to take them to Anarkali Bazaar petrol pump. He indicated to Noor and

Gurdev to sit in the seat and himself got on the back, standing up on a crossbar the whole way, about twenty minutes. They couldn't put up the shade because Imran's head came through the accordion folded shade, peering between them as they sat in the narrow seat. On slight inclines, Imran got off the rickshaw and pushed to help the puller along. At the petrol pump, Gurdev paid the man whatever he asked. Once again, Imran whispered in his ear and Noor strained to listen. This time she knew he was probably telling Gurdev to bargain.

Anarkali Bazaar was like Liberty Market in terms of the sights and sounds, but they could tell immediately that the roads were a little wider; the women who wandered from shop to shop were older, better dressed. The shops themselves were larger, much like their Nilibar in Khan Market. She realized what they had modelled after but a look at Gurdev's face gave no indication of reflection or nostalgia. He had never been associated with this business. Nirmal had been the only one. Nirmal had first convinced Sangat whom he knew already. They were both from Lahore. And then they convinced Gurdev. She wondered if there was a reason why they went after Gurdev. Conspiracy theories swirled in her head like bits of mango in lassi. They were here only because of Nirmal's embroiderers. He had convinced them all. And then Nusrat saying that the two had got into trouble…

'Bibi, Bibi, come follow me or you will get lost,' said Imran loudly, to be heard over the noise of the street. Noor followed the two men blindly, not looking at anything, mind still in a jumble. The three partners had come a long way. Whatever had happened had been a natural progression. It was only natural that they would aspire for more. There was nothing sinister in their single-minded search for the best embroidery in the region. She was slowly convincing herself that Nirmal was indeed the eccentric, slightly crazy artist and craftsman that he presented to the world. He was nothing more, unless … there was more to his relationship with these two boys than he was telling them, unless the boys meant something to Nirmal's wife, Amrit, and not to him. The two didn't have any children. She wondered why. Thoughts entered again, bumped against the walls of her brain and gave her a headache. She reached up to her head with both hands, as Gurdev looked back to check on her progress.

'I'm coming, I'm coming. I'm not looking at anything else…'

'Why are you holding your head? Is it the heat?'

'No, I'm fine. Although a cup of tea…' She looked ahead at Imran. 'Never mind.'

'This market will have nicer places. Let's find one and do that first, okay?'

'Imran Bhai, we are going to stop at this small restaurant and eat something. Can you wait for us?' said Gurdev as they crossed a passable place with pastries in a glass case.

Imran waved them on and kept walking, indicating that he would be back in ten minutes, flashing his wide-open hand twice. Noor and Gurdev opened a glass door and were hit by a blast of cold air; the café had a small air conditioner humming in the back wall. Noor smiled gratefully. Her thick forest of thoughts dwindled once she saw the beautiful tea set at a table before an elegantly dressed older woman.

'Ah! This is what I need,' she said in her perfect English, tired of talking in chaste Urdu, making sure she wasn't making any mistakes, while also making sure Gurdev wasn't making any mistakes.

'One pot of English Breakfast tea and an order of scones, please,' she said to the young man serving them.

He responded in good English, 'Yes, Madam. Anything for you, Sir?'

'I'll share her pot of tea, if she'll let me, and maybe eat one of her scones as well, thank you.'

As she drank her perfect tea, Noor's head cleared up completely. She began to focus on the task again. 'So, are you going to ask him?'

'I already did. He knows about them. But he doesn't know where they are. He's going to ask around. For a crazy lady who wants the best embroidery,' he said with a laugh. 'It's fine, it's a good reason.'

They finished, got up and paid the bill with more Pakistani rupees and walked out into the heat. Imran was waiting outside, leaning against a wall, downing a small cup of tea in a paper cup. He threw the cup down on the side of the street and came striding towards them.

They went into the bazaar, this time, Noor closely following and listening intently to the running conversation between the two men. Gurdev's Urdu was colloquial, of the common man, probably from his years of living on farms and talking to farmhands. He spoke fast, without hesitation. Noor's was more measured, as she had learnt it in Delhi and spoken it at home. Mostly, she had grown up speaking English. But she had noticed that the Pakistani woman in the café spoke

Urdu like she did, in a crusty accent that said that she'd prefer to speak in English but she appreciated that Urdu was her mother tongue so she must speak it.

After walking for about ten minutes, they went into a shop, a near replica of Nilibar, and sat down on the low stools. Imran, the whisperer went and whispered something into the owner's ear. The owner called one of the young men huddled in a corner and asked him to show Bibi the best.

'Finest quality only, huh, Mukhtiar. Don't show her anything ordinary.'

Mukhtiar began taking embroidered suit pieces out of a large plastic box, one by one, each wrapped in tissue paper that he gently unfolded to reveal the craftsmanship below. To each, Noor shook her head, too much, too bright, too mellow. The young man took out another box; this one was red leather, like a large jewellery box. The pieces in this box were wrapped in satin cloth. He took out each one as if he was a father holding a newborn baby, gentle, tentative, uncertain – but to each of these, Noor said no – not right for her, not intricate enough, too heavy.

Then the owner called Mukhtiar to him when the young man turned to his boss to ask what was next. He returned to Noor with a tin trunk, much like the box that Nirmal carried his precious embroidery pieces in. The box lay under the platform that Mukhtiar stood on. He parted the mattresses with another young man's help and lifted a wood door below. While the other man held the door, Mukhtiar took out the box and laid it to one side. Once the platform was all settled again, he laid the trunk before Noor, sideways, and opened it. In it were pieces of work, once again, wrapped in tissue-like paper but it wasn't. It was even finer onionskin paper. These pieces were only embroidery. They didn't include the fabric to make the outfit.

Young men who were sometimes employed by these shops but often were freelancers did the other pieces. They would bring a sample of their work to the shop. If approved they were given the fabric on which to embroider. Technically, this was the better way, and it was the way almost everyone worked. Almost. The only person who didn't work that way was Abida Bibi. She created the embroidery on plain pieces of silk or khadi or linen and so covered the fabric with her coloured skeins that not a millimetre of the fabric below showed through. This piece could then be expertly stitched on to new suit fabric. The advantage of this method was that when a suit didn't fit any more, the embroidery could be removed and reused on a new piece of fabric. But Abida Bibi's reason for doing pieces was her independence, Mukhtiar surmised. She didn't want to work for anyone, he said, and anyone willing to pay the price for her work was welcome to have it.

'Where is she now, this Abida Bibi? Her work is exquisite.'

'Yes, this is her original work, old, you can tell by the paper it's wrapped in. We don't take it out too much. People don't like it. They say it can barely be seen and no one can tell the difference. But Bibi, Abida Bibi is gone. She died many years ago.'

Noor looked at Gurdev, who was sitting with his head resting in his hands, a bored husband. He shook his head gently.

'Is this all that is left of her work? Nothing else?'

'Yes, Bibi. What is in this trunk is what we have. Other shops will have even less. Maybe Imtiaz Brothers will have a few more pieces but us two, we bought her work the most,' the owner said, entering the conversation.

'Are these all neck and sleeves or are there some sari borders as well?'

'Bibi, where are you from? No one wears saris in Pakistan any more. It's not our dress.'

'Arre, we live in America. I still wear a sari sometimes. And the beauty of this work is such that no one will have anything like I have.'

'America, Bibi? You are lucky.'

It was a blunder, Noor knew by the look on Gurdev's face but then he settled down and bobbed his head from side to side. The word had the right effect. The owner came and sat down before them himself, asking Mukhtiar to carefully unwrap each piece and lay it on a piece of matching fabric, holding it up for Noor to examine.

'Bhaijaan, what will you charge for the whole box?' Gurdev chimed in from his seat.

'Oh … that … I'll have to work it out.'

'Will one thousand dollars in cash be enough?'

'Oh … oh … yes, I'll have to … no … yes. That will be enough.'

'Noor, do you want to see anything else?' Noor shook her head. 'Imran, let's wrap up the box, carefully.'

Imran looked at this man who had hired him for fifty rupees and was now pulling out a tightly rolled wad of hundred dollar bills. He cursed himself. Gurdev put his hand in his pocket again and took out a twenty dollar bill. He handed it to Imran. Everyone in Pakistan knew dollars. It was the currency of the rich. If you had dollars, you could go anywhere, buy anything.

As they were walking out with the trunk, Mukhtiar came after them and asked them to come back. The owner wanted to talk.

Gurdev and Noor came back in. Gurdev asked Imran to sit holding that thousand-dollar trunk close to him. The owner indicated to them to follow. Just like in their own store, this shop had a mirror that opened when pushed, but behind the mirror was not a workshop but a plush sitting room. It was probably for special, regular clients who didn't want to shop with anyone else. The owner indicated to them to sit.

'Bhaijaan, what is your good name? And Bibi yours, too?'

'Shakirullah and Noor Hasan. And yours?'

'I am Sajid Maulvi. My shop's name is Maulvi Brothers, but I have no brothers, only three sisters but they have nothing to do with the shop. My father also had no brothers but he didn't think to call the shop Maulvi and Sons like many do – he started it, you see. He thought that maybe if he said Maulvi Brothers, it would feel more long lasting.'

'Okay. Good.' Gurdev was looking around for an exit on this side of the shop. He knew the shop owner was also buying time.

'Shakir Bhai, what is your occupation in America?'

'I am a businessman, Bhaijaan. Many things, this and that. We are in a little hurry now ... so...'

'Wait for a few more minutes. I have someone you should meet but it will take a few minutes. Tea, coffee?'

They both asked for tea, but Noor looked perplexed. Gurdev could see that she was worried, about her slip up about the sari or about the dollars or about whom they were going to meet. Her hands went to her forehead, which glistened with sweat, then to her hair that was plastered to her head.

Gurdev said, 'Sajid Bhai, can you switch on the air conditioner. My wife finds the heat here difficult to bear.' He then looked at Noor with his eyes circling her face, slowly, unblinking, telling her, wordlessly, to calm down. She wanted to run from there, but that would make it worse.

They had tea and bakery biscuits that tasted like butter. Everything in this country tasted the same yet so different. It was as if the soil was different and the water had a better flavour. Gurdev savoured the taste and smiled at Noor. She smiled back but barely. He picked up a third biscuit and offered the plate to Noor. Noor shook her head, one shake to the left, her chin down, eyes on Gurdev. He blinked several times and smiled again. 'So good, so fresh,' he mumbled.

'Here they are. I think you will get great pleasure in meeting the grandsons of the great Abida Bibi, Sultan and Samir. She taught them everything she knew, you know. They are now treasures of Pakistan and they are my responsibility. They suffered for some time after their remaining parent, their father, died tragically in the riots of 1947, but now they are with me and will soon start working again.'

'Oh! Hello, young men!' Noor was suddenly alive again and relieved. Gurdev could see it in the way she flipped back her hair and made it fluffy again. Imran had told him that the boys had been seen at Maulvi's shop. He had also told him that they were followed each time they came. The two boys looked to be about fifteen and seventeen, both with soft fuzz on their chins and under their noses. Samir, the older one looked right at Gurdev but avoided Noor's eyes.

The younger boy, Sultan, looked straight down at his leather shoes, scruffy and worn down, his skinny, dirty ankles bare below the too short salwar of his Pathan suit. Both boys were light-skinned with light-brown hair, partly because of the Northern Frontier influence and partly because they had been indoors so much. For all their skills at embroidery, their own clothes were rough like Gurdev's Pathan suits and well worn. Neither spoke.

'Bibi, forgive them, they don't speak too much, but their work, I can say it is even better than Abida Bibi's. She always told me that. My boys, my jigar, my soul – they will carry my name forward.'

Sultan, the younger of the two, reached into a cloth satchel he was carrying and took out a carved wooden box, about eight inches by ten inches and about eight inches deep. He passed it over to Noor. In it were pieces much like his grandmother's but even richer, and there were rolled pieces, borders for saris – five metres by six inches, sometimes eight inches of dense embroidery, as neat on the back as on the front, not a loose thread, not a stitch out of place. There were Parsi gara borders and sequin borders and cross-stitch borders with minute Xs in an endless, beautiful flowering vine, all laid down on one side of the box, one on top of the other. Noor reached out to touch one but Sultan waved her hand away. 'It'll get soiled,' Sajid told her.

'We have clients for your work in America, both for Asian dresses and western dresses. Are you willing to come with us? New York City, boys! It's the land of opportunity,' Gurdev asked. While Gurdev spoke, Noor put the wooden box down on the table, took out a small notepad from her purse and scribbled something on it. She tore the page out, slipped it in her hand and put the notepad back in her purse. Then she picked the box back up to stare longingly at the contents again.

'Arre, Shakir Bhai, these boys don't care about money or big cities. It's people like you and me whom money serves. These people are slaves to their craft. But why should they leave Pakistan? They can make whatever you want and we'll export. Don't worry; our government will not stop anything like this. They'll encourage it, in fact. They are happy to see our people settle in London and America, they take our country's name forward.'

'But they have to see the proportions – the measurements, you know, the sizes. Even neck and sleeve embroidery will be measured differently. American women are bigger, taller...'

'Don't worry, Bhaijaan. These boys have worked with English ladies. They are all the same, no? Tell them Samir.'

'Yes, Uncle, we used to give our work to Nirmal Uncle, a tailor here, from our biradari only. He went to India. He was a Sikh so he had to go. He took us with him when he went to his clients. Big, tall English ladies. We embroidered their big long dresses.'

Gurdev stiffened at the sound of Nirmal's name but not visibly.

'Okay. As you wish.'

'Where are you staying in Lahore, Shakir Bhai?'

'We are staying in Model Town, close to the big white house, number A-8 I think, in a smaller house with a beautiful front garden. It is much better than any other garden on the street. Do you know that area, Sajid? It is so well planned, like a foreign country.

'Bhaijaan, I've heard of it but we live in the city. That place is a little far.'

'Just ten kilometres on Firozepur Road, buses run all day and late in the night. The last bus goes at 11:30 p.m. Very easy to reach. Not even half an hour away, with the bus making many stops. Anyway, we thank you for your kindness.'

They said goodbye to the boys. Noor was still holding on to their box till Gurdev pried it out of her hands and returned it to Samir. Imran carried the trunk filled with the old lady's work to a rickshaw and they made their way back to Liberty Market, then through the maze of shops and out on the other side where Akbar and the LaSalle were waiting.

31

GURDEV STRODE UP TO THE CAR AND FOUND THE DOOR open, Akbar asleep on the upright driver's seat, flies buzzing around him, the heat stifling, but the car parked under the shade of a tree made it bearable. He knocked on the windshield. Akbar woke with a start, wiped a bit of dribble down the side of his mouth with the back of his hand and said, 'Salaam, Saab. Sorry, so sorry.'

Gurdev ignored him and opened the back door for Noor and then went around to the back to help Imran load the metal box into the trunk. He banged it shut, paid Imran his promised fifty rupees, which the young man waved off.

'Shakir Bhai, it has been my pleasure to take a real American around the bazaar. If I can be of any further help, you know how to find me. I'm at the chai shop night and day.'

'Don't you ever sleep?'

'There only, Bhaijaan, I sleep there. I have nowhere else to go.'

Gurdev made a note to help this young man. Maybe he could come to India with them too. He thought about mentioning this to Noor, who was already sitting in the car with her head heavy on the back seat but decided against it. She was nervous enough. Now, they had to let the boys know who they were. He had dropped many hints about where they were staying. Maybe they were smart enough to catch on.

Once they were in the car, Akbar began whining. He was probably not going to be popular with his handlers tonight. 'Arre, Shakir Bhai, you were inside that Liberty Market a long time. Only some bangles and that metal box, huh!'

Gurdev responded with a grunt but stayed quiet till they were inside Model Town and passing Ali Zafar's home. He couldn't help but strain his eyes to see his parents' old house as they sped past. There it was, in all its old glory, except for the bright garden that his mother had planted. Now, it was mostly paved, with a few generic bushes here and there. His thoughts returned to the present, and his anger came along.

'Akbar, the slip of paper you had in your hand said 'Baig'. Riaz Baig didn't speak to you when you arrived. He simply looked out of the window and told me that my car was outside. How did you know my name was Shakir and my wife's Noor?' Gurdev said this quietly, despite his anger. 'You can tell me. Maybe we can help each other.'

'Er … Er … Bhaijaan, I was told your names and told – report on all you went and all you met. I don't know why. Tourist business slow, Bhaijaan. What to do?'

'Tell them whatever you saw today … you still have to live here. But after this, you tell them what I tell you to tell them, understand? We are tourists from out of station, that's all. And come back tonight at midnight. Wait outside. Sleep till I wake you up. Tell them that we are going to Ajodhan. Madam is a big believer in Baba Farid.'

When he rang the doorbell at the Baig house and Shakeela answered the door, he knew instantly by the look on her face that something was wrong. It was too late to turn back. He had to go in. He went back and helped Noor out of the car and picked up the tin box from the trunk. He followed Shakeela into the drawing-room and saw the room that looked so inviting the night before look menacing now. There were four men, in almost identical dark Pathan suits, sitting, two facing each other. They stood up when Gurdev and Noor entered. Gurdev walked in first as Noor held the door open for him and the metal box.

'Shakeela Bibi, what a long busy day we've had. Remind me to send you shopping with my begum next time. I can't do it again. We didn't even have time to eat anything. Oh, you have guests. We can go for a drive and come back after some time,' Gurdev said, indicating with his hand behind his back to Noor to stay silent.

'Shakir Bhai, these men are here to see you. I tried to tell them that you were out shopping, but they insisted on waiting.'

'How was Liberty Market, Hasan Sahib? Anarkali is much better. You should have gone there. Better quality for better people like you, if you know what I mean,' said one of the men, addressing the second part of his remarks to Noor.

'We will go to Anarkali also, but tomorrow we are going to Ajodhan to the shrine of Baba Farid. My begum is keen and no man can ever disappoint his begum and live to see another sunrise, don't you agree Baig Sahib.?' Gurdev looked over at Riaz Baig, sitting in one corner of the room, his face twisted into an expression of physical pain, his hands on his lap as if his testicles were being squeezed. Gurdev knew that if they were taken in, they would all be taken, including the women, but it was the men who would be tortured. He sat down on the one remaining sofa and indicated to Noor to go inside. He placed the tin box before him on the floor.

'Janab, you haven't told me who you are or what you want from us.'

'Hasan Bhai, we want nothing from you. This is a friendly visit. We want you to tell us what you like so much about India that you decided to stay there and not come here to your Mussalman homeland.'

Gurdev's eyes opened wide, comprehending what was going on. This was why they had got their visas so easily. A Muslim couple, seemingly rich – why should they be contributing their talents to their enemy – India. Why shouldn't they be bringing riches to their own nation?

'Brothers, we come here in peace to see our old friends. We have left our two sons behind. We must get back soon. My wife had never even been to West Punjab, I mean Punjab, I mean Pakistan's Punjab…' he quickly added, 'and neither had I. Both of our families are long-time Delhi dwellers, also a city that has been popular with Mussalmans for generations. Now, if you'll excuse us, we have had a long day of shopping in your remarkable city and would like to rest before dinner.'

'You know that if we put the word out that there are two Indians staying in this house, none of you will live to eat breakfast tomorrow.'

'Is that a threat, Bhaijaan? Don't you think we've killed each other enough for now? We are not harming anybody, spending money. What more could you want?'

'Our orders are to bring you in. If you are not Indian spies, we'll want to make sure, then we will welcome you into our …

your country. We'll give you a home – better than what you have in India. You can even go back and bring your sons.'

'Janab, we are at your mercy now. Give us a few more days to think this over. Then you can do what you want. My begum, she wants to do some more shopping for friends and relatives and it is her wish to go to Ajodhan. Your offer is a good one. You can check all you want. We have nothing to hide. Once we finish everything, we can go back, say our goodbyes, bring our children and come here to our country.'

The four men stood up and moved away from Gurdev to talk to each other. Gurdev had thought that if things went wrong, they would be shot in the street, no drama, no pondering. This civil and polite threat shook him. He cursed himself for having brought Noor, who on cue walked in changed and refreshed. She had sprayed on more of what made her smell so good, her hair was pulled over to one side, her clothes were crisp and her step slow but with purpose. She walked up to the four men in a huddle and whispered something to them. There was a respectable but loud guffaw and the four men, palms to forehead, backed out of the house.

'What did you say, Noor? Have you got us into more trouble? What did you give them?' asked Gurdev but Noor was silent, her mouth stretched out in a tight smile, a triumphant but controlled smile.

'You don't need to know what I said. Just know that I've bought us a few days. We'll probably still be followed but not bothered. After that we need to leave without them knowing and without that Akbar driver saying anything to them.'

Riaz Baig finally straightened out his face, stood up and rushed over to Gurdev. He put his arms on Gurdev's shoulders, a stretch because the two were about eight inches apart in height.

'Arre arre, Bhai Saab! We were so scared. I thought we were going to jail now, for sure. As it is, they think we sympathize with India because our daughter still lives there, and that Ali Zafar, he's no help, no help at all. In fact, I wish your sister had married someone else,' he said, turning to Shakeela. 'Anyone but him.'

'Now how is this Ali's fault? He had nothing to do with all this. You don't like him because he's rich and you are not. That's all.'

'And how do you know he had nothing to do with this? He can't stop talking about how great Pakistan is and how great our films will be and how wonderful everything is. Let me tell you, everything is not wonderful. I wish … I wish I could go back to Shahdara.'

'You go back, Riaz, and live inside a locked door making khadi. I'm staying here where I'm free.'

'What free, Shakeela? Free to see our daughter when we want? Free to be watched, people checking who's coming and going from our house – I know, Shakeela. I know that people sometimes look into our windows – probably these same four goons that you were giving tea and biscuits to. I wouldn't offer them a glass of water. They are making us look like criminals when our only crime is that we came here. We will always be refugees, Shakeela. What you call free is bondage, it's being second class for the rest of our lives.'

'And what about these Indians you are keeping here? Who knows what they are here for, who knows what mischief they are up to, what if they are spies, then what? I never wanted them here even though Umrao asked. She doesn't know our life here. She doesn't know anything. She's nicely gone and become a Hindu – Urmila – how can she know?'

Gurdev and Noor stood quietly at one end of the room listening to the husband and wife argue. They tried to back into their room but got an angry look from Shakeela and stayed where they were.

'I told them that I wanted to move to Pakistan but Shakir didn't want to. I told them that I would convince him in a few days, I told them that even if I couldn't convince him, I would leave him here and get the children,' said Noor.

'And that worked? They are stupider than I thought. It worked for now, anyway. Let's eat dinner.' Everyone began talking at almost the same time.

'Yes, let's eat dinner,' said Noor. 'Shakeela, I'll help you.'

Shakeela had made dinner earlier in the day. She was still sulking but Gurdev was hungry. All he had had all day was those scones at the café and two cups of tea. Noor must have been hungry too. When Shakeela laid the table and brought out the food, the four people said nothing, simply sat down and began eating.

Later, in their room, Gurdev sat scratching his face where his beard used to be. He had a feeling. And his feeling was that they were going to leave Pakistan soon and suddenly. Whatever Noor said to the men and whatever they thought, they would be back. Their superior officers would not permit them to lose this opportunity to bring back prominent Muslims. And when they found out that he was a Sikh, the story would be in all the newspapers and India would be accused of espionage and he would be shot or hung.

'Noor, I think you should pack up and be ready to leave – anytime. I can't put you in any more danger.'

'Without the boys!' shrieked Noor. 'Never! I didn't come all this way, with all the preparation we did, to go back without them.'

'Noor, your safety and the safety of the Baigs is most important. They could lose everything and be deported to India. As it is, Ali Zafar thinks of Riaz as an Indian sympathizer. And you, I wouldn't want anything to happen to you.'

Noor turned away from Gurdev. 'Why?'

'What do you mean, why? You are all my responsibility. I've brought you into this. I have to take care of you … all.'

'But why do you not want anything to happen to me, Gurdev? It's all right. I came here knowing what could happen. I don't hold you responsible. I am an adult Muslim woman with a valid Indian passport who came to this country legally and legitimately. There is nothing they can do to me. You on the other hand … I think you need to worry about yourself more than us.'

'Don't be like that, Noor. You know what I mean,' said Gurdev.

'Actually, I don't know what you mean, Gurdev.'

'You know, I'm responsible…' said Gurdev.

'I said, you are not responsible,' said Noor

'I mean you are my friend and I don't want to get you in any more trouble, okay?'

'Oh, I'm your friend?' said Noor

'Yes, wouldn't you say you are my friend? Noor, you are acting strange. I don't know what to say to bring you back to me,' said Gurdev.

'Where have I gone? I'm right here,' said Noor.

'Noor, stop being obtuse. You are not with me. You are somewhere else, all disgruntled and cranky, and I can't understand why,' said Gurdev.

'Gurdev, I want you to look within yourself and tell me why you are so concerned about me. Is it because we are friends and because you feel responsible for bringing me here or is there something else? Because there is something else for me. I haven't said anything but I can't believe you don't know, you don't feel … I won't believe it.'

'Noor, I don't know what you are talking about. What else could there be?' said Gurdev

Noor, still sitting with her face away from Gurdev and looking down at the floor said, 'Get out of this room, Gurdev. I don't care where else you go or what you tell the Baigs but get out.'

Gurdev walked over to Noor. He pulled her up. She turned away from him. He put his arms around her stomach from behind and smelt her hair. It smelt of sweat and fumes and dust and recently sprayed jasmine. She turned around and put her head on his chest, slowly taking in the moment. Gurdev held himself up straight, not ready to let go. This was not what he had planned. He was not done with Simrat. She still came to him in his dreams, chastising him for his neglect. He had neglected her but that was because she had asked for so little. She should have demanded his attention, like Noor was doing now. She should have insisted on using the dollars as he was now. But she hadn't known about them. Gurdev liked secrets. He liked to have things that only he knew about. Now Noor knew about the dollars. He didn't want to explain any more than he already had. He could feel a small hill of belligerence building up in his forehead.

'Is this what you want, Noor? Is this what you want to know? Why I'm worried about you is because I care about you in this way? Is that what you want?'

'I … yes, but … I wanted you to say something…'

'And now what, Noor? Hopefully we get back to Delhi soon, but Delhi is not England or America. We can't be boyfriend and girlfriend.'

Noor giggled at his terminology.

'I'm not joking. Where do you think this will go? Or do you want me to sneak into your house after dark every night and leave before dawn?'

'I want to marry you and be with you, in your ridiculous shack or wherever. Is that okay?'

'What are your parents going to say to that, your in-laws, if they are still involved – they must be?'

'I was living in their house when we got the news. It didn't make sense for us to get our own house when war was imminent. I moved out to live on my own because I didn't want my parents or my in-laws telling me what to do, who to see or not to see. They have no say in my life now.'

'That's easy to say as long as all you are doing is learning about Sufism and sitting with disturbed women all day.'

'They are not "disturbed", by the way. They have issues … but yes, I see what you mean. A man poses a different problem, any man, of any religion. If he's Muslim, they'll check to see if he is Sunni or Shia, reformist or conservative, who his parents are, what they do, his family members, siblings, everyone will be assessed – even though this would be my second marriage and all this has already been done before. If he's not a Muslim, it could be difficult. But could anyone predict what would happen to my husband? What was the use of all that checking and counter-checking and matching religion and class? He died, and they want me to start all over again. Well, this time I'll chose my own man.'

Noor held on to Gurdev. He had loosened his arms around her but tightened them when she did. This was not the time to lose her. He needed her. He loosened his grip around her and gently put her arms by her side. He sat her down on the bed and looked at her as tenderly as he could.

'Those boys, Noor, they will come. I think they'll come tonight.'

'Why do you think that, Gurdev?'

'I saw you, Noor. I saw you slip in a note with the box, the box you wouldn't let go. Well done. They'll come. I know they will. Let's nap for a while. We'll leave at midnight, after everyone has settled in, and wait for them near the main road. We don't want to get the Baigs into any more trouble.'

'I wrote the word "Nirmal" on the piece of paper. Nothing else. But tell me, how will Jagtap know that he has to pick us up tonight?'

'I asked him to come every night. Wait for one hour from 12 to 1 a.m. and then leave. It was a lot to ask for but he agreed. A chance to drive his car on empty roads, maybe.'

Noor slept. She was tired. Gurdev stayed awake. At 10:30 p.m., he got out of bed. There was something else he needed to do before they left.

Quietly, he put his shoes back on and slipped out of the bedroom. Noor was snoring softly. He could hear voices in the Baigs' bedroom but they were drones, not an animated conversation – either a pre-bedtime recounting of the day or possibly the radio. They had one, he knew that and they didn't keep it in their living room like many people did. He walked out of the front door, leaving his bunched-up handkerchief at the bottom of the door to keep it from locking but not looking open.

Outside, even this late, it was still warm and dry. He went down the street and turned on to the larger street, walking briskly with arms swinging, like a resident walking off a heavy dinner. Yet, he took care to avoid the bright streetlights and kept himself in the relative dark. When he got to his parents' house, he went around the back, towards a small gate in the fence. He reached over the top and unlatched the gate. It was high, almost six feet and the latch could have been lower but the person who installed it was probably tall, so it was high enough for him to get to it. He walked into the back of the house, a small brick courtyard criss-crossed with lines of rope on which still hung a few not dry clothes or clothes that were washed that evening because they had to dry out of the harsh sunlight. He ducked his head under and walked towards the servant's quarters. He remembered that his parents had employed a man named Raheem and his wife, Sitara. They had a son whom he sometimes played with when he was not out playing with his school friends; the same son his father had said had taken over the security of the house.

Gurdev called out softly, 'Raheem, Sitara, Raheem, are you there?'

An old man came out of the house, tall, bearded but with close-cropped hair on his head.

'Raheem is dead. What do you want with him?' he said in Urdu.

'I wanted to meet him, ask him about the fire ... the fire that killed my ... the owners of the house,' said Gurdev.

'Who are you? Why are you asking so many questions? Get lost from here.'

'I knew the owners.' But as he spoke, he sensed something familiar about the old man. He was tall, tall, taller than the average Muslim, taller than the average Sikh ... was it...?'

'What is your name, Uncle?'

'I told you, get lost.'

Gurdev switched to English. 'I'm here to enquire about Mr and Mrs Pritam Singh. They lived here until the fourth of September 1947, when they were killed in a fire. Do you know about them?'

'I don't know...' the man responded in English so clipped, so familiar, that Gurdev forgot who he was and where he was and went and put his arms around the bony old man.

'What are you doing? Who are you?' Without his turban and beard, Gurdev had also changed. But the old man's eyes blinked in recognition.

'My son, my son, Gurdev. Beant, come and see who's here, your favourite son. The one you've been slipping money to all these years. We have nothing more to give you, son. See what they've done to us. They've taken our property and imprisoned us here. We have Muslim names now, can't even practise our faith. My hair is gone, my kesh...' The old man cried large round tears, but silently. He pushed Gurdev towards the covered structure, a shack much like the one Gurdev lived in, back in Delhi. His mother had got up, draped her dupatta over her head and come towards the door. She wore a faded salwar kameez, shapeless and ordinary. His mother had never been ordinary. It was his mother who had handed him wads of American currency the last time he had visited, in early 1947, to ask his father what he thought of the situation. His father had said to stay put, nothing was going to happen to them. Despite the riots in Rawalpindi in late 1946, Lahore and the upper reaches of Punjab would be okay.

He bent his knees and hugged his beautiful mother, face drawn, no makeup and hair white as a cloud, tied up in a stringy braid.

'Tell me everything. There isn't much time. I have to leave at midnight.'

'Where are you going?'

'Back to India.'

'They let you come here ... okay let me tell you what happened.' Gurdev's tired father had suddenly got a second wind. He sounded like his old self, even sitting up perfectly straight and ordering his wife to quickly make them a cup of tea – for no serious conversation was possible without a beverage. He would have preferred a scotch, neat, but he had forgotten the taste, he said.

'Old man Raheem's son, Farid, it was his idea. He and his wife had started working in the house because Raheem and Sitara could no longer manage. He hatched this idea of burning us alive and taking our house. He knew about the fire-safe cupboard where the cash was. For so many years, I said let's invest the money, but no one listened to me. When we had a chance ... that lovely girl ... anyway. It was your life.'

'Go on,' Gurdev prompted.

'Raheem tried to talk his son out of the plan but Farid was as if possessed. We had no one to go to. We should have left when you asked. Raheem locked us in the servant quarter and wouldn't give Farid the key. So, Farid came up with another plan. We would live as servants, and if we ever tried to complain, he would expose us as Sikhs. He locked his own father in the house and left town. He hired some goons to set the house on fire. That fire, it burnt for three days, bringing everything down with it except the fireproof cupboard. Farid and his wife came and emptied it into suitcases at night while the embers still burnt and no one had gone through the remains.'

'I saw the fire. I was here. I thought you were inside … I went and did something that … I have to live with. I took revenge, Papaji, I avenged your death but you are still alive. I can't leave you here. You come with us.'

'We can't child. We have nothing. No papers, no money, no jewellery, nothing.'

'You don't need anything. Come out when you hear a car's horn. Bring anything you value. You can't come back here – and neither can I. Get ready.'

Gurdev touched both his parents on the shoulders, one right and one left, and walked out the way he had come, latching the gate from the top. He walked rapidly back to the Baigs house and entered the front door, still propped open with his handkerchief. He roused Noor and asked her to use the bathroom or whatever she needed to do. It was time. He checked the clock. It was five minutes before midnight. Gurdev lifted Noor's heavier suitcase and the metal trunk, and asked Noor to carry his small suitcase. Slowly, quietly, they made their way out of the house and on to the road. Gurdev left the handkerchief in the door again, in case they had to come back. Akbar was waiting in the LaSalle, engine off, no lights. Gurdev tapped gently on the windshield. This time Akbar was awake. He opened the trunk and loaded it. And gently brought it down and pushed it shut. They all got into the car and Akbar started it, driving slowly down the lane.

'Go slow after you make the turn. Go close to the big white house. Slowly … honk once when you are outside.'

Gurdev asked Akbar to stop outside his parents' house. A minute later, he saw the gate opening and the two people walk slowly out, the old man carrying a small satchel, the old lady nothing at all. They walked to the car and Gurdev opened the door with a finger on his lips, and a wave of his hand indicating 'later'.

He got into the front seat with Akbar and they waited for Sultan and Samir, the embroidery boys, out of the glare of the streetlight. Noor and Gurdev's mother dozed off. The three men sat uneasily as time walked by. Gurdev got out of the car and went out to the entrance gate on Firozepur Road. It was past 2 a.m. Local buses had stopped running hours ago. They could have walked, but Gurdev didn't think they had the vigour or the confidence to attempt the ten-kilometre walk from the city. He walked back to the car and got in.

'Take us back to the Baigs' house, Akbar,' Gurdev said.

The three people in the backseat were all awake now.

'Son, we can't vanish from our home like this. These people will come looking for us,' said Gurdev's father.

'Gurdev, who are these people and why are we taking them to the Baigs' house?' said Noor

'Puttar, I have not left that house for five years now,' said Gurdev's mother.

Before Gurdev could answer any questions, Akbar had parked outside the Baig's house, got out of the car and opened the trunk. Gurdev got out too, put a finger on his lips to silence the chatter, took the luggage out of the trunk and walked it back into the house. His handkerchief was still in place and the house was quiet. He indicated to Noor to take the elderly couple to the bedroom and came back out to Akbar. On the way, he took out two hundred dollar bills from the roll in his pocket and folded the currency double and then double again. Akbar was waiting right outside the door. Gurdev put his hand on the back of Akbar's shoulder in a side embrace and walked down the driveway with him. He stopped at the road.

'Bhaijaan, I don't know what you are doing but I…' said Akbar.

Gurdev faced the man, lifted his hand, pried open his fist and put the folded bills into the still rigid hand. Akbar brought the pieces of paper to the light and smiled.

'Now, no talking to anyone about this. Come at 9 a.m. We will go to Ajodhan tomorrow as planned,' said Gurdev. He walked the man back up to his car in the driveway, opened the door for him and then shut it. He gave him a mock salute as the car reversed out. He walked back into the house, this time letting the door lock, and went into the bedroom. Three question marks greeted him as he opened the door slowly and let himself in.

'Noor, these are my parents. They didn't die in the fire as I thought they had. Biji, Papaji, this is Noor Hasan, my … friend. For now, let's rest for a while. In the morning, I'll explain everything to the Baigs. Akbar is coming back at 9 a.m. We are all going to Ajodhan to learn more about Baba Farid and the Sufi movement.

'But, Gurdev, how will we all sleep here?' said Noor.

'Gurdev, what is this utter nonsense? If we were leaving, why didn't we leave? Why did we come back here? And whose house is this? They might know those people and then everyone will know we are Sikhs. And where is your turban and beard? We didn't sacrifice our lives for you to give up your faith,' said his father.

'Puttar, I'm with you. Do whatever you need to. Our lives can't get any worse,' said his mother.

Gurdev smiled at everybody, a tired smile.

'Biji, Papaji, you take the bed. Noor, you take that side of the bed and I'll take this side. Let's lie down for some time. Papaji, we are waiting for two boys who we came to take with us. They didn't come last night, but I think they will come tonight. If they don't come tonight, we'll have to go back to Anarkali Bazaar and get them. Let's see. Other things you will have to wait for. For now, only that my name is Shakirullah or Shakir and this is Noor. We are husband and wife, but only for this mission.'

'What mission are you talking about, Gurdev? Who do you work for? The Indian government? Are you a spy?'

'No, no, Papaji. I am a ladies' tailor. I mean, I am a partner in a ladies' tailoring business. The mission is to bring the best embroidery boys in Pakistan to India.'

'Puttar, what boys? I knew one Abida Bibi. She was the best in my time. She took months on a single piece but what work, what detail, what talent,' said Gurdev's mother.

'These boys are the same Abida Bibi's grandsons, Biji. I think you understand now why we must take them to India.'

The old lady nodded resolutely. 'Puttar, if that is your business then you need those boys.'

'Ladies' tailor, is that what I heard? You, Gurdev Singh, are a ladies' tailor. When I offered you a hotel to run, you turned me down and became a peasant instead. Now, you are a tailor, for women?'

'Pritam, you and your sarcasm. Do you know where we are now or was your brain cut off along with your hair? Keep quiet and support your son for once.'

The old man looked at his wife, his eyes round and large with rage and then looked down, his head bobbing up and down. He looked up again, tiny tears in the corners of his eyes, and held his son's hand. He shook it hard and smiled without uttering another word.

32

THE NEXT MORNING, GURDEV SLEPT LONGER THAN everyone else. In his corner of the room, with one frilly cushion for a pillow, he slept through everyone else waking up, bathing and getting dressed. When he woke up, he saw that Noor was wearing one of her suits from Delhi, Biji was wearing another one of Noor's suits and Papaji was wearing a pair of Gurdev's new trousers and a shirt. The older couple was thin, with age and with circumstance and the fancy clothes looked awkward. He heard mumbling around him, shuffling and even a little giggling and woke up. He saw his mother putting on makeup, lining her eyes and colouring her lips. He opened his eyes fully and gazed at this frail old woman inside whom lived the mother he had known. He didn't get up till he felt a swift kick in his side.

'Get up, Shakir. Time to go. Akbar will be here anytime. How do you want to handle the Baigs?' said Noor.

Gurdev got up, went straight to the bathroom and came out several minutes later, in the same clothes that he had slept in but freshly shaved and clean. He found his mother gazing at Noor, a distant look in her eyes.

'Puttar, this is not the woman you married? Where is she? Did you give her what I had sent for her? That was a special gift, one for each ear. She would look like a princess even if the rest of her clothes were rags.'

Gurdev noted that Noor was listening attentively to the conversation. He wondered how his mother knew that he was not married to Noor. She had never met Simrat.

'We'll talk about this after we are all safely out of here. For now, Noor, you need to distract the Baigs while I get Biji and Papaji out of the house. No breakfast today. I'm the most sorry for that because that Shakeela Bibi can cook. Unfortunately, she is also a traitor. I am certain she is the one who has been informing on us. But because her husband told us right up front not to tell them anything about why we are here, she hasn't been able to say anything to the Pakistani agents.'

'I think Mr Baig knows that his wife is an informer. That's why he said what he said, and that Ali Zafar definitely has something against him, and us. They could be informers together,' added Noor.

'I think you people know nothing and have no proof. You are making things up. We will now eat only after we are home, in India,' said Papaji.

Gurdev looked at him through the corner of his eye but said nothing. Noor went out breezily, her dupatta and her sandalwood smell wafting behind her. He heard her greet the Baigs and opened the door slightly. He didn't know if Akbar had arrived. It was 9:15 a.m., so he should have come. Gurdev indicated to his parents to slowly follow him through the narrow corridor towards the living-cum-dining room. He peeped outside to see that Shakeela Baig had gone into the kitchen with Noor but Riaz Baig sat on a sofa looking directly at him.

'Come, come, Shakir Bhai. Have some breakfast. Aloo paranthas this morning. My favourite and probably yours too. Probably well favoured by the two people right behind you too. Who are they, by the way?'

'Riaz Bhai, how did you know? We came in quietly. Your lights were off. They are Noor's relatives. They also want to go to Ajodhan but live in the city. Better they came here, I thought … I should have asked you … please accept my apology,' Gurdev whispered.

'I had got up to go to the bathroom, some problem down there, old age…'

'It's your prostate. Get it checked,' said Papaji from the corridor.

Gurdev shushed him and asked his parents to wait. He went to the window, parted the curtain and peered outside. The LaSalle was there, by the side of the road, Akbar sitting in the driver's seat, awake. He opened the front door and ushered his parents out and to the car, shutting the door behind them. He parted the curtain and watched them get into the car. He came back to Riaz Baig and shook his hand.

'This isn't goodbye, Bhaijaan. Noor and I will be back tonight after our pilgrimage to Ajodhan,' Gurdev said loud enough for his voice to carry into the kitchen.

'Thank you, Shakeela Aapa, I will personally make these besan laddoos and feed them to Urmila as soon as I get back and then make sabudana laddoos after delivery, for abundant milk production, I remember,' Noor chattered and made her way out as Gurdev blinked his eyes rapidly. That had become their sign for 'beware – danger ahead' now.

'Chalo, we will see you in the evening, upon our return from Ajodhan. If it's not too late, we'll wake you up and tell you all about it,' said Noor.

Gurdev wanted to shove her out of the door to stop her from talking but had to politely wait till she finished, then mutely walk behind her. They waved to the Baigs from the driveway and got into the car. Gurdev's parents had crouched down in case anyone was watching.

They set off, out of Model Town and on to the highway, both old people crouched down but peering out of the window as they passed their former home. Gurdev had to gently push them down again because if they hadn't already found out, the present residents of the house soon would, that their forced tenants had vanished. The car picked up speed on Firozepur Road, towards Lahore City and soon came to an intersection, right towards Okara and left towards Kasur.

Akbar turned right towards Okara and continued rapidly on the highway. The journey was long, everyone sitting up now, Gurdev turning around every now and then to look for a tail. He didn't see anyone till they were about an hour into the drive. A black car, American, but he didn't recognize the make, drove on to the highway from a side road and stayed behind them for a while. Gurdev asked Akbar to pull over on the side. He got out and hunched down by the front tire away from the road and peered up but with his head down.

The black car passed them, driving fast. He waited for two minutes till they could no longer see the car on the horizon and got back in. They drove on and only stopped to fill petrol once. Gurdev didn't ask anyone if they were hungry, no one said that they wanted to eat. There was tension in the car that Gurdev knew he had created. He hadn't told anyone the plan. Noor, he knew, was quiet because of his parents' presence and because she couldn't guess what was on his mind. He also knew that she did want to go to Baba Farid's grave and pay her respects. It was for nothing but the spiritual specks that she probably thought still floated around the place he had lived the longest and the place he died.

When they were about four hours into their journey with Akbar stating determinedly that they were only an hour away, Gurdev saw the black car by the side of the road. There were only two occupants. Both stood outside, smoking cigarettes, doing little to hide. They jumped into the car and followed as soon as Akbar raced by. Gurdev was making this as easy as possible. He needed to keep them believing that they were doing exactly what they had planned to do.

The group reached Ajodhan a little after 2 p.m. Akbar parked as close to the city gates as he could. Gurdev looked around but didn't see the black car. It would be waiting outside the city on the main road, the occupants certain that the group would go back the way they came. Any other way was long, the road not as good.

Gurdev ushered his parents and Noor into one of the gates into the city and towards Baba Farid's shrine. Akbar had told him that there had been six gates around the walled city but only four remained. They first found a place to eat. Chapli kabab, haleem and nihari – all mutton dishes, all Gurdev's favourites, his mouth watered as he stood outside two small dhabas, both with menus written in chalk on a small board behind the cashier and owner of the establishment.

He picked the second one and they ate, Gurdev constantly looking at the time. Everyone was hungry and the food was like he remembered frontier food to be. This food was not available in Lahore and not in Delhi, although enterprising businessmen had begun selling Mughlai food, a combination of Punjabi and frontier food in street stalls.

After eating, Gurdev rushed the group through to the Nuri Darwaza, the Gate of Light at Baba Farid's tomb, and gave them five minutes to gather all the spirituality they could find. He pushed them back to the car and called Akbar aside to talk to him. Akbar nodded at everything he said but shook his head violently for one thing. Gurdev patted him on the back and whispered something in his ear even though no one was listening. The two men got into the front seats of the car, and Akbar pulled out of the busy streets and back to the edge of the city.

'This is not the way we came,' Noor was the first to notice.

'No, this is definitely not the way we came,' said Papaji.

Biji didn't say anything but she, too, looked perplexed.

'We are going back a different way. Those men following us, they will be waiting for us on the road we came in because that is the safest way back. This other way goes through Kasur. The road is rough and it will take us more than seven hours to reach Kasur. We can stop for toilet and petrol on the way but nothing else.'

'But why are we doing this? All we've done all day is drive. You didn't even let us stay at the shrine for ten minutes. You know, Guru Nanak also came to Baba Farid and talks about him in his teachings,' said Papaji.

'Papaji, you can do whatever you want once we are back. You can put your forehead on the cool marble at Harmandir

Sahib in Amritsar and you can wash your feet on the steps of Bangla Sahib in Delhi. You can do whatever you want but not now. Now, I'm in charge,' said Gurdev in a tone he had never before used with his father.

The group settled in, the three in the back dozing off and on but no one for too long because they didn't want to miss anything. Several hours and three stops later, they reached the outskirts of Kasur.

'Drive into Kasur village, keep driving till you reach the end,' Gurdev told Akbar.

'Bhaijaan, what are you doing now?'

'Akbar, drive. You will not regret it. And no one will know.'

Akbar drove, his hands shaking, his mouth quivering with religious verses that he never thought he knew. It was past 11 p.m. Jagtap wouldn't be there till midnight.

'No, no, don't stop, Akbar. Keep driving. I want to go through to the end of the village.'

They saw no one on the road, no trucks, no cars, no bullock carts nothing. Akbar drove right through on a village road, bumpy and rocky, tossing the occupants of the back seat side to side.

As they approached the end, there was a single sign that said 'Pakistan-India Border Approaching.'

On the other side, there was no checkpost, no gate, no wall, no fence, only a shiny Dodge DeSoto, with its lights off, engine off parked one hundred metres away. They all got out, looked around, saw no one. Akbar got out too. He smiled. 'This is how it should remain.'

But for now, the group walked towards the car. The driver remained inside.

Gurdev indicated to the rest to wait as they crossed what appeared to be the border while he went on to the car. The driver lowered the window.

'Jagtap Prahji, you came early? We could have waited for some time. Now, there is a small problem. That old couple with Noor, you have to take them with you and come back for me again, same time, same place, every day. If I don't come for three days running, you can assume I am finished and send the couple to Delhi with Noor. She'll know what to do. Or you can call Sangat and let him know they are coming. He'll pick them up from the station or airport – whatever is possible Prahji.'

'Gurdev, I have been coming early because Sangat told me that you are never late, always early. Who are these people, Paaji? Are they your parents? You look like their child. I'll be here every day. You do whatever you have to do. Although, you have done the important job, no? This even I would have cut my hair for and come.'

Gurdev indicated to his parents, and Noor to walk over and opened the front door and the backdoor. He leaned into his parents, then Noor.

'I'll be back as soon as I can. Till then, take care of things. Wait for me in Amritsar unless...'

Noor helped Biji into the car. Papaji got into the front seat. Noor shut both doors and turned to Gurdev.

'I'm staying here with you and coming back with the boys,' and she turned and walked back towards Akbar, who sat inside his car, engine running.

Gurdev didn't argue, he waved to the car on the India side and walked back to the Pakistan side.

'Let's go back to Model Town, Akbar. I don't have to tell you...'

'Janab, what time shall I come tomorrow?'

'11 a.m. Give us some time to rest and rest yourself. Only rest. No talking. We have to go back to Liberty Market tomorrow morning. Noor Madam wants more bangles and other things. These women, when they have one of something, they want two, in case the first one breaks. Why not break the first one and then buy more, I ask? But how will she get back to Pakistan, she asks. And nothing from Pakistan will ever go to India, she says. Maybe someday some things will but they'll be so expensive. These ladies, they have everything worked out. I don't know when they do all these calculations, but they do and they are so precise, so certain, at least the women I know are. Are all women like that, Akbar?'

Noor kicked the back of Gurdev's seat as he sat beside Akbar chatting away, trying to take his mind off other things. His parents for instance. He had abandoned them so readily so many years ago but had risked what he had come to do to get them out. That's how things worked, he reasoned. Sometimes not as per plan. He was glad they were alive – more than glad, he was relieved. As old as he was and as long as he had been on his own, there was something about a sarcastic father and a doting mother that took his breath away.

As they approached the intersection where they had, that morning, turned right, Gurdev noticed a car by the side of the road, the black car with the two men in it. Gurdev asked Akbar to turn his lights off so that he could better see into the car. As they slowed down to make the turn, he saw that both men were asleep. They had come on the good road and reached several hours before them. He knew that they would be watched more closely the next day.

33

WHEN GURDEV AND NOOR WALKED UP THE DRIVEWAY, it was past 12.30 a.m. Gurdev realized that he had neither taken a key nor done his handkerchief trick – he couldn't have done the latter because they had left in the morning. They would have to ring the bell and wake up the Baigs. As they approached the front door, it opened. Mr Baig stood before them in white pyjamas with a long kurta, crisp, not crumpled as if he had just woken up.

'What took you so long? We have been worried. Did you come back on the Okara road or did that foolish driver take you some other way? And where is that old couple? You didn't leave them in Ajodhan did you? People do that sometimes, to old people, people they don't want to take care of any more.'

'Riaz Bhai, what can I tell you? These women have their own plans. Noor wanted to feel the spirituality of the place – not for half an hour or one hour – for a whole two hours. Then we had to drop the old couple back to the city. Don't ask me where. That's between Akbar and them – if you ask me, we were going round and round in darkness in a city that's beautiful during the day but at night is filled with shadows and apparitions of times past.'

'I know what you mean, Gurdev Bhai Saheb. The city frightens me too. Let's sleep now. My begum will be up early to cook breakfast. Whatever she says, she will always take good care of her guests. Don't pay too much attention to her words. She's also scared, like I am. Those men in our house, we've never had that happen to us before, and once that Ali Zafar finds out, he'll be taunting us even more.'

Gurdev played back Riaz Baig's words as he and Noor walked into the house. They said good night softly and walked to their room. Noor looked at him, then shook her head and fell on the bed diagonally, fully dressed, eyeliner smudged, dusty hair and feet, and slept. Gurdev thought about moving her to one side but decided that morning would come and with it a beginning of many new questions and a continuation of what they had already started. He pulled the same frilly cushion off the bed, put the fan on full speed and lay down in his corner, asleep in not more than three minutes.

The next morning, Gurdev woke up first. He went into the bathroom, this time with a change of clothes, his old clothes, a dark worn out Pathan suit that he had put in along with the suits that Nirmal had made. He smelt like he had in the village, like the animals he had tended and the oil he had pressed. He shaved and bathed and braced himself for Noor's questions. He opened the door to find her waiting outside, clothes in hand, ready for her turn. He stepped aside, packed up whatever he had taken out and left the room. They had eaten one meal yesterday and he could smell puris frying, zeera sizzling and ghee roasting. He swallowed his spit and quietly walked through the narrow corridor and into the living room. The table was laid for four. Riaz Baig sat at his spot, the head of the table with the newspaper. He nodded at Gurdev as he sat down in the same place he had been sitting since they had arrived, his chair facing the window on the side of the house. Today, the curtains were pulled open and tied back with silken cords, unlike all the other times when they had been drawn tight with just a little bit open on one end.

Shakeela came in from the kitchen and greeted him. 'Good morning, Gurdev Bhai Saheb. I hope you slept well. So late you got last night. We were wondering if you were even coming back. India is so close, no? And safe. No one comes to your house to question you about your guests or peeps into your windows or threatens your family if you don't tell them things.' She looked down as she said this. 'They told me they could get to my daughter and kill her, and the Indians would suspect nothing. They told me they could make it look like an accident if I didn't tell them all about what you were doing. Riaz told me that you came with an old couple yesterday. They also told me that. They want to know who those people were. Who were they, Gurdev, and where are they now? What are you here to do? Please tell me something so that I can save my daughter, Gurdev. I beg you for her life,' Shakeela Baig said all this as she ladled soft potatoes into Gurdev's plate and placed two perfectly round brown puris alongside. Gurdev's finger had almost cracked the crispy exterior of the puri when he caught Riaz Baig's eye and held back.

'Shakeela Aapa, you are an aunty to me. I am fond of both your daughter and your son-in-law. They have become dear friends, and I wouldn't want anything to happen to either one. As far as I can tell, the facts are like this. The Pakistani secret police or whomever it is that is bothering you has no leverage over you. They cannot go and murder an innocent person simply because her mother is not cooperating with them – and for what? There is no espionage here; there is no deceit or any effort to undermine this country. This was our home, Shakeela, we were forced to leave it but that doesn't imply that we mean the people here any ill. They or this government did not cause the upheaval; the British caused it. We are only here for a simple reason. And if I tell you, you will laugh. But I cannot tell you till we have successfully accomplished our mission. I hope you understand.'

Gurdev looked down at his deflating puri, eager to eat it but waited. Shakeela looked at him, face drawn.

'Bhai Saab, if that is the case, you do what you have to do and I will do what I have to do. But who was that old couple? At least tell me that much. That will keep them quiet for some time.'

'That old couple, Shakeela Aapa, they are the Sikh couple who used to live in that house close to your sister's house – A8. I know everyone believed they had perished in a fire – but they hadn't. I felt it my duty to send them home. Surely your government won't have a problem with that.'

Shakeela was quiet for a moment.

'And have you? Sent them home?'

'No, no. How could I? Your hawks have been watching us. Call them off, Shakeela. Let me do this good work.'

'And what about your "mission"? What about that? What if you are lying? What if you are a spy? I can't stop them from following you, how can I? And I can't help you. That would make me a traitor to my country. Ask Riaz to help you. He wants to go to India anyway. He'll do whatever you want.'

Gurdev was wondering where Noor was. He felt another family squabble rising up through the marble floor. It can't have been easy for this couple, leaving their only daughter behind, struggling in this young country where they were refugees, a country that welcomed them but had little to give them but the detritus of those who had fled.

'What do you mean, I can help them? I'm not a traitor either. I only miss the old days that everyone does, I can tell you. You do too, don't you?' he asked his wife.

'Riaz, look at this house, look at this neighbourhood and look at the people we meet because of Ali Zafar. In India, we lived in Shahdara where the only way to find our house was to ask someone on the street. There was no culture, no class.'

'Class ..., you want class or you want neighbours who will take care of you whatever happens? At least people on the street knew where you lived. We've been here for almost five years and the only thing anyone knows about us is that you are Ali Zafar's wife's sister.'

Noor came out then, fragrant and flowing, her hair still moist, her bare feet padding almost soundlessly on the white floor.

'Oh puri aloo, my favourite. Gurdev, your puri has completely collapsed. Why aren't you eating?'

Gurdev looked at her and without any further comment, broke off a piece of fried flour and scooped up as much potato as he could get into it. He put the small roll in to his mouth and let it roll around. As expected, the spice combination was like a circus in his mouth, acrobats and trapeze artists and clowns and elephants all elegantly directed into a beautiful dance. This lady may have betrayed them and she was cranky, but her food was the best Gurdev had ever tasted.

Shakeela went back into the kitchen to get fresh puris and finally sat down with them and ate quietly. She was always one short breath away from an outburst, and Gurdev was afraid of her. She could easily plant false evidence in their luggage or claim some other lies about them and turn them in. He wondered if Urmila knew what a temper her mother had.

'So, Noor, Gurdev is not telling me anything but I think you are smarter than he is. Where is that old couple who went with you to Ajodhan and what else are you here to do? You don't look like a spy, more a shallow, self-obsessed, rich princess is my guess. Are you in love with Gurdev? You are aren't you? That's why you are here. Well, he's using you. Just like he's using us. I can get you back home safely, he can't. So, tell me why you are here. And Gurdev, don't give her any signals or anything. I am watching you both.'

'Shakeela Aapa, you are right, I am a shallow, self-obsessed princess but I'm not rich any more. My parents are rich and my in-laws, but not I. I live on my dead husband's pension and that's all. I like beautiful things, and I am interested in Baba Farid. I came because I had never been this side before Partition and who knows when the next opportunity will come. That's all. Gurdev, I'm not in love with him. He's a married man with two children. I'm not that type of woman. And those two old people, didn't Gurdev tell you that we dropped them back home yesterday? We want to take them to India because their lives are in danger here.'

'Nobody's lives are in danger here. Everyone is welcome. That is what our founder Jinnah promised. But I'm not blind. Nobody is left. All the Sikhs and Hindus are gone,' said Shakeela wavering a little. Gurdev urged Noor on silently.

'Let us go, Shakeela Aapa. Let us finish our work and go home,' said Noor.

'Your work is the problem, Madam. Nobody knows what you are here to do. But now you go. I tried my best. They can do the rest,' said Shakeela.

Noor and Gurdev got up quickly and left the house. Akbar had not arrived yet so they began walking towards the entrance of Model Town, past A8. It was hot, the sun bright even at 10:30 in the morning. They walked slowly, finding shade wherever they could, crossing the street for a long patch. When they made the turn on to the row of A bungalows, Gurdev felt a quiver at the top of his neck. Ordinarily, his turban would have covered that part and he would simply tuck in some imaginary loose hair with his finger and feel better. Now, it bristled and burnt, not because of the hot sun but because of what he might see as they walked passed A8. A car horn made him jump up, grab Noor's arm and pull her as far back on the sidewalk as he could.

'Relax, Gurdev. It was Akbar. He's gone ahead to turn the car around. Here he comes. Let's get in before I vanish into the ground like a melted ice cube.'

They drove by A8 instead of walking past it. Akbar sped by and Gurdev couldn't ask him to slow down, which was probably better because there was a fair amount of activity in the big house. People were running around: the back gate, the gate that Gurdev had unlatched and gone in through was open, clothes and other items were on the ground in a small pile. Gurdev was sure the new owners didn't care too much what happened to their forced tenants but it could be a matter of pride. They could call the police if they hadn't already – but then who would they say the couple was? They were too old to work and usually when servants got too old, they were sent to their village, sometimes with a nice lump sum and sometimes nothing but what the servant had managed to save. No, there would be too many questions. Their existence could be questioned. Hadn't Ali Zafar said that the other neighbours had filed a complaint? They wouldn't call the police.

Akbar took Noor and Gurdev back to Liberty Market and parked under the same tree he had the last time. He opened all the windows and settled in for his nap even before his clients had begun walking towards to bazaar. Gurdev looked around to see if their tail had arrived. He didn't see anyone. The two retraced their steps, walking into the same bangle shop, buying some more bangles then walking out to the teashop where Gurdev had another cup of tea. Noor politely declined with her hand, palm out, held up by her chin. Gurdev looked around for Imran but didn't see him. A different boy brought the tea, holding it on the side but his thumb clenching the top of the glass. Noor looked at him and made a face.

'Noor, you are not drinking the tea, I am. I am immune to anything that might be on the glass or on his hand.' He turned to the boy and asked him where Imran was and was told that he was in the back, washing glasses. He knew he couldn't come out till he was done or he would be beaten, and Gurdev had no interest in going to the back. His immunity only worked in the front of the house. They waited, Gurdev sipped his tea slowly, licking off the cream and savouring the deep overcooked flavours of milk, sugar, ginger and cardamom. And tea – deep-flavoured tea from Darjeeling or Assam. A few minutes later, Imran came to them, wiping his hands on the back of his shorts, the muscles in his narrow arms flexing a little with the stretch.

'Dollar Man and Madam, I am happy to see you here again. What do you want to see now? More embroidery or something else?'

'Imran Bhai, you know what we want, I think. So take us to them without too much drama. We don't have much time.'

'Samir and Sultan, that's who you want, no? No, no, I can't help you. They are being watched by ... people. I don't know who, *gorment* people, they say.'

'Okay, but can you take a message to them? I'll tell you what to say. Nothing on paper.'

Imran looked around furtively. 'Okay. I can do that. But you come with me to Anarkali. Same as last time. Leave your big car here. That driver, he is sleeping when you go and when you come back. Who knows what he's doing otherwise. There are two men here, looking for you, I think. I saw them from the back. A big black car. They looked like police but not in uniform.'

Gurdev stood staring at Imran for a minute. He knew Akbar was his, that the $200 was a down payment. They hadn't discussed anything but after that money exchange, Akbar had become cooperative. He didn't say anything about Gurdev's parents or about the stop in Kasur. He could still be playing both sides. Maybe he had to in order to survive. Gurdev felt trapped. At home, there was Shakeela Begum, who was itching to see them in jail; here there was Akbar and then the actual agents.

'Janab, we have to go now. This time they will not wait outside all day. They will come in to look for you. And this market is not so big and people talk. You are easy to describe.'

Gurdev and Noor scurried after Imran. Gurdev wondered if Imran was leading them into a trap, if he too had been paid off, but he followed anyway. They went the same way, past the dupattas that Noor stroked once again and through the narrow streets with the clothes displayed as before. Once outside, Imran hailed a rickshaw and they got in, the same format as the last time. This time, no one was talking and there was no time for tea once they reached. Imran jumped off the back and without looking to see if they were behind him, went into a narrow lane parallel to the main path they had gone down before. It was the back entrance to all the shops, the workers and owners' entry. Many shops had small rooms in the back for the workers. These looked out into the back lane. Imran moved fast, dodging people and slop that lay about, mostly garbage and not raw sewage, Gurdev hoped as Noor lifted her sweeping pants high enough that they didn't touch the ground and not too high that her ankles showed. Gurdev slowed down to let her keep up but Imran rushed along. He turned right and then left, Gurdev just about catching his brown arm as he turned. He came to a stop outside a small door. Gurdev felt disoriented. Was this behind the cloth shop that they had been to or was this somewhere else? The word trap entered his head again. He shook it away and knocked on the wood door. He turned to ask Imran if Samir and Sultan were inside but the boy had run off, vanished around the corner. Gurdev would never see him again. He knocked again, louder this time.

He heard footsteps coming to the door and a voice call out, 'Kaun?' from inside.

'Open the door, Sultan. It is us, the couple from America.' Gurdev heard more scurrying and another set of footsteps approach and the door unlatching. Sultan and Samir stood before him but they were not alone. Behind them stood a man, not one they had seen before, but he was dressed in a dark salwar kameez, much like the four men who had come to the Baig house.

'What do you want with these boys, Janab? How did you find this place?' the man said.

'Arre Bhaijaan, we only want their work, nothing else,' said Gurdev.

'Who brought you here?' The man walked out and looked around.

'No one brought us here, Bhaijaan. We asked for the home of Sultan and Samir, the embroidery boys. Everyone knows about them.'

'You know why everyone knows them? Because they are our treasure. We like to take care of our valuables so they are not stolen,' said the man as he re-entered the house. 'If you don't tell me who brought you here, I will find out myself.'

'Listen Bhaijaan, I have a lady with me, my wife, so no need for these threats. We met the boys before at Sajid's shop and then thought, why not cut out the middleman and find them ourselves. My wife is interested in making a small business of this.'

'What? Stealing our people to make them do your work?'

'No, Bhaijaan, not stealing your people, only their work, and at a fair price,' said Gurdev, but he could feel the conversation slipping away from him. The man knew everything. Next he would ask him what he said about America to Sajid and the dollars he had. His hand went to his belly; he rubbed it, as many Indian men are prone to do when thinking.

'Okay, listen, if you don't want us buying anything from them, we'll go. My wife will have to manage. But now, how to get from here to Liberty Market? Our car is parked there you see. The driver didn't want to come through these small lanes.'

'I know your driver Mr Hasan, and I know where he is parked. I also know what car it is – a mint-condition Buick LaSalle. Samir will go with you. He'll show you. His brother will stay here with me. Now go.'

Gurdev and Noor walked out with a look at Sultan who had gone back inside the house without paying them any more attention. Samir walked out and began walking at a brisk pace, expertly dodging passers-by and the detritus in the street. After they turned the corner, Gurdev kept walking but put his hand on Samir's shoulder, indicating to him to slow down. He caught up with him and put his arm around the boy's shoulder, a common enough gesture in the subcontinent. Noor stayed a step behind, glancing around constantly.

'Samir, did you get the note that day? Did you hear us tell you where we were? Why didn't you come? We could have been long gone by now, before anyone had noticed anything,' he mumbled under his breath. Samir looked at him – somewhat defiantly, thought Gurdev.

Samir spoke loudly; Noor could hear him even though she kept falling behind: 'Bhaijaan, this is our country. These gullies are familiar to me. I saw the note. I know Nirmal sent you.' Gurdev noticed Samir's use of Nirmal's name without a 'ji', 'bhai' or any other indication of respect. 'He wants us there for his own welfare. That is not our country. This is. Now we are getting the same respect as before, even more, actually. People are coming to Sajid Brother only for our work and all the money is coming to us. Nirmal was keeping most of it, giving us barely 10 per cent. Did you know that? Now we know. Definitely, without us, he has no embroidery, only what some second-rate karigars can give him. That serves him right. It will teach him not to exploit children.'

Gurdev couldn't believe the words coming out of Samir's mouth. This didn't sound like a naïve boy who didn't know how to come out of his own house. It sounded like someone who had played them. He had wanted Nirmal to come; he had wanted to punish him. All the letters had been a charade, the pitiful motherless children persona a farce. Gurdev caught Noor by the elbow and pushed Samir away. He walked purposefully down the narrow road, not as deftly as Samir had done but made it to the end. Samir stopped by the side of the road and watched them scurry along, a small tear rolling down his right cheek that he couldn't lift his hand to wipe off because he didn't want Gurdev to see him crying.

Gurdev and Noor stumbled down the lane and out into the main bazaar. They hailed a rickshaw, the same way Imran had done, and sat down. The man looked back questioningly but Gurdev didn't see him. He couldn't see anything. He heard Noor say 'Liberty Market' and felt a slight breeze on his beardless face as the rickshaw moved forward. Gurdev rubbed his face, his head and thrust his head in his hands. He felt Noor's hand on his arm but brushed it away. They rode in silence till Gurdev heard Noor ask the man to stop in the back, the way they had gone out the last two times. He couldn't help but admire her; she hadn't frozen, she hadn't screamed, she had gone on.

Once Noor and Gurdev got into Liberty Market, they slowed down. Gurdev settled himself. Noor took her time browsing through the tiny shops that lacked the shine and sparkle and the closed doors of Anarkali but shone with warmth and craft and folklore instead. She went inside one shop, sat down on a rickety bench and asked to see phulkari dupattas. She got into a long conversation with the owner about phulkaris for weddings and the colours used and the fabric underneath. The man brought out his secret treasures, old phulkaris that families had sold for extra money. Gurdev was getting restless but he settled down. He owed Noor this time because they both knew this was the last time they would come to Pakistan. He was not worried any more. His parents were on the other side, they didn't have to attempt a midnight border crossing; they could cross at Wagah, the way they came but they would have to work out a way to get back to Amritsar. Jagtap would be waiting at Kasur village tonight like he probably had been the previous night. Gurdev rested his head on the wall behind the bench, with eyes half closed, and listened to Noor talk to the shop owner, small exclamations, low-voiced questions about the piece, then more personal conversations about the man's origins, then cups of tea all around.

Noor bought several things, two large bags full. Gurdev didn't see what but he paid without complaint with Pakistani rupees that Riaz Baig had given him in exchange for dollars. The dollars would remain hidden from now on. He gathered up the bags before Noor could bend down to lift them and carried them out into the narrow lane. They walked along slowly, Noor pausing to admire fabric and parandas and jootis as they walked. She stopped again to try on jootis and bought a couple of pairs. Then they were back to the teashop and searched around for Imran. He was not there. Gurdev wondered about him. Had he led them into a trap? Finally, they reached the bangle shop and Noor browsed again. Gurdev was losing patience, not because he was in a hurry to get anywhere but because he was a man and he couldn't understand how women could wander from shop to shop, touching this and stroking that and then do it again and again and again.

When Noor was done, she loaded Gurdev with more packages and they made their way to the car. Akbar was asleep, mouth open, drool dripping down one side, loud snores out of his nose, one fly sitting on his cheek and one on the bridge of his nose – no, Imran didn't know anything. This man had not met anyone while they were gone. Gurdev banged on the hood of the car to wake Akbar up and shoo the flies out. He put all the packages on the back seat next to Noor and got in the front seat next to Akbar.

'Let's go. Time to go home,' said Gurdev.

Akbar drove them back to Model Town. No one in the car said anything. Gurdev and Noor both glanced at his parents' house as they drove by. The place was quiet. They pulled up outside the Baigs' home. No black car anywhere in sight. It was dusk, about 6 p.m. Sunlight was dimming on the city of Lahore. Gurdev and Noor brought their bags and the steel trunk out of the house. Shakeela and Riaz Baig followed them out. Shakeela and Noor hugged closely. Shakeela gave them a large package, things for her daughter. Riaz shook Gurdev's hand. No one said anything. The luggage stayed by the side of the car. Akbar stood by the driver's door. Gurdev indicated to him with his chin to load up.

Akbar opened the trunk, turning the lever to the right. It was unlocked. He probably hadn't locked it after Noor and Gurdev returned from Ajodhan late in the night. Lying side by side in the large trunk, broad smiles on their faces, were the two embroidery boys, Sultan and Samir.

Acknowledgements

~

Close to eight years ago, I resigned from my job at IBM and began writing. I was helped along by Amal Chatterjee, my online writing teacher at Oxford Continuing Education, my Goddard College advisors Jane Wohl, John McManus, Sherri Smith, Reiko Rizzuto and Elena Georgiou, my Pune writing mentor Randhir Khare and my early draft editor Daniel Castro. I'm grateful to all of them for getting me ready for this writerly life.

I am particularly grateful to Mrs Manju Khan, my English Literature teacher in school. She ignited a love for the language and sent me off to make my rounds of the business world and to circle back to this wondrous world of fiction.

I am thankful for my first readers, Raj Hajela and Nirupama Krishnaswami, both of whom read my manuscript attentively and quickly, giving me that gentle nudge to keep going.

My agent, Mita Kapur, is an utterly no-nonsense presence in the literary world. She knows everyone and their assistants and I am grateful she was able to sell my book to the publisher it's with.

Well before Mrs Khan, it was my mother who first got me reading the simple stuff, the fun stuff. I am grateful to her for making me a reader. And I am grateful to my father for being there for me.

My children, Ashad and Nishka, have graciously listened to plot lines and sections of my manuscript. They've cheered me on through this excruciatingly slow journey, one even using me as an example of resilience in her college class.

Aman, my sister, also a writer, has inspired and encouraged me in that silent, somewhat stern middle-school-teacher way that says: the rope is yours – take it as far as it will take you.

My paternal grandparents Bakshi Pritam Singh and Beant Kaur, both long gone from this world, lent me their names and their extrapolated stories for this book. They gave me love, attention and a quiet place to read in their home in Simla, one that I will write about soon.

Finally, a big thank you to Prerna Gill, my editor at HarperCollins for pulling *Ladies' Tailor* through to the end.